Adlucinor Chronicles

Book 1

K. Graham Sutherland

So dear June

Thank you for all your support. It means a great deal.

Love

K. Graham Sutherland

Dream Big Publishing
Byron Center, MI

Dream Big Publishing
A publication of Dream Big Publishing
Byron Center MI
Copyright 2015 by Karen L. Graham Sutherland
All rights reserved, including the right of reproduction in whole or in part in any form.
Dream Big Publishing is a registered trademark of Dream Big Publishing.
Text of this book is set in Garamond text size 13.
Manufactured in the United States of America
All rights reserved.
Cover photo © Can Stock Photo Inc. / curaphotography

Summary: 'Muscles poised and clenched to run, I turned but his strength overpowered mine as easily as a spider would capture a fly. It is how I felt at that moment; caught in a web of my own making. I should have left- I didn't.'
When Becca meets her new neighbor, the life she worked so hard for begins to unravel, until it disappears entirely. Swept up into a world of Somnias Vagus, better known as wanderers of the night, she finds herself embroiled in the midst of a continuous battle for her mind…and her soul. One wishes to save it, another destroy it by any means possible.
They were referred to as Elders. The five best of the Creator's children who were chosen to pass through the entry gate from their dying world to earth. For centuries the elders dwelled within the shadows of night, feeding, satiating themselves on the private and personal dreams of humans as they called out in their sleep; searching for their soul mate. Becca, unbeknownst to her, was a siren caller; the most powerful and rare of any human for a Wanderer. Night after night she calls out, screaming her need through visions as she sleeps. So powerful is her sonnet she draws the attention from more than just the Elders. Every young wanderer responds with unbridled need. Unfortunately the naked desire reveals a sixth elder. One who had slipped through the gate mere seconds before it closed. The five elders must join together to save her now, not only from the young ones but also the sixth, ravaged by madness and determined to have and control Becca. Her gifts, combined with his, would offer the ultimate control he desired and craved.
Will Becca forgive the intrusion of her mind, her soul, and her life; push aside resentment and find love within the embrace of his arms ... Should they ultimately survive?

[1. Fantasy – Fiction 2. Romance 3. Paranormal]
978-1514149737
K. Graham Sutherland
Copyright 2015 by K. Graham Sutherland
All rights reserved.

DEDICATION

To my family, I love you, thank you for all of your support and love

To my family physician, thank you for helping and guiding me through the good times and bad while writing this book.

To my best friend Mona, love you, thank you for being your beautiful witty self

In loving memory of our beloved Uncle Ed who unfortunately never made it to see the publication of this book.

Book One: Robert

Chapter 1

The irises of his cold dead eyes began to flicker with life. A shimmering almost horrifying color of crimson stained the black, expanding until all that could be seen was red, as he straightened and sniffed the air; a cruel smile pulled at the corner of his lips. Six hundred years it had been since he had last sensed this presence. Benjamin turned towards his almost lifeless puppets, executing a grand gesture with a sweep of his arms for them to rise from their kneeling position before him. His eyelids closed as he travelled towards the sensation that had very nearly been his downfall upon his arrival on this world.

"Ah yes," Benjamin's voice was as abhorrent as was the manner in which he treated those that he had created. "Finally, finally someone worthy of me," he leered with excitement as his heart began a crescendo that had happened only once before. "This time she will be mine." His eyes travelled over the hundreds of unwilling followers that had slowly risen to their feet, their bodies thin, their eyes desperate for life-or death. Captured much like a fly in a web, they had suffered for centuries, neither living nor dead. Hope had long since been forgotten, their one sole purpose- to have their piece of soul back that had been stolen so they could rest in peace.

He sat back in his elegant black wing tipped chair, his throne he often called it, his long tapered fingers caressing the leather as he crossed one well-muscled leg over the other while glancing down with complete disdain towards those who served him. "Enter my mind, feel the path I now follow. That call-that whisper of sweet infinite need that beckons me." With an exaggerated flair for the dramatics, he raised his arms in the air, the black of the designer suit that had been created to match his chair fluttering against the white of his skin. "Embrace your new queen. She is to be found immediately my slaves. I shall guide you to her via her dreams and I will finally claim what should have belonged to me all of those centuries ago. Once she is here, I may just release a few souls to those that follow my instructions- those who prove themselves superior." There was no shifting from the Wanderers he had created; no lingering hope that flared to life. It was something they had heard, had envisioned; had believed one too many times. Each however knew that they would do all they could to find her because to fail would be far worse than the existence they now had. Finally he turned to the three he had chosen to be the closest to his equal, paying little notice to the tinges of red within their irises, trusting in his power over all he claimed.

Benjamin embraced the touches of his mind as they drank in the flavor and the essence that none had experienced before. Sweet and sultry, a mixture that was more heady than the finest wine and far more desirable than the most beautiful of woman any could remember. Desire touched every wanderer that dared enter the evil that was Benjamin. Hope warred with despair. Perhaps she could be the one that might just have the power to release them from this torturous half-life they had been forced to live. He forced them from his mind before they had a chance to feed on hope instead of helplessness, thrusting them back, relishing the moans and whimpers as they yearned for what he had shared. A ruthless smile curled his lips as he nodded to the three he had chosen before rising and leaving the room. Quite frankly, the sight of his growing army made him nauseas and he was much more content to be away from their stench. Now they were mere mindless slaves, easily disposable and meant for one purpose; bait.

He led the three to his chambers, seating himself on the bed with regal grace, the bed that had once carried the dreams of the woman stolen from him. Now she was dead. He had claimed her house though no part of her lingered within the walls or the fabric. They had taken that away from him; taken everything. Anger and need fueled each motion as he spoke.

"You three will feed those sloths only enough to ensure their fidelity towards me, to ensure they are successful with my mission. Failure will be dealt with swiftly and brutally. "Benjamin turned cold eyes towards those he had chosen. "Be very sure in your words and actions lest I decide to demote you back to their status. Go now, I must focus, seek her out and find her for you. Time is of the essence."

They bowed, shielding the venom and hatred within their eyes, hiding the knowledge that they grew stronger with their bonding. Now was not the time to display such for they were far from ready; but soon... soon it would be they whom Benjamin would bow to.

Becca leaned against the wall as she felt the pain begin to rip through her head again. All day she had felt the stinging sensations while trying to finish her work so she could get the hell out of this flea bag hotel and away from the three stooges. Sleep had been nothing but quick drifts here and there during the last few days as they waited and watched. The tip she had received was that the drug bust would be going down within seventy two hours which by her calculations was anytime now. Swallowing a few tablets to try and ease the pain, she turned her gaze back towards the window.

All she wanted at the moment was her home, her bed and the mystery man that had visited her dreams nightly for the past few weeks. She shivered at the thought, feeling an easing in the pain that had erupted and threatened the dinner she had wolfed down.

"There!" She pointed, hearing the others rush to the window, cameras ready. Adrenalin washed through her as she spied the vehicle pull up to the abandoned warehouse. The clicking of the cameras was the only sound heard as they focused on the men emerge seeing their shifty eyes watching as they looked suspiciously around before backing towards the entrance. Focusing her camera she took clear, concise shots of each face as the sounds of sirens approaching at high speeds indicating the gig was up. Before they could flee, they were surrounded by dozens of officers shielding themselves behind their car doors, guns pointed. She smiled. It was over. Gathering her gear she slung the pack over her shoulder and left without a goodbye. Checking to ensure the recorder was on she raced down to the scene. It felt good to be the first reporter there, even better to receive the exclusive as promised. Now it was just a quick trip to the office to put the entire story to bed and she could go home to rest. Looking a final time back towards the scene she thought she noticed a shadow lurking to the far right of the crime scene. Before she could lift her camera to take a picture, the shadow had disappeared. "Must have imagined it," Becca shrugged her shoulders as she jogged to her car.

Becca was itching for a shower after the long captivity in the flea motel room with the others, who were nothing less than vulgar and unkempt. Perhaps I'm being unkind towards them, she paused a moment to think… "Na, I'm not," she laughed as she stowed her pack in the trunk of her car before slipping into the driver's seat.

It took less than an hour to write up the remainder of the story, adding the pictures before sending it down to the editors who would ensure the writing before putting the paper to bed. Becca looked forward to the byline that would be in tomorrow's paper but not as much as she would enjoy seeing the large shipment of drugs taken off the streets. That was her focus, her goal- to rid the streets of as much of the crap as she could. Becca's editor had warned her to be cautious, knowing the danger she placed herself in each time they managed to bring down some flunky doing the big man's job. Each time Becca would smile and promise to be careful. This was not just business to her however. It was personal. There were too many young children out there becoming hooked on the stuff before reaching teenage years and Becca had decided when she became a journalist that it would be her goal to do all she could to throw as many obstacles in their path as she could.

Waving goodbye to the security guard Becca stepped out into the cool night and hopped into her vehicle, more than a little anxious to head home.

Benjamin stood, anger and desire etched on each feature of his scarred face. She has been touched by a wanderer. How was this possible he seethed while pacing the luxurious room, moving back and forth in rapid furious motions? He was beyond furious now as the weight of the situation fell upon his shoulders. The feel, the sense was that of an extremely powerful wanderer. Perhaps one as strong as he, but that could not be possible. He was the only one left. The others he had left for dead upon their arrival. There had been no impression of their presence for more than six hundred years. Could it be one, or more had survived? "No!" Benjamin raged as he drained the life of the nearest and newest member of his army. Kicking the body aside, he continued his path of destruction until sated, though no less calm. Sinking into his chair he called the three chosen with a ringing of the antique silver bell that sat upon the table to his right. His plans had to be changed. They would have to begin his plan more quickly than anticipated. He needed this woman- wanted her almost as much as he wanted the one kept from him all those years ago. This time he would not fail.

"Ready your groups," he spat the words. "You leave tonight for her place. Delve into my mind and see where she lives. Bring her to me- alive!"

As Benjamin closed his flaming eyes to allow entry, the others reached out to touch their hands together, binding themselves as they fed from their leader. Each felt the power grow exponentially as it flowed and was shared directly between them instead of individually. Their sneers were hidden, though their hearts rejoiced that soon they would kill Benjamin and lead the army themselves, with far greater success and far less leniency. Quickly pulling apart as they witnessed his eyes flicker open they bowed once more to him before exiting.

Exhaustion, complete and utter exhaustion- Rebecca sighed as she let her briefcase fall from her hands. Kicking off her shoes she moaned deeply, whispering, "Damn it's good to be home." Bending forward she gave Felix, her Persian cat a cursory pat; ignoring the hiss she received for the lack of attention. Willing her fatigued body into the bedroom, she flipped the switch, illuminating the bedroom as weary eyes glanced towards the inviting bed. The white duvet spread across the double sized mattress. Multi coloured pillows strewn along the top by the oak headboard. Another exhausted whimper escaped. Every muscle in her body screamed to crawl under the blanket and sleep; a long peaceful sleep; maybe a day or two. Although tempting, the repugnant smell of the last three nights in the same clothing assaulted her senses, making the decision for her. A shudder of disgust propelled her into the bathroom to discard the clothing, dropping them in a dirty heap on the floor. A long soothing bath would have to wait. Instead she chose a quick shower, washing the scent and grime from her, every muscle craving the plushness of her bed. Becca loved her job and wouldn't trade it for the world; though times like the last three days made her wonder why. Shrugging into her favorite 'I'm not going anywhere for the next night pajamas', she blocked the thought of the inhospitable accommodations left behind, instead choosing to savor the enjoyment of being home, the feeling of comfort that had filled her from the moment she unlocked the door. The first real smile graced Becca's lips since she had left the hole that passed for a hotel. It erased a few lines of fatigue as she poked her fingers through the holes in her pajamas.

Being a reporter; a good one, was all she had ever wanted to do with her life. Never had she regretted a moment of work or struggle. Finally having achieved her goal had made all of the sacrifices worth the effort. Even the personal ones she had made, like- maybe a life. She returned to the bathroom to brush her teeth. Becca couldn't help but wince at her appearance as she glanced into the mirror while brushing, finally seeing the effects the last few days had bestowed on her face. Weariness prominently showed in her eyes, dark purplish circles that shadowed beneath the long fringed lashes, marring her slightly tanned skin. "Ugh, "she groaned as she leaned forward, holding the brush in her mouth, foam and bubbles coating her lips as her fingers traced over the fatigue lines. From an early age she had always thought of herself as nothing more than ordinary. Her face was oval, much like her grandmothers, with high cheekbones, and unmarred creamy skin. Graced with full lush lips and eyes-when not marked with racoon circles, were a vibrant green with golden flecks that sprinkled along the deep set color-perhaps her best feature. Rinsing out her mouth, she quickly ran a brush through her thick waist length russet hair, finally turning out the light before moving wearily to bed.

"God this feels good," she whimpered with pleasure as she stretched out fully, noting the tension in her muscles beginning to unwind. People say sex is pure bliss but nothing could top this moment. Silence graced her ears and after three days of being confined in an all too small space, with three of the rudest, most unkempt, and altogether far too extremely flirty reporters, Becca savored each moment of her new found peace. Fatigued eyes began to close, her mind drifting as she visualized the article just submitted. More than a few people were going to be extremely upset when morning dawned. It was definitely one of her best pieces of work. Yawning, her mind quieted as her body became languid. "Night Felix," she stroked the cat as he snuggled against her. "Maybe my mystery man will be waiting for me in my dreams again," Becca felt slight tremors weave through her at the depth of emotions the mere thought stirred. She had been visited by this stranger-yet not a stranger for some time now. Faceless and voiceless yet her heart yearned for him nightly with a painful intensity.

A high pitched nails down the chalkboard screech developing in depth and annoyance barrelled its way into her dream, abruptly waking her from the deep sleep she had just blissfully succumbed to. Felix jumped and hissed at her quick movement, glaring indignantly before settling once again. It sounded like the air brakes of a rusted out eighteen wheeler transport truck. No, she thought, a rusted out truck with an idiot driver that had no idea what he was doing, that was the sound. She buried her head beneath the pillow, praying the truck would pass quickly. Bright lights illuminated the entirety of her room as though daylight had made an early entrance. Impatiently she waited for them to dim- to move from the blinding direction they were pointing; to offer back the darkness, but of course they didn't.

"What the hell?" She growled while clamouring out of bed. Becca stomped to the front entrance, muttering, about no need to turn the lights on- there was enough from that transport to signal the arrival of an approaching UFO.

Gently moving the curtains aside she yawned while peeking out the window at the offensive moving truck noisily grinding its way down the street to her neighbour's home. A quick glance at the clock had her bristling. Midnight! "Don't these people understand normal working hours?" She shuffled from foot to foot on the cold floor, while doing her best to hide behind the thin fabric of the curtain. Having just completed a three day investigation for the newspaper with Larry, Curly and Moe, she was dead tired and had the patience of a cornered tiger; none zip-zero. Loud transports were definitely not on her agenda tonight. All she wanted was sleep. Admittedly, her curious nature which made her the best reporter at the newspaper had her puffy eyes transfixed down the hill to the only house within miles from her. A hint of red tinged her cheeks upon realizing she was perhaps a little too curious. "Oh well, one time can't hurt. I mean really." she mumbled as she kept looking. "We need to see what type of person would purchase a place like that, right Felix? With my luck it will be some weird version of the Adams Family," a show that portrayed vampires and other non- earthly beings living in a normal neighborhood. Tapping her fingers impatiently she waited, anxious to see the type of person that could tolerate living in that monstrosity. The waiting was making her crazy.

She would never have admitted how much the house fascinated her. There was something surreal about it; something that seemed to cry out to her. Hell, it's why she eventually succumbed to purchasing her home. Slowly she parted the curtains aside to glance again. Two sets of lights began to flood the long circular driveway damn near blinding her. She cursed while blinking, attempting to rid herself of the stars circling her eyes. Once she was finally able to see amidst the bright flashes of light her eyes became transfixed on the beautiful car trailing the banged up transport.

Felix brushed up against her legs as she resumed her position. "Wonder what type of neighbors they will be. Not too friendly I hope" Felix purred in agreement. The lights of the vehicle shone once more along the side of her house, illuminating the darkness before slowly dissipating- leaving it shadowed. It gave her the opportunity to peer once more at the dilapidated house that had remained empty for as long as she could remember. "There goes the nude sun bathing" she groused while straining to ogle the occupants of the gorgeous mustang. She whistled in appreciation of the black sleek car. The sound changed to a long low wolf whistle directed towards the man emerging from the vehicle. Suddenly she felt wide awake as she blatantly stared.

"Jesus, have mercy" she fanned herself as she searched intently for an equally exquisite female to fit the arm of that delicious man. "Please let there not be a woman with him; please let there not be a female with him," chanting as she unabashedly ogled the fine form emerging from the driver's side. "Hmm," she mouthed, no ring apparent, and better yet, no long perfect legs exiting the passenger side. "Well what luck, Felix," she cooed. "Perhaps I will have to sunbathe after all." She had the decency to blush at the wayward thoughts even as her belly flip flopped with excitement. Heat flooded her senses swirling through her veins, finally making the trek downwards to the nether parts of her anatomy. An audible gulp was heard as she swallowed. He had just bent over to retrieve items from the trunk of his car. "Well hello Cousin It'," another mental reference to the Adams Family blushing as the words spilled from her tongue- slowly, sensually, huskily. Desperately she tried to remember how to close her mouth as she stared at the man from the bottom and worked her way up along his muscled body. To hell with the curtains and hiding this was far too great a sight to ignore. "Now that is what I call a great ass, Felix." Becca's subconscious was busily wiping the drool from the sides of her mouth.

And then he rose. A stunning face turned in her direction. Dark hair that appeared recently hand tousled, settled messily around his unnaturally pale face. A strong gust of wind blew the messy ebony hair back, revealing a strong chiseled face, and those oh so kissable lips. Odd, she thought, how pale his flesh was, almost translucent-pasty and thin though no other part of him looked anything other than perfect. Her eyes met his and the sudden hammering of her heart had her fingers clutching the pajama top. Deep set, wide eyes, long fringed lashes that any woman would kill for. Not only beautiful-but black. Forget dark brown-or chocolate melt your heart eyes, dark midnight black, accentuating the whites circling the irises. She was sure he was gazing directly at her-no...in her, with those black fathomless depths that were his eyes. What's more, that sinful look was completely intentional; and purely sexual. She found herself held motionless, excitement and fear stirring her blood. The blushing effect highlighted her cheekbones, setting off the vivid green of her wide curious eyes. She was helplessly mesmerized; even breathing seemed to be a chore as those devastatingly haunting eyes captivated and held her. Willing herself to turn away had no effect. Spellbound, she surmised; bewitched- entirely his fault.

And then he smiled. Her world tilted on its axis. Everything changed in that one vital moment; nothing, absolutely nothing would ever be the same. He touched her-without a touch; without a sound, without any nearness, he had stolen his way into a place no other had ever discovered. It was almost more than she could bear; the tangible change stirring deep within. Some instinct warned her to be afraid-to use caution, to flee yet nothing had ever felt quite so right. Except her dream man of course. Arousal swift and powerful washed over her. She whimpered as sensations plowed inside before spiralling down a path there seemed to be no control of. Her sub conscious was dancing with glee, urging her to rush out and meet him.

Moments- or a lifetime later had passed; she wasn't sure, but finally he severed the connection. She knew it was he that had done so because she couldn't. There was no strength of will to break the bond they had shared. On quivering legs she retreated until the hardness of the wall pressed against her back. His image flooded her mind. Volcanic heat scorched her body... she sure as hell knew something monumental had occurred -though she had no idea what. It was as if

16

she could feel him. Her breathing began to match his; the caress of warm breath physical against her sensitive flesh. It took every ounce of self-control to temper the panic welling inside. "Balls," she cussed, "I must be more exhausted than I thought."

Sure, she had enjoyed evenings out with a few very handsome men even dabbled in some heavy petting." I mean really who hadn't these days," she thought to herself as she toyed with her hair finding herself blushing again. There was however, something about this particular man that spoke volumes. No, that wasn't right. It screamed- run now… run fast, and yet she was purring like a well-oiled machine, and her sub-conscious was rifling through lingerie, trying to find the sexiest one. It was all she could do at the moment to remember to breathe-in through the mouth, out through the nose; or was it the other way around? "Crap," gently banging her head against the wall she moaned" now I can't remember how to breathe!"

It was impossible to relinquish the vision of him as she edged along the wall to her bedroom. Dropping her robe onto the floor she wearily climbed into bed. The last few days of work had been strenuous, and at the moment she was feeling every ounce of fatigue. Reaching to turn the bedside light out she curled into a ball. "Get out of my head," she shouted mere moments later as she felt the same enticing sensations that she had from their last encounter. Frowning in annoyance she turned over, unable to rid herself of the image of pale flesh, dark eyes and that sexy tousled hair. The ache increased ten-fold and heat raced through her veins like wildfire, rendering her with a new sensation – need.

Closing her eyes did nothing but compound the rising inferno that had become her libido. Punching her pillow she rolled over again, blowing stray tendrils of hair that tickled along her flawless cheeks while doing her best to ignore the late night antics of her body.

Counting sheep; I could try that, she thought. Innocent fluffy little sheep jumping over a fence should serve to lessen the demands her body was making. By the time she'd reached thirty nine the sheep had turned into "Mr. sexy new neighbour" bounding over the fence towards her. Trembling, she flipped over again on the now rumpled sheets.

Snapping her teeth together in frustration mutated the growl as she covered her head with the pillow. She was going to be one bitchy woman tomorrow.

As tired as she was, sleep was far from instant before finally claiming her. Eventually the drugged sensation one feels as they walk the line between slumber and wake enveloped her. Sounds grew muffled-distant, her body becoming languid once more, melting into the bed. Becca never dreamed; well rarely, but tonight she could feel her body floating- a beckoning shroud encompassing her.

Would he visit her tonight, Becca wondered as she drifted. The voiceless, sightless invader of her dreams that had brought to life each wish she had ever shelved. How many nights had she wondered if this would be the night he would emerge from the shadows, embrace the light and welcome her gaze upon him.

He appeared instantly, the man who tempted her for weeks while she slept. He entered her room as mind and body finally succumbed to fatigue. His focused gaze wandered along her lithe frame while his dark cloaked form merged amidst the shadows already clinging to the wall. He estimated her height to be approximately five foot, seven inch; curves in all the right places and legs that stretched forever. The ache to reach out-to caress the flawless pink tinged flesh that softened with the peacefulness of sleep cut through his stationary form. It was becoming increasingly difficult to stifle the primal urges bubbling forth. Seeing the bluish shadows beneath her long lashes troubled him. Tonight would not be an evening for feeding; she would require all her energy. A half smile curled the upper corner of his lip as he listened to the whispered coos that escaped with each breath. Tilting his head, he inhaled, memorizing the scent that was purely his Rebecca. Gently he probed her mind to ensure she had not been touched again, the strain of worry etched along the corners of the fathomless black eyes. A whoosh of air escaped. He felt a recent contact. It was time to call in the other Elders. "Damn," he growled with concern. And then she spoke. He knew he would linger just a little longer before taking care of business. She called to him-she was his siren.

So close, Becca mumbled as she slept; so close all she had to do was reach out to feel him. Confusion blurred her thoughts enough that she reached out. Nothing; her arm dropped once again to her side. Damn it, Becca knew someone was in the room with her. A frown creased her forehead. Comfort sang within her as it always did when he was with her. Just one look, one touch and she could sleep peacefully-or not. Riddles; all of these riddles were quickly becoming frustrating. Never having been one that enjoyed mysteries-not in her waking hours, certainly not in sleep, she resolved to search for the answers in the following days. Having come to some resolution, her mind relaxed into sleep again. Images of intensely beautiful yet unusual onyx eyes stole into her dreams.

He was calling to her with a deep sensual voice, urging her sleeping form to find him-desire him. "Crazy dream- his fault," She murmured before turning over.

He bit back the laugh as he listened, tenderly watching her sleep as he brought to mind the image upon her face as he exited the vehicle. Robert had basked in her gaze long before she would have been able to see him. To see the vision of her awake, watching him caused a deep shuddering sigh to escape. The emotions it had stirred. His blood boiled, and he had left impressions of his fingers in the leather steering wheel to stop himself from bounding out of the car to her. She couldn't know yet. Soon however…Once he could tell her-show her,-live outside of her dreams with her.

She didn't know; couldn't know that every deeply hidden need, ache and dream she coveted or wished for had begun to seep through her dreams, fluttering along the night breeze to those that hungered most for the music. She inadvertently began creating visions; haunting images and sounds that were the exact hunger filling sounds a Wanderer lived for… All those years of shelving her desires; her true yearnings had opened a pathway that was now destined to change both of their existences. He couldn't say lives as he did not live but merely existed. For weeks the call had grown stronger until its depth; its urgency could go unanswered no longer. And now with another invading her mind, probing her soul-time had run out. The utter desirability of her thoughts had created a road now travelled by both; one neither would be able to stray from. Never had a soul matched his as hers did. It seemed to be a perfect symmetry; an exact synchronization of their deepest core. Nightly, as she writhed in slumber, her heart and soul searched for a fulfillment she was yet to realise. One only he could provide-her perfect match, now to just have the time to convince Rebecca.

Robert understood the dangers of committing himself to one. More than the pain and suffering he would willingly inflict upon his body to enable himself to spend short periods with her during daylight hours- it was a union of souls; plural- a concert of two- a joining, where one would no longer be able to live without the other. Shimmering eyes rested directly on her peaceful face. Rebecca needed to accept what and who he was; how he had found her, and… he cringed, somehow find it within her to forgive the number of times he had intentionally invaded her dreams- and fed from them. A tall order for someone with the feisty and courageous attitude Rebecca buried herself in.

Somnias Vagus or wanderer; the name chosen for those of his kind- Robert shook his head at the terminology, though if confession was indeed good for the soul, the shadowy apparition; the ability to blend within the night, and how they fed made the name associated more than appropriate. He and those like him wandered and dwelled beneath the blanket of dark, basking in the blackness, alive within the shadows. Night after endless night with their acute hearing, they, the wanderers, would listen to the needs of humans who inadvertently released their inner most desires via their dreams and seek them out. No secrets could be hidden from them as they merged their silhouette with the stillness that came after dusk. It was quite comforting to feel those humans who were content with their lives, their dreams embracing what they had. Robert envied those as he continued his search. For more than six hundred years, the world had been his to wander; to feel, to feed and to seek the one that would complete him.

His knowledge as an Elder was vast and he knew a caller of her magnitude-her undeveloped skill, would have others seeking her dreams- her soul, as one had begun to do already. This one however felt different. It felt old, as old as he and he was sure it was not one of the other four. Rebecca was now a magnet, unintentionally touching the emotions of every wanderer that remained hidden on this planet. Her sweet lingering melody would stretch out to encompass every continent, offering a gift so pure- so alive that it would be next to impossible to prevent the chaos he was sure would ensue.

Onyx eyes had grown vigilant night after night as Rebecca tossed, feeding on dreams; her innermost longings, hoping to quiet the strength and unequalled depth within her calls. Though he was nothing more than an eclipsed illusion along the wall each evening he slipped into her bedroom, the fascination; mesmerisation of the frail being that writhed beneath the crisp clean sheets never abated. His fingers contracted as he begrudgingly forced his hands to remain stationary. He could image wanting nothing more than to tangle them deeply within her tousled, vibrant red hair-to feel the luxuriousness of those enticing curls. To smooth the stray webs that fluttered along her creamy flesh, absorbing the warmth that settled beneath her skin caused a smile to turn the corners of his lips upwards. Would her temper match the rainbow of russet highlights that flowed along her cheeks to spread across the white pillowcase? Anticipation galloped through him at the prospect of discovering each and every emotion held within her. There was no doubt in his mind that this woman bore a strength that few would ever realize, and a kindness that made her exceptionally unique. He yearned to erase the lines of confusion and desire. Robert ached each moment

Rebecca did, whispering words of comfort that he knew she would be unable to hear, while watching over her-feeding from her energy, absorbing her flavor.

One so powerful in the tranquility of rest would almost certainly arouse and summon more than just him. Robert exhaled as his fingers weaved through his hair-hell it was going to invite every damn wanderer. Danger, most likely at this very moment was closing in on her; and yet as she slept, her lips slightly parted, tinges of rose swirling beneath the surface of her skin as it shimmered beneath the moons glow, she seemed the vision of lovely sweetness. For his kind, Rebecca was a temptress-a siren caller. She came with gifts of her own that, once united with a wanderer, would create an unimaginable power. It was this unexpected union that had been the birth of his kind. It was that very same devoted and loving mating that each wanderer searched endless nights for; feeding on lesser dreams to satisfy their hunger- holding it at bay as each sought the one they were meant to bond with. Finding a true Caller however, was beyond rare… yet was every night wanderer's ultimate dream.

The temptation to possess the potentiality that lay dormant within Rebecca would be far too great for most to resist; so much raw untouched power…again Robert shifted towards Rebecca. Just the sonnet alone was so breathtakingly simplistic- yet astoundingly intricate and haunting, it would mesmerize all but the Elders. He was sure none aside the five elders would be capable enough to prevail against the depth of perfection each note promised.

Joining-a union of souls on this planet was extraordinarily rare. Robert himself was over six hundred years old. Only now had he felt the compulsion to seek out the one who tugged on his soul with each lyrical note. Only one of equal or greater power, such as an Elder could withstand the bonding of not only souls but a collaboration of powers as well. The actual formal uniting would become a testament to both their strength and commitment. Surviving after hovering along the edge of an endless, black and empty abyss while their souls entwined, was the closest either would come to death. It would beckon, waiting with bated breath for one to reject the other, whilst their souls mirrored the others motions in perfect symmetry; a dance of unimaginable love until reunited with their bodies, satiated; complete-home

Though for it to be a siren whose song was so sweet it melted the hardest of hearts, was unheard of. Hundreds of years had passed without sign of one. Truth had become myth, a legend. Perhaps only one existed; the one meant to create their kind. Robert smiled as he gazed admiringly down at her, his caller.

He wondered just how much of her dreams she recalled. The thought fascinated him as he stretched along the bay window, avidly watching each intricate motion she made, each facial expression. She fascinated him. Little coos when a pleasurable thought rolled through her mind, to whimpers as thoughts grew more vivid, more real- less imagined. His gaze never wavered- need growing stronger by the moment as her hand would reach up to grasp what she could feel but not see. Color would stain her cheeks as her dreams turned to visions of passion, of desire and completion. Her sweet scent permeated the room, and he drew in large quiet breaths- memorizing the intoxicating aroma that was purely physical, mingled with a soft scent of a sultry perfume. A heady combination that was totally she, Robert smiled at the thought.

He knew it was his presence that now compelled these visions. Their connection had become so strong that need fueled each thought; each motion. It was this same need that had Rebecca frustratingly kicking the sheets from her heated body as she struggled to find the answers- to find him.

Oh there was just so much to teach her-to learn together. He glanced out the window, the worried frowns returning as the pin prickles of the other probing settled again in his mind. This woman was most assuredly not timid; in fact he suspected she had a bite that would make many weaker people think twice about any confrontations. She was strong and vibrant. Just as alive in her sleeping moments as she was awake. Perhaps more so, he mused as his eyes fixated on her. Through slumber Rebecca could release the visions-the dreams she harbored. Letting go of what her world considered normal, freeing her thoughts to possibilities, to the needs that had carved the path they were now destined to share. The desperate desire to allow; to reveal- bring to life the total completion she ached so deeply for, had been the catalyst to the emergence of her calls. Rebecca projected all that had slumbered- dormant within her mind since birth.

Robert had been staggered the first time he felt her beckon. It was a harkening he could no more push aside, than he could ignore feeding. That very evening he took to the freedom of the night, his large shadowed form hidden beneath the cloak of darkness. His essence was humming with anticipation, with wonder at what could be so utterly powerful, for he had given up the idea of finding a caller more than three hundred years.

As he weaved between the shadows, Robert tilted his head up, inhaling deeply of the chilly breeze that brushed along his already cold flesh, savoring each new scent as he closed the distance with a speed no human could ever understand... Having an incredibly hard exterior; and a strength few would comprehend had its benefits certainly, but internally, the structure of a wanderer was, at times, very vulnerable. Transitioning was the time Robert would be at the greatest risk from attack or injury.

"Ah but to obtain the ability to remain outdoors in daylight for greater periods of time," Robert fantasized aloud. "To touch and feel and breathe in her scent not only in her dreams." He was more than willing to risk everything.

Barely noticeable, he turned his head, glancing out into the night; his home-his prison. A wanderer's vision was better than most humans during daylight hours. He had known only shadow, only the inky darkness as his essence was caressed by thousands of mortals, crying out their needs-their desires. Many of his kind thrived on this. Indeed they sustained themselves with the energy projected through dreams;

their most desperate desires. Misguided young ones; or those particularly cruel, enjoyed touching the humans that called, offering fragments of fulfillment before leaving them hopelessly lost. Night after night the wounded soul would scream for more; for what was once attainable, until finally they existed, only half alive. Strength was gained within the shared visions. It was how a wanderer normally fed. Generally it was a brief connection to the human's mind; a touching of their soul and the soothing of nightmares when discovering their souls did not match

The new ones however, those below the age of two hundred had no such compunction. Night after night they rose to the call of others, sharing their most intimate thoughts, feeding on them before leaving them wanting and aching for more. Those were the humans that became almost helpless willing victims, seeking time and time again to find one more moment of all they desired. In recent years the new ones had begun to feed further on the vulnerable sleepers, feeding until they would wake no more. The stronger the call, the more the human had to share.

Feeding until draining the body of its soul was against their rules. One that had been abided by far longer than Robert's six hundred years. He sighed. The time was quickly approaching that he and the other Elders would need to step in; to take control of the situation and those who chose to deliberately break the rules.

Becca moaned, causing Robert to turn from the window towards her, his thoughts forgotten as he watched, absolutely enthralled. He could taste the love, the lust- the desire and ache in each of her thoughts. More than a touch of confusion flitted through her mind; visions of completion stumbled headlong through her fantasies, causing the ache to grow. But the deepest, the most fervent desire was true, lasting love. She arched on the bed, still in her dream state, a soft cry of need escaping as her fingers rolled over her belly.

Oh to be able to soothe her. Robert felt the pangs of need as he inched closer. He halted as she stirred before turning in his direction.

His senses heightened as she inhaled. An incredulous look crossed his features as he realized she felt him. It couldn't be. Robert blended into the background, torturing himself with fanciful imaginings. "Of course she can't feel me," he chastised himself, pushing past the pain the words created.

Long ago, Robert shifted through memories as he watched each minute motion she made, there had been talk of a rarity within a siren. A vision; he paused, seeking the correct phrasing, frustrated with himself, the ability to view reality in both waking and sleeping hours. Shock held him immobile- not daring to breathe as she hesitantly reached out again.

A longing deep within him stirred something more powerful than anything in all of his existence. Dryness coated his mouth and it took every ounce of self-restraint to remain in the shadows. The urge to brand her as his, to claim her before every god damn wanderer left on this planet tried. Robert gently probed within her, surprised that he felt no fear, just a rapid pulsing and throbbing need for completion. Almost begging as her arms lifted again. "Damn" he murmured as he moved back to the bay window. Her projection, her thoughts of sexual need, of trusting unending love would bring the entire lot of the young ones with or without scruples. Anger, deep and hot welled within him, pouring out as his eyes began to glow at the thought of another near her. He sighed again as he reigned in his temper, knowing it was taking all of his self- control at the moment to remain apart; to not become one and consume what he knew would be the mating of their souls. Lust rose as she tossed the sheet from her. He ached to ravish her right here, right now. To take her as she wished to be taken; with dominance and the love that went along with it. But in the cold light of the day as he rested, he knew it would not be the enough. She was dangerous, not only to herself but to him. To mate with her, to make her his; she would have to be willing to join him in both daylight hour and her sleeping state. No easy feat from what he had witnessed of her thus far. What he was sure of however, as the sun began to rise and he slipped from the shadows into the night, making his way to the house next door was that were he not able to claim her there was more than a good chance it would end up killing them both.

It was interesting that she had purchased the house next to this one. Robert wondered if her dreams had become more active since moving in. Most people in the sleepy little town of Woodstock Ontario avoided being anywhere near the place. They felt a presence, something more than they wished to know, shrugging it off as superstition though they were basically correct. The house he now entered was the gateway for his kind. It had remained empty and neglected for many years. Those in town studiously gazed past it, willing it to just decay-to crumble and be gone forever. Robert however could still feel the lives of those that had used the house before him. A smile crossed his features, content with the knowledge that perhaps at some time the house might be active again, the portal opened. Robert felt a fiery need stir inside, his body aching for fulfillment. He knew where he belonged. It would not mean taking a portal, finding another place. It was resting in a house mere feet from where he sat.

His fingers tapped along the old wooden staircase, thick with a layer of dust as he looked back over to her house. What had drawn her here he wondered when all others pretended it didn't exist. Was it part of what made her visions so strong? He believed she was one of the rare humans in the world that could feel both in wake and sleep and she was pure in her heart, another rarity.

It was painful to watch and feel her night after night as he waited, wanting and aching to fulfill her dreams, to taste her and to make her his. It was not just the pain that had caused Robert to wait until now; until she called so loudly that it could no longer be ignored, it was something much different.

Should they unite and their souls not match, it could kill one or both of them. This was generally why the young ones chose to feed from lesser dreams before moving onto the next. The calling, the sensations, the knowledge that their souls would unite was the only thing that could bring on the change. Already his days had been spent in agony as his flesh thickened; his body adjusted. They had to be able to exist within both worlds in order for completion. A wanderer could spend no more than an hour in daylight. Even that amount of time cost them greatly both in power and strength. The change, almost complete would allow him to see her world-join her within it or have her join him within his world.

Chapter 2

Life for wanderers began with the setting of the sun along the horizon. Leaving in its slow descent the final glimpses of vibrant pink and orange glowing edges, giving way to the more subdued though equally exquisite luminous streaks that blanketed the earth with its caresses. This was the time that Robert and the others of his kind awakened. The naturalness of their melding into the darkness, sightless and soundless to those who would have mistakenly crossed their paths as they hovered within the misty darkness had maintained the secrecy of their presence for many hundreds of years. Though to be honest, humans were quite unobservant as they dashed here and there with their lives a chaotic mass of meetings and chores. But it was more than that. Most human's instinct was to shy away from what they didn't understand. It was a source of amusement to the wanderers as they were glanced at before the pair of eyes would go blank with denial. They were always there- searching-always searching.

His powers had grown exponentially beyond measure after six hundred years of existence. Perhaps it also had something to do with this planet the gateway had sent them to, he wasn't sure. What he did know was that he and the other four elders were far greater than any wanderer they had ever known; on either planet. Though, he thought as his head tilted, the almost ripping of her mind had the flavor of one just as old as he. Robert was confident that few-if any had the courage, or strength to challenge him. He was one of the original five-an Elder, existing within the sanctuary of dark. Elders had always been the strongest; the most talented, and the very best their kind had to offer. Sent here by their Creator as their world crumbled, becoming nothing more than a reminder of how precious life was. Death and destruction left the once beauteous planet in tatters. Individually they were a formidable adversary; together-indomitable-

and right now, he needed indomitable. No wanderer would be reckless enough to engage in a full on confrontation-until now. Rebecca's calling was far too potent to ignore. He was confident that small groups of young ones would band together, tossing down the gauntlet of challenge, or worse, simply taking what they desired-Rebecca. A low deep feral growl emerged at the image he could foresee. She was his and no one foolish enough to cross his path would live to see another night.

The girl must be guarded until Robert was ready to meet in her world and then to draw Rebecca into his world-if she would. It was time. Slowly closing his eyes he reached out with his mind to the other elders. The final talent gifted upon reaching the status of an elder, telecommunication; one he was now grateful for. While seeking them, calling up their visual images, the resonance of her calling recoiled back to him by those he considered friends. Naturally they would be drawn to her sonnet, not nearly as strongly as he, but enough to have garnered their attention. Already assembled, they had been anxiously awaiting Robert's connection. Answers were required-decisions made without preamble.

"We are here, Robert," the second eldest responded. He grimaced as he listened to the choked sound in his friend's husky voice.

"Yes my old friend, she is that powerful. "

After all these years, there were still moments it felt awkward to address one by a given name rather than simply elder. He would have chuckled at the familiarity humans had towards one another had he not been so concerned with the danger Rebecca was in. Perhaps in some facets it was far more evolved-less structured than their origins, but to have been witness to the ending of their beloved world he felt obligated to hold onto large parts of his heritage.

The opening of the portal was a rarity that only the five Elders remembered. Having earned the right to bear the title, it was reasonable that those of lower status refer to he, and the others as Elder, regardless of which planet they resided.

Only the five that had borne witness to the mass destruction; the hatred, could document the occurrence in the pages of their history journals. The Youngers- those created on this earth; or those who had found the means to cross through the portal were vastly underpowered. Without the memories of their world; without training, they often needed to reside in groups to eke out survival. On many occasions they had reached out to those younger, offering their teachings. But to no avail. It was different here; less structured and far less formal.

The elders had no need to converge in groups. They fed less. It took much less energy to sustain them opposed to young ones. Contentment flowed within them; aside from their search, with life spent deep in the shadows. It had been more than five years, Robert counted back, when he last saw his old friends. It would be good to see them again, to feel their powers combine.

"I need you to come here, to the median house, "Robert spoke to each. "It is," he paused, an unusual feeling to be back where we first entered this world. She is far too powerful right now. You can all feel her; almost as strongly as I, but as elders you will have the power to resist. The young will not. I believe she is a rare- we must care for her until our souls unite. "

"I have said for some years now, Robert," Markus chided, "that we would sooner or later have to take to task the young ones for their misdeeds. "

A sigh escaped. "I know. Though you and the others have understood the reluctance, Markus," Robert paused. "With so few of us left, we had all remained optimistic that they would reach out to us as others had. Allow them to be guided instead of becoming soulless feeders. Those that we have trained are functioning well. The sharing of our memories with them-the methods and structure from our world has garnered amazing results. They grow in both skill and intelligence. "

"It has not happened, not with the newer ones." Another voice echoed in his mind, this one sounding almost weary.

"I know Giles," Robert responded. "We will hold council when you all arrive," Robert heard the affirmatives. "Come quickly. She has been touched, probed by another Elder, my friends, one that appears to be as old as we. This however was not a gentle probing. He has" Robert paused, "it seems as though he has tried to strip her mind, to pull it back and absorb it."

"We are leaving now," Jerard reassured Robert though he himself could never recall having felt a siren song so strongly. She was indeed a caller, he was certain of it, which meant until she and Robert united, there would be nothing but discord and mayhem.

The moment Robert gazed upon her innocent sleeping form, he knew. This was the one; he was sure enough to stake his life on it. His mate was here; he felt it deep inside.

The danger was real. Those like him, and there were very few left, knew the risks a wanderer took when they have found their mate. It was all or nothing. One or both would cease to exist were things to end badly. Robert believed however, that he was finally, after more than six hundred years, willing to take the risk. He had waited far too many years, drifting through others dreams, seeking and searching, to not be with the one that was his mate. The question was- would she also be willing. Was Rebecca strong enough to accept what he was, who he was and what he had done? Could she accept the invasive manner in which he had found her? Only now was he beginning to comprehend the power that lay dormant within her. The combination between his power and hers was incomprehensible to him. Just how they would combine he wasn't sure, but he did know there was no escape for her from his kind; should she reject him, the young ones would find her.

Drawn towards her house as she whispered silent pleas for fulfillment, he allowed his gaze to linger as he recalled her reactions this evening. Easily he could see the tiny figure barely hiding behind the curtain, brimming with curiosity. Robert chuckled as he pulled up in his all too fancy vehicle. Driving seemed incredibly sedate in comparison to his usual mode of transportation. All the boredom of driving melted away as wide beautiful green eyes settled on him. Fatigue showed within the shimmering depths- but oh the secrets they held. They spoke to him, volumes of hidden layers wrapped tightly inside the saucy veneer she presented. A smile etched across his lips as he exited the vehicle, stretching to his full six foot two height, deep hypnotic eyes never leaving hers. He rendered her motionless with his dark compelling look, gazing deep inside; seeing what she was, and feeling her needs and desires as they echoed his own. His smile grew as he saw the pink hue creeping beneath her pale flesh, her throat muscles convulse as she swallowed. It was definitely her. She was the one, and she was very, very innocent. Complex, Robert shook his head. To the world she presented a somewhat jaded exterior, yet inside, tucked securely away was an innocence that spoke of a desire to learn; to find the goodness she believed people had. He glanced back, wondering just how susceptible she would be to him since his nightly visits began. Would she realize the connection?

"You are mine Rebecca," he whispered into the night. "Know you will feel every ounce of pleasure you seek; from me-only me." Inky bottomless eyes held hers for a moment longer before releasing them. With each step towards his house, Robert could feel the palpations of her heart, the pulsing of her blood.

The movers had turned on the lights in the old house. He was quick to dim them, finding a slight irritant to his sensitive eyes and flesh. He had no need for the bright artificial lighting. He saw more clearly without false illumination or sun, and after six hundred years, Robert preferred the shadows.

"Red," he scoffed as he drank in the gaudy coloring along the walls. Slowly he turned, inspecting the large room with its beautiful original hardwood floors. This well preserved charming space deserved far better than red. "I wonder what the elders would think about picking up a paint brush and a mop." He laughed out loud at the thought before quieting, his thoughts returning to Rebecca and the danger she was in. Everything else would have to wait.

Reluctantly he stepped aside as the moving men struggled in with the heavy furniture. It would have been so much easier; so much quicker were Robert to do it himself, but oh the questions it would raise. Inhuman strength came with many advantages. Unfortunately it also had its downside. Hiding his capabilities was a necessity, not a choice. Some five hundred or so years back, a young wanderer; one without thought or knowledge displayed feats no mortal could possibly accomplish. It came with a price. He was hunted. Night and day a target; finally captured and burned at the stake. For years the rest of his kind were searched for. That legend had served as a warning for all new wanderers, now displaying complete control amongst those who mingled and shared this planet.

He was not, nor had he, or any wanderer, been comfortable around humans. They had a tendency to stare openly, knowing they were different-sensing something before ignoring their thoughts and leaving with a quickness that bordered on rude; wise judgement on their part, perhaps. He preferred life in the shadows, where his thoughts were at their peak and his senses on high alert. Having any other in his home was tantamount to feeling invaded. He had to hold back the laugh at the thought. Invasion, something he and those of his kind did naturally as they wandered from dream to dream, called by the sleeping whispers, the chance, the hope that they would find whom they were meant to be with. As they set his black leather couch, matching chair and ottoman down, Robert wrinkled his nose in disgust. How cliché, he shook his head. Red walls and black leather, add this to the top ten lists of don'ts when seducing a woman, unless she preferred life in a bordello. He moved though to sit in his chair, long thick fingers stroking the pliant cool material.

Oh there was no doubt that Rebecca belonged with him. Robert envisioned her; lying beneath him, bearing the four marks that would bind her to him for eternity. Their souls united, dreams becoming reality; their needs assuaged. It was true that his taste in the bedroom were not those that led to the tame side. Knowing Rebecca dreamed of the same thing only increased the pulsing desire.

He seated himself in his chair once the men left and unfolded his long legs before crossing them at the ankle. As he leaned his head back he closed his eyes, walking the path to her place in his mind. He could hear the whimpers of need, the pull she could sense. He blew a kiss into the night, as soft as a whispered breeze yet with the force of strength that would enter her subconscious.

The language she used would definitely need refining, he chuckled. But that combined with her anger told him all he needed to know as he relaxed one more into his chair. He closed his eyes and imagined her at his side, smiling that radiant smile up to him. Feeling her warm fingers stroke his chilled flesh, his fingers pressing her against his body, sharing a union that would last a lifetime.

He let his eyes drift closed so he could meet her in her dream, to find her, learn about her, train her and finally claim her with his four marks. The fear had dissipated somewhat knowing the others were well on their way. For now he would be able to sense any other presence but it irked that he had to do so. Taking time away from her was not something he wanted at this moment.

He had thought only the shadows would touch her. It was meant to be thus unless he chose it to be otherwise. Rebecca, he rolled the name around in his mind before continuing his thoughts. He would not allow her to hear nor see his face until he was sure she was ready. Robert was risking his life and hers on this. Until she wanted him for what he was. Already she felt him there, this connection, this heady knowledge that within her dream was the man she was meant to be with. He reached out to her. Just a hazy vision for her, and he watched as she jumped slightly in her sleep, startled, afraid yet, something pulled her towards him as though she had been waiting for his arrival.

Robert left her then, somewhat disoriented as he straightened. It has been many, many years since he had created a dream for someone. This one he knew would be difficult. Her subconscious was strong but the need within her even more so. Dawn turned into morning and his body succumbed to the slumber the first rays of light brought.

She woke the next morning as needy as when she had fallen asleep. Becca brushed her hair back from her face, moaning at the pounding in her head. "I had the strangest dream, Felix," she scratched him beneath his chin as he pressed against her. "Can't figure it out though; some man was there, he touched me I'm sure, without touching, and "she paused. And I'm talking to a cat. "My friends are right, I do need a life.'

A long hot soak did nothing to cure the thumping in her head, or the bitch mode she could feel pulsing alongside the headache. She remained in the shower until the water turned cool before finally feeling human enough to step out. Goose bumps covered her flesh and Becca clenched her teeth together while vigorously drying herself to warm up before looking into the mirror. She looked the same, her eyes a little more feverish, but aside from that, rather, uninteresting. Same old as usual she thought, with the exception of her long wild mane of red hair. Quickly she brushed her teeth and hair before opening the cabinet. Tossing back a few Advil was sure to help she thought as she padded back into the bedroom.

After dressing, she bypassed the cat, making her way into the kitchen, calling Felix as she filled his bowl with fresh food and water. "Be good today. No more claw marks or I swear I'm having you declawed... and neutered." Turning the lights out she locked the door and headed to her car. She couldn't resist looking towards the house next door. The curiosity was damn near killing her. She still felt the pull that had held her captive last night. It was the house of course that she stared at. It had nothing to with the tall handsome man with the incredible fuck me eyes; nope not at all. Purposely Becca turned her head away as she fumbled with the keys to her car. "Don't look, don't look" she coaxed herself while doing her best to ignore her sub conscious as it drooled and whispered look, look. "

A chill raced up her spine as she moved to insert the key into the lock, hearing the deep and oh so masculine voice from behind. It startled her enough that she jumped and dropped her keys. "What the hell!" she exclaimed as she spun around, her mouth opening wide before snapping shut. It was him. Glorious in the morning as well as night she noted. Becca swallowed; once-twice and then a third time before remembering how to speak. "Get a grip, girl" she scolded herself as she pasted a smile on her face. Risking a quick glance upwards, wanting nothing more than to see if she had been correct in the deep onyx color of his eyes that had held her immobile. Instead she found instead a pair of reflective dark sunglasses that shielded not only his eyes but downwards along the upper curve of his cheekbones. "Damn it." She blushed as she looked down again.

His laugh was as mesmerizing as the rest of him, Becca mused as she tilted her head. What did he find so amusing, she wondered; quite sure the answer would be she. She couldn't' help the blush that stained her cheeks as she bent to retrieve her keys, shivering as his fingers glided over hers as he bent to do the same. She rose quickly, knocking him under the chin in her haste to put some distance between them. The image of jumping the man in the middle of the street was growing more delightful by the moment. The thought of feeling this incredibly hot man against her caused the blush to grow even more deeply. She leaned against the car, an awkward smile turning her lips upwards as she fumbled for the door to the car, opening it as she choked out a thank you.

"Robert is the name" he held out his hand as he introduced himself. Becca looked at his large hand and then down to hers, wondering how it would look if she wiped the sweat from her hand first. God she felt like an idiot standing there. It was of course entirely his fault.

Bastard, she mused. The thought gave her comfort and some spirit. She placed her hand in his for just a moment, pulling back when she felt the electricity flow through her. It felt so familiar to her. Something she just couldn't place. His hand felt so cool to the touch she noted. Not clammy, just. Cool, thin, and much unexpected. She had assumed as tall and muscular as he was, that his grip would be firm, hands and body, she had to add the latter in there, warm and the skin roughened from work.

"And you are..? " Robert prompted, stifling a laugh as he watched her squirm. He could smell the familiar scent that was Rebecca, and he felt the same electricity as it flowed between them. Her rapidly beating heart pounded a thundering that spoke of need and desire. His nostrils flared to inhale her scent again as he waited.

"Becca, well Rebecca but everyone calls me Becca". She snapped her lips closed, frowning as she tried to figure out where her senses had gone. This was not turning out to be a good first impression meeting. She had rather hoped it would have included margaritas in her back yard while sunbathing, or having sex, whichever came first. She blushed again at her wayward thoughts and looked away, fervently wishing he would remove those dark sunglasses so she could see those beautiful eyes again.

"I'm your new neighbour," Robert stepped a little closer, invading her space intentionally. She nodded as she backed up, pressing against the car, wincing at she felt the heat against her pert ass. She held herself there, pretending not to notice the exterior of the vehicle had a temperature far hotter than was comfortable. "Stupid sun" she muttered as she began to wiggle slightly.

He couldn't contain his laughter. She was priceless, she was perfect, and she was without a doubt going to be his. Tongue in cheek he enquired. "Is something wrong, its Becca, right?

"Hot," she mumbled, blushing as she inched forward, "the car I mean, not you, well not that you aren't hot, but…" Becca clenched her lips tightly closed She already felt like a blushing virgin. Any thought of pressing her body against his was not a good idea at the moment. "Asshole" she whispered under her breath as she turned her head up and offered a fake smile. "Pleasure to meet you, Welcome to the neighbourhood and all that," She was babbling again she noted as she opened the car and entered. "Have a great day. "She called out as she opened the window for air. It was stifling inside.

Chapter 3

As soon as he was out of sight, Becca desperately tried to compose herself. Flushed, aggravated, and burning with humiliation in regards to the unexpected confrontation, she reached forward, pushing the button on the air conditioner to high. Frigid air blasted her face, easing the redness though she doubted anything would lesson her internal temperature. Images of pouncing the 'oh to sexy for his own good, neighbor' flitted through her mind again. Becca lifted the thick strands of hair that clung to her neck, shivering as the icy air whispered against the thin film of perspiration like a gentle breath, her sub conscious continued taunting her with tempting reflections of him, in oh such delicious positions. She increased her speed exponentially, not allowing for the opportunity to turn the car around and return home. "Nope, not going back, maybe never," she grumbled, wondering how big a fool she had actually appeared this morning. "Well shit," she dropped her hair, feeling it swing loosely around her shoulders and down her bare arms. "Maybe sell the house now," she mused while tapping her nails on the leather steering wheel. "Certainly can't meet him again. " Becca spoke the words aloud, while focusing through the painful twisting in her gut at the notion of never seeing his beautiful face again.

"What is it about him that makes me squirm like a long tailed cat in a room full of rocking chairs?" She wondered. Okay, sure, he was gorgeous and jumping him, a few dozen times had crossed her mind, but that was no excuse for losing what was left of her mind when he was within sniffing distance. Becca shuddered. He scent really was unique though, unlike anything she had inhaled before. It smelled as if summer reflected from him; like sunshine if, you could describe the aroma of sunshine.

She grunted as flooding sensations of heat reignited, circulating inside again. Lord, she wanted the man; even just for a few hours. Shoe shopping, Becca purred. What could possibly be a more agreeable distraction than finding that new pair of "do me" shoes? Nothing soothed frazzled nerves more quickly than inhaling the scent of leather in a shoe store, and feeling the suppleness mold itself to your feet. Becca sped to her favorite shoe store. Relaxing now that she had a destination in mind; a plan, she grinned, feeling very pleased with herself, knowing the purchase would be frivolous , would put a dent in her savings account, but a girl could never have too many pairs of shoes. After finding a parking spot, she almost bounced into the store, taking her time to peruse the shelves before deciding on a pair that comprised of all the qualities she had been thinking of. She stroked the black leather, savoring the well worked material against her fingers before slipping her feet into a pair of beautiful patent high heel open toed shoes with a gorgeous bow centered along the top by the toes. Balancing herself on the far too high of a heel, she pivoted while standing in front of the mirror. Glimmering eyes wandered downwards taking in the length of her legs, the nearly perfect shape the heels provided her calves. Becca felt all the tension melt away as she pirouetted slowly, glancing at the reflection from each angle. This was definitely one of the most enjoyable forms of stress relief. So what if she could only wear them for an hour before regretting the purchase. That hour would be more than worth it. Especially if "Mr. too good looking for my sanity" happened to see her in them, she blushed as her sub conscious whispered, "And only in the shoes, perhaps with your legs draped over his shoulders.' She grimaced and blushed at her wayward thoughts while paying for her purchase.

As tempting as it was to wear them home, she placed the bag in the back seat and continued with her errands, pausing occasionally to chat with acquaintances she happened to bump into. Finally finished, Becca parked across the street from her favorite little coffee shop. Smiling a greeting to the sever she ordered the usual, strong black coffee, and a muffin. Nodding her thanks, she sat at the table closest to the air conditioning vents. Picking away at the muffin Becca glanced at her watch, hoping she had been able to stall long enough to forgo a repeat meeting of this morning. With any luck, he would be off doing who knows what with who knew who. Becca snorted at the thought, placing the remainder of her muffin back on the plate, suddenly losing what little appetite she had.

"Damn it," Becca growled, "He is ruining my day." Tucking spiral curls behind her ears, she grabbed her purse, frustration displayed in each simple motion; bracing herself she left the shop, still staggering slightly as the hot, humid air assaulted her. "Ugh, "she muttered, "It's never this hot in Timmins." Suddenly she really missed everyone. Perhaps it was time for a visit. A smile lit up her face, imaging everyone sitting on the large dock at the cottage, staring across at the waterfalls, sipping on a drink. Just laughing and talking, catching up with all she had missed. Longing surged through her for home. Soon, she promised herself, soon she would go home. Digging the keys out of her purse she crossed the street, quickly unlocked the doors, sliding in, eager to start the car and the cool air "Why him," she muttered a word that would have made her crass fellow reporters proud of her. "Why, what is it about him?" Leaning back, Becca closed her eyes, shuddering as the sensation of Robert enveloped her again. The unique aroma was all she could smell. It invaded her senses as it crawled along her flesh.

"Get the hell out of my head!" Becca yelled furiously, suddenly realizing someone was watching her. "Ugh Jerk! It was of course Robert's fault. She just didn't know how yet, but Becca was quite sure she would find a reason. Offering an awkward wave towards the man staring, fighting waves of embarrassment at being caught talking to herself. "Could this day get any worse," she shook her head while putting the vehicle in drive.

"So odd," Becca took a quick glance over her shoulder, seeing the long progression of vehicles passing. Putting on the signal she waited, and waited. Glancing sideways, she gazed unobtrusively at the man, trying to figure out what niggled at her. There was something eerily familiar about him- Robert! A shiver flowed up her spine as she whispered his name. He reminded her of Robert. Tall, the same pale flesh and the same damn dark glasses that allowed no glimpse of his eyes. Pushing the button on the side of the door, she locked the doors, feeling somewhat comforted with the loud click. The man was quickly climbing the list of her creepy scale. "Shoo," she waved him away while trying to ignore the quickly increasing flash of concern that bellowed huge warnings inside.

Becca nibbled on her lip as she rubbed the goose bumps that covered her tanned flesh. Angry green eyes narrowed. Now she was getting a little pissed. The thought of giving him the finger popped into her mind, but she hesitated. Better not to provoke the motionless interloper that continued to stare. Choosing instead to ignore him, Becca turned to check the traffic again, lifting her foot from the brake pedal, relieved at the slight break in traffic, only to slam it down again as the man positioned himself directly in front of her vehicle. The creepy meter began to chime loudly in her head. Naturally, it had to be the "I'm creeped out feeling" that would be the first sensation within the past twenty-four hours that had absolutely nothing to do with her new neighbor- and finding out if he looked as good naked as he did dressed.

She offered her best 'get the hell out of my way or I'll run you over, look' while lifting her foot to let the car roll forward an inch. Did he not realize how close he had come to being a part of her fender? Thoughts of Robert were making her a little mad; enough that she had acted like a start struck virgin this morning. What was surprising, she noted, was the surge of anger now directed towards the stranger. No, Becca thought; she was straight up pissed. He was killing her buzz Damn it.

The stranger began to inch closer; his steps slow and purposeful, his stance predatory-menacing causing her to shiver in fear. Becca swallowed, her foot still depressing the brake but itching to move to the gas pedal. A quick glance around let her know there was no other witnesses in the vicinity. Perhaps he did want to become a new hood ornament, but she was quite sure the insurance company wouldn't find it fitting. Again she waved, this time signaling for him to step away from her car.

In the few seconds it took to gesture to the man, Becca tensed and then screamed at the sense of total invasion. A battle had begun to rage within her mind. She could feel the tension rising exponentially. An image of threatening stances, black eyes and frightening growling noises rolled through her, knocking her back against the headrest. Fresh stabbing pain inside of her head had her clutching her stomach before doubling over. Nothing made sense, just paralyzing fear and pain. Both crashing inside, working in tandem to overwhelm her. From a hazy distance, she could hear pain filled echoes of screaming. It took a moment to realize it was her. Terror caused shaking through her tense limbs. Panicked, Becca reached to open the door, listening to impulse that yelled run. Bile filled her throat as pain encompassed her head; harsh needle like stabbing that increased in precision and volume as she began to thrash. The car rolled forward as she curled into a ball, rocking in her seat. Her face blanched, tears streaked down, mingling with the sweat that dotted her flesh. Opening her wide terrified eyes did nothing to help. Becca's vision was hazy, barely able to see a foot in front of her, but she felt the jolt as the car struck the man standing in front of it-she didn't care.

Robert's scent filtered inside the car, filling it with a reassurance that she was not alone. She struggled against the nausea to inhale, finding it strangely comforting. She reached to brush the tears that streaked down her cheeks, shrieking as another stabbing pain pushed through her mind. Shaking hands clutched at her head, tugging on her hair, doing her best to create a different sensory pain. "What's happening?" Becca whimpered, "Please, someone help me." Her throat was dry, her voice nothing more than a pitiful ragged sound as she pleaded.

Movement to her left caught her attention. The stranger was trying to take another step forward. Anger etched along his features, turning what she had thought was handsome to a hideous pale opposite of what he first appeared. Gaunt, rigid with frustration, his cheeks hollowed as he inhaled. He stopped abruptly as though hitting a brick wall. The needle sharp pain in her head began again, this time less centered. It felt as though she was being probed from all directions. Passing out became a distinct possibility as she began to sway in the seat. "Shit." Becca moaned at the agonizing, invasive sensation travelled. "Help," she tried to scream. The word croaked from her aching throat nothing but a tormented scratchy sound escaped. Her head rested on the console, swollen tear filled eyes closing. Becca was succumbing to the pain. Darkness crept along the edges of her mind before she felt a sudden insight, a brief clearing of her vision.

Pain filled eyes quickly turned upwards as blissful emptiness soothed the thundering misery within her head. It took mere seconds to realize the man she had hit was gone and her vehicle was rolling forward straight into the car parked in front of hers.

Drive, a strong dominant voice commanded. Immediately she complied, needing no further prompting. Her foot punched the gas pedal; she ignored the angry honking from behind her as she weaved into traffic. The further from the stranger, the less powerful the pounding became. Home, just get me home, she prayed as she forced herself to drive.

Becca rubbed her head; still feeling the remains of the excruciating sensations that had engulfed her just moments before. Wiping away the wetness from her eyes, she slowed the vehicle, realizing how far over the speed limit she was. Fatigue plagued her as she drove on auto pilot, following the familiar route that would take her to safety. A thick fog hung heavily within her mind; all she could think of was getting home. She would be making a doctor's appointment first thing in the morning. Having never felt such an instant, agonizing pain before, Becca firmly believed she was dying. The trembling began to subside as the stabbing sensations finally abated. Maybe it was a stroke; worriedly she chewed her lower lip.

Still dazed and more than a little disoriented she parked the car and trudged into the house. Weaving, each step more painful than the last. Her legs quivered and her head felt like it was about to explode. Dropping the packages on the floor she staggered towards her bedroom. Felix purred at her feet and she reached down to pick him up, thankful for the distraction. Nuzzling her nose in his fur, she carried him with her, curling up in a ball, not even bothering to undress. Exhaustion claimed her- she just wanted to rest. A few more tears slipped unnoticed from her eyes as she closed them. Sleep held her in its soothing grasp in moments.

The growl escaped as Robert felt her body succumb to sleep. She had been lucky today. How the young one had the power to remain out in the day, to act so brazen, so open had him very confused. It had taken much of his self-control to keep the lad from claiming her. Now he paced, waiting, his senses on high alert. Onyx eyes shimmered with a ferocity that lay deep within him, turning them a disturbing, threatening black, the irises disappearing.

"Thank you Jerard," Robert felt weak as he spoke. "Your quick actions spared her. I don't know how much longer I could have kept him from finding his way inside."

"We come," Leonard, thought the words having no need to whisper.

"He was not normal," Jerard spoke softly, his breathing even as he raced to the house.

"The girl must be marked, Robert. You know this. "Giles's voice was softer, more compassionate, which was ironic as he was the more hardened of all the elders.

"No," Robert hissed. "She must come willingly. This must be her choice. I cannot take her fully and bond without her consent. You all understand that she would only have half a life." He curled his hands into fists as he worked to control his emotions. "She would forever remain in the flux she is now. Neither content in waking hours or sleep."

46

"Does she mean this much to you, Robert" Markus questioned, "that you cannot settle for being with her at night? We have all felt the desire and the need," he continued before Robert could respond. "The possession she craves touches us all."

The loud growl cut off the remainder of his words though a soft chuckle clearly rang in the background.

"There is nothing amusing about this Leonard," Robert snarled.

The chuckle grew in sound and he was grateful Leonard was not within close proximity at the moment.

"You have it bad, my friend," Jerard worked to control the tone of his voice though it was anything but easy. Six hundred years of weaving through dreams, searching, seeking the specific woman they were destined to bond with, to control, and Robert finds a seeker, a caller "Only you, Robert" Jerard whispered as he streaked between the shadows, moving more quickly than a normal person could comprehend, or see.

Like a door closing, Robert shut off the others, feeling calmer knowing they would soon be here. His attention turned back to Rebecca. He whispered her name, savoring how easily it trailed from his tongue. He could almost taste her and arousal stirred as he saw her restless dream state. Going to her as natural as breathing to him and he needed her right now. To know she was alright. To know she was unharmed, untouched by the events of this afternoon.

Even in sleep, Becca felt like she was not alone. He was there-waiting for her; in the dark, shrouded by shadows- alive within them. Her heart began to hammer, a husky whimper escaped as tingling fear spread through her. Memories of earlier, of the pale man, watching; waiting, wove their way into her dream, remaining no matter how hard she tried to break free. Finally a more powerful image replaced the haunting memory; Robert's beautiful perfection. She didn't care why-or how, she was simply grateful for a slice of peace.

Gut instinct prodded Becca, advising her of another presence. Shaking fingers clutched at the sheet, drawing it up to cover herself. The sense of modesty was touching to Robert while confusing at the same time.

"Why do you hide your beauty?" A voice spoke from the darkness.

It was the first time the entity she felt had ever spoken. "Who are you?" Becca thrust aside fear to seek that which she needed most-answers. Screaming would come after, once she could comprehend the meaning of her dream.

Straining to see beyond the shadows; searching for what she felt yet could not see, tested what little patience remained. Growling with frustration, Becca turned over, studiously ignoring what she now thought of as a disturbance in her dream.

"I am your darkness. I am what you crave the most, little one. I am what you really dream of yet hide from reality.'

"Okay wake up; anytime now, wakie, wakie," Becca urged her subconscious, guessing correctly that this dream scenario would be far too intriguing, far too dangerous- far too stimulating for her to walk away from.

"Why are you here?" her voice though meant to sound firm and controlled rolled past her lips as the exact opposite. It was erotic, laced with undertones that belied the deep torrent of emotions that overwhelmed her senses.

"You called me to you, Rebecca. Every night you screamed your needs as you slept, allowing them freedom within your dreams. Even now, you don't fear me, Rebecca. I hear the wild beating of your heart, feel the quickening of your pulse, and I can taste pleasure within your mind. You seek what I am- what I know." Again, Robert inhaled, parting his lips as though he were able to capture each scent, each essence on his tongue. "You wonder what I am, Rebecca, ahh yes, it intrigues the spirit lying dormant inside. Danger lurks; you sense it Rebecca, and yet you are doubtful it is from me. Will I kill you- am I a monster, a beast? Though you lay clutching the sheet you ask yourself, is he cold to the touch, or will you feel sensual warmth wrap around you?"

"I," she stumbled and blushed, pulling the sheet up to her chin. "Show yourself- or will you forever lurk amidst the intricate web you have created in shadow? "Becca replied with false bravado, captivating him with the sheer will in which she carried herself. Boldly turning to stare into the darkness where she felt him, offering a smug look as she waited. Always in control Rebecca, now speaking to shadows on the wall-in her dreams. The satiated part of her dream state was joyous at his presence; the logical side was confused and unsure. "Will I wake if I pinch myself in my own dream?" she spoke aloud, turning towards the deep throaty chuckle he responded with. The sound inched along her flesh, touching- breathing life into every crevice. Uncertainty directly followed the spine tingling chuckle. Bracing, she willed her mind to waken; half hoping her pleas were ignored

"I haven't called anyone."

Black eyes now looked upon her. An enigma, he mused, shaking his head in amazement. Rebecca was a caller, one of the rarest in the world to find, and yet she found the strength, the will to refuse in her dreams. He smiled crookedly, enjoying the resistance, knowing when she came to him; it would be because she ached for it as well.

Robert twisted on the seat of the bay window, his senses heightened. Sharply he inhaled, searching for the scent of the young one. He growled, deep, low and long, a warning to the man to leave. As his head tilted, he listened for sounds, direction, motion of clothing that may flutter in the wind, carrying with it the scent and number of young ones.

Restlessness filtered into Becca's dream, a sense of insecurity that caused a hushed whimper to escape. "Please," She whispered as she reached outwards again, somehow knowing where his presence was though still blind to his form.

"Giles," Robert called almost urgently to him. "Outside-I don't know how many but at least one is outside."

"We will search," Giles responded, sensing the real danger.

"Robert,' Markus spoke softly. "She is too powerful. You must mark her tonight. We will be here to help protect the one that matches your soul, but even then, she may be too powerful, her call to pure and sensual to stop the young ones from returning."

"NO" Robert dismissed the words as they slammed through his mind. His shimmering eyes turned back towards Becca, a fierce protective instinct fueling him. He wanted nothing more than to jump out the window and seek the young one. "She cannot be influenced."

"Perhaps," Leonard paused before speaking, choosing his words wisely. Never had they witnessed or felt this level of ire that radiated from Robert. "Perhaps, because of her strength, the first mark will not take away her choice or freedom, Robert. She is a caller, a siren. If I remember correctly they have a resistance."

His knuckles turned white against his already blanched flesh as he closed his eyes, drowning out the sound of their voices and their increased speed. Outside, maybe one hundred and fifty feet from Becca's window was the young one from earlier. Robert could feel him-see him, though he suspected that the young did not have the power yet to feel. Robert turned in the young one's direction, purposely letting his presence to be known, allowing the foolish wanderer to see the ominous, dangerous glowing eyes that were filled with every thought of what would happen if he moved any closer.

"Son of a bitch" he drew his hand through his hair while watching the man step back slightly; giving space without any intent on leaving. Robert cursed again, deep inside he understood, hell, he couldn't resist the call either- though for different reasons. Exasperated by the fool with the death wish, Robert allowed the night to touch him, the moments between him and Becca sullied by the intrusion. Again, he heard her pleas and turned towards her.

The sheets were tangled, and she was writhing. A piercing scream was followed by her fingers dragging through the air at an unseen enemy. Within seconds, he had moved from the window to the bed, reaching forward to grip her by the shoulders. The choice had been taken from him. He could smell the essence from an ill- fated attempt at invading Rebecca's mind-to claim her- albeit a clumsy, foolish and soon a deadly mistake. Becca fought the fear evident as she lashed out and howled.

The sound of his anger echoed through the night. The scent began to dissipate though Robert knew it would be only a short period before he returned. The pull, the need to feed from one so powerful was too great. Still he hesitated. To invade her dream instead of her offering would place the first mark on her. It would bind her to him in ways she would not understand.

"She will be strong enough," Jerard spoke, his voice much closer now. "I can feel the resistance she has to the young one, Robert, and the need and desire for you." He paused. "Robert, the flavor, the scent, it mingles with one as old as we. He is being led, you cannot hesitate any longer."

Robert mulled over the words.

"Listen to us," Markus urged. She will not become half a soul once you give her the mark. She is far too strong, far too sure of her needs and desires. The only thing that will happen is she will be more attracted to you. "

His fingers reached out to tangle in her hair, marveling at the differences; his hand, so light in color, hers so strikingly vibrant and alive. The last word cut him, for it was indeed the crux of the matter. Would she become only half-aware? Would she be one that chose to live life in her dream instead of finding pleasure and joy in both with him? Alternatively, would she hate him and simply leave. The possibility was strong given the determination, the fortitude within her, unfortunately, if that was to occur, they would both suffer the consequences.

"You are not alone," Giles warned. "The young one is not alone. I smell two others flanking either side of him. Mark her now or we will never be able to protect her, Robert. Mark her now as we go after them."

A soft sigh escaped as he nodded. "You are right. Get them, kill if you must be try to bring one back alive. We must know what we are dealing with."

He could almost hear Markus smile as he spoke "on it." The man lived for moments like this. He was a force to be reckoned with, even more so as they crossed the portal to this world.

Robert shook his head, feeling the exhilaration that flowed through the elders as they closed in on their prey. His attention was back with Becca. He soothed her, calming her with gentle touches as he slowly invaded her dream. This time it would be he that guided-she would follow. Resistance was instant as he took control-to push a little harder. Wide ocean green eyes met his, a questioning look. A defiant look, and finally a look of acknowledgment almost saying, what took you so long.

"I am sorry my little one, "he whispered, the words heart felt as he leaned closer to her. "This was not supposed to happen like this but for your safety, I must mark you with the first of four. These you will wear as protection against others."

Words swirled inside her mind, she caught some of them but others were instantly forgotten. Sinfully sultry eyes became half lidded; she offered a beautiful smile, so familiar. Marked? What does he mean marked? Though his nearness calmed and soothed, she was eager. Having never seen; nor touched, anticipation pulled deep inside, pushing past the pain. Lifting her hand towards him, trembling for different reasons now as his chilled flesh closed around her wrist, dragging it above her head.

Held captive, she felt more alive in this dream than she had ever felt in her day hours. He was cold- yet hot, and his scent lingered in her mind as it had in the car earlier that day.

"Those that try to touch your mind through your dreams will feel and see my marks, little one. I am hopeful that will keep you safe until... "He cut the words off as the noises from outside captured his attention. A grim smile replaced the frown. They would wait for him; he knew this as he turned back to her angelic face.

His eyes remained opened, focused on her breathing while merging his entire form into her dream. He heard her gasp and pull away, trying to turn from the invasion. "I will not harm you, nor hurt you, little one, until you wish to feel my full marks. " He leaned forward, placing his lips to hers.

Hunger rose like a tidal wave, washing over them both. Only six hundred years of self-control stopped him from consummating their union right there. He tasted her, invaded her mouth with his tongue, moaning as he felt her eager response, the way her body rose in surrender as she succumbed. The kiss lingered; long, passionate-filled with promise and hidden delights that had taunted her so many nights in her dreams.

Finally, he pulled back, his breathing ragged. Lowering his head again, Robert trailed his cool tongue down to the slope of her breast, causing goose bumps to prickle along her flesh, warring with the streaks of heat that flowed through. Parting his lips, Robert suckled on the flesh just above the perfect mound. "I'm sorry," the words mumbled as he increased the pressure until he left a perfect circular shape on her flesh-teeth marks clearly imprinted in the center.

It was done. Reluctantly he pulled back from her dream, feeling her fighting to keep him there before the weightlessness of fatigue consumed the remainder of her strength. Morning would bring some reminders but for now, she would sleep peacefully while he tended to... Other matters

Chapter 4

The distinct sound of male laughter echoed through his mind before he snapped the door closed to them. At the rate they were going it would be fifty years before he saw any of them again. Robert smirked, hoping they heard that particular thought as he lifted the latch that led to the basement.

Stairs that would normally creak from age were soundless as he launched himself downward. There was afresh eagerness to speak with those that threatened Rebecca-his beautiful Rebecca. He could smell the stench of fear but another essence also lingered in the air. He tilted his head and inhaled- arrogance that was the flavor. His brows furrowed as he turned his gaze towards the other elders, those who for more than six hundred years he had considered his friends.

Handshakes ensued-a custom they had mirrored from witnessing others.

"Have you learned anything useful?" Robert tilted his head towards the three young ones, skillfully bound and silent. Intimidation was a powerful tool when dealing with those who were hundreds of years there junior.

"Unusual," Leonard replied. "They were more than a little surprised to see us. It appears their senses are limited to feeling dreams-or taking orders. They had no clue we were approaching. Though its true we closed in quickly, any of our kind should have been able to pick up our scent or feel our presence. It's almost as though they are a wanderer and yet-not one."

"It wasn't until we were close," Giles continued, his eyes almost blank as he recalled each movement the three young ones had made. "And it was instant, Robert. Not individualized 'get the hell out of here' motions, but a clarity of insight apparently gifted to the three at once." His eyes cleared as he turned. "They couldn't sense us- we were sure of that; remaining upwind so our scent was undetected. Even so," Giles looked confused, "they should have been able to feel us. I would judge them to be at least one hundred and fifty years, yet they exist without senses, and suddenly in synchronization they moved as though one person.

A derisive snort sounded from Markus. The young ones glanced over; strangled fear etched across their already ashen faces, though within the depth of their inky black eyes, there was still something more. "I am far too old to be chasing down these children," Markus's thoughts leaned towards simply killing them, and being done with the entire mess.

Robert paused for effect before turning towards the three. It appeared they had a mystery on their hands. Rummaging through the garbage would take more time than he was willing to give, not when Rebecca's life was at stake. This would take more than any of the three young ones expected or anticipated-death. His eyes blazed, the charcoal color seeping into the whites of his eyes until nothing more but raw intimidating black anger remained. An ominous glow erupted from them as a low feral growl escaped passed his lips. Anger; raw and unleashed filled the room. He could taste madness on his tongue, savored each ounce that radiated from deep within, spreading outwards, engulfing the three, lashing them repeatedly as the furious rage swirled menacingly around the small windowless room.

Frightened, glazed eyes widened as dawning understanding seeped between their arrogant exteriors. Finally, only now at the end did they realize these men were exceptionally powerful, unbelievably more than they had been led to believe. All but one young refused to feel the inevitable panic that filled a body when the inevitability of death gripped them. Though the elders could sense his confidence slip a few notches, he clung to an attitude- one of superiority. Robert found this very confusing. Did he not realize how easily any of the Elders could annihilate him?

He turned menacingly towards the young wanderer who had ruthlessly attempted to capture Rebecca's mind, inching closer-purposely controlling each motion, his steps slow, purposeful; predatory, fueling the fires of fear he could sense buried within the lad. Blazing eyes scrutinized as the young one blanched and swallowed, but made no attempt to retreat, or even lower his stare from the Elder. Stopping mere inches from him, he sneered, revelling in the fresh scent of fear. Betraying no emotion, he digested the confusion finally emanating from the youngster. Some distant memory niggled along the back of his mind; a memory long forgotten. Filing them away for study when they had completed the business at hand, Robert pushed his mind forward into the man he had already fought once-inside Rebecca's mind. The resistance pushing back was weak at best. Levels below him in training and skill, it took mere moments before seeking entry, probing his mind; discovering the world he had originated from

Shocked murmurs echoed through Robert's mind. Instinctively he drew the other Elders in alongside him, reaching out, sharing the vital information he had gathered. One, almost as old as they, had created this young one, granted him marks-enabling him to reach out and speak, to seek guidance.

"Who," they all seemed to question at once. "Who has this power?"

"Separate the other two from this one, "Robert ordered. "Let us see who will be the first to talk- or die." Burning, ruthless eyes remained focused on the three fearful men, wondering which would be the first to break. Such a waste of his kind, he shook his head while watching the Elders manhandle the two, escorting them into another section of the sub-basement. A labyrinth rested beneath the basement. Built hundreds of years ago with layer upon layer of greyish stone, chipped away to fit together. Long forgotten, the walls showed the years of abandon, cracks allowing slivers of light to pulse through, along with infrequent breaths of fresh air. The hinges on the doors had long ago rusted, and spider webs now decorated the ceilings, angling downwards to cling almost lovingly to the weathered stone. Along the right wall were antique wall sconces their contents, half used hand crafted candles, now covered with thick layers of dust and webs. The historian in Giles took great interest in the making of the house, the craftsmanship- but more than that, the very essence of it. The walls all but screamed with the desire to reveal its secrets. He found it more than a little interesting that Becca would choose a house near this one. Any normal human with an ounce of sense would have quickly fled.

Granted the area was beautiful. He could imagine it back a few hundred years, horse and buggy riding along the dirt road with sunlight filtering through the multitude of weeping willow trees that bent their limbs forward to create a canopy. A sense of nostalgia filled him. He longed to go back to those days. Life was simple; a hard day's work for a hard day's pay with family and friends surrounding and helping one another.

He left his revelry as they reached the bottom of the stairwell. The musty odor filtered through before they had opened the latch. Shuddering with true terror, the two men vainly attempted to free themselves-a futile though valiant effort. As Jerard lifted the rusty latch, he pushed the creaking door open with his hip while continuing to grip the young man by his neck. A distinctly foul odor escaped as the door inched slowly open. Dead rats, he presumed, his face scrunching in distaste.

Tossing the new wanderers inside they closed the door quickly, eager to stem the flow of obnoxious fumes that had their eyes watering

They chuckled as they made their way up the stairs, racing up them without taking a breath. There was no need to strain to hear the faint echo of cries and pleading to be released, though it grew faint as they took the last steps to the door. Physical strength and stamina was something vastly different on earth as it was on their world. Here they were vastly stronger than the humans. The Elders could be powerful and deadly when required, which was rare. For the most part, their preference was to remain amongst themselves, searching the nights for their one desire; a soul mate-their soul mate. And right now it was one very powerful siren, the caller that was in jeopardy.

"They are in the very last room in the tunnels," Markus's normally handsome face contorted with a grimace as he continued to hear the distant pitiful sounds from below. He had no compassion for young ones that refused to be guided by the elders. Those that chose to become nomads without training, following barely understood instincts instead of learning their true power and calling deserved nothing from him.

Robert nodded, continuing to hold the gaze of the one young one that remained. He could now sense the fear, taste it, and drank deeply of it. Separating him had worked to an extent but not enough. Whoever controlled him was still managing somehow to maintain contact. Dawn was lurking, and he could hear Becca moaning in her sleep, tossing and turning. He took a moment to enter her dream, ensuring her safety before exiting.

She wasn't safe. All five of the elders grasped the severity of the situation as they listened to her, their stares fixated on the young one. Robert paused and tilted his head, his lips parting as he drew in a breath. He could taste the presence of another. Interesting.

"Did you taste it as well?" Robert questioned while stepping forward to invade what little space had remained between he and the inexperienced wanderer.

"Yes," Markus's brows furrowed as he responded. The scent is old, almost as old as we, but different somehow- as though he controlled not guided. "

Robert nodded as he leaned over the young one, his presence more than a little intimidating, once again breathing in deeply. The scent grew in strength, viler-more hateful. With fingers spread, almost talon like he ripped away the shirt of the young one, inspecting his body, searching for something, anything that would define the mark.

Along the lower left side of his abdomen was the scar Robert sought. It was not ordinary, but one made only by the mark of their kind. He smiled, victorious as he stepped back for the others to inspect.

"He may be almost as old, but it is obvious he has much to learn. His mark is weak and can be easily broken. "Robert declared as he crossed his arms over his chest.

"It would be best to have him speak first before cutting him off from his Master. Once the tie is broken, the young one will not live. Giles spoke in an even tone. He was very matter of fact with the young one's fate.

"Leonard" Robert motioned him forward. You are the most sensitive and knowledgeable in retrieving information before rendering them useless. Is it possible that you can invade his thoughts without sleep, find out whom, find out where and how many are coming for Becca?

A sinister smile played along his lips, turning one side up as he rubbed his hands together to create a friction. Once he began there would be no stopping until it was finished.

"You have one chance, and only one chance to speak and reveal all that you know before being taken to task for the part you have played in this. " Robert turned back to the young one, waiting.

"You can't stop him," the young voice trembled as he straightened in the chair, no longer slumping, almost as though anticipating the end. "There are too many"

Leonard stepped forward, his hands rubbing together so fast it would be impossible for any others to see except those of their kind. It was not something any of the elders enjoyed doing. Ending the life of one of their own kind when so few remained, but rogue young ones, untrained were far more dangerous and would most assuredly turn every rule they were governed by upside down. Wreak havoc, well more havoc than they have already by flitting from dream to dream, feeding, leaving the humans defenseless and without the desire to wake but to feel them again and again in their dreams.

Robert felt Leonard clear his mind of all thought before placing one hand on the side of the young ones face and the other on the center of his chest. As his fingers rested against the temples he began to pour his essence into the man, searching for answers. The hand on the chest, covering the heart would free the soul, or souls that resided within him.

They watched as the young one closed his eyes trying to resist, pulling back. He had the option. He did not have to cease to exist but Leonard knew immediately that whoever controlled this young one would destroy him, should they not do so. His eyes closed as inch by inch he invaded the space within the controlled man, searching through memories, dismissing those that were of little value, and those that were simply revolting to any elder. The abuse of power, he shook his head as he fought to control the urge to simply end it here and now.

"The other Elder that slipped through the portal behind us; just as it was closing," Leonard paused as he pressed his fingers more deeply against the side of his face, "this has to be his work. "I assumed he had died after what happened."

Already the young ones face blanched even more than was natural to them, his eyes turning from onyx to a lighter color as life began to drain.

"The man; he is a collector," Leonard continued. Disgust filled him as it filled the others as they read his thoughts. "It's he that has amassed so many young ones and set them free to do as they wish among the humans." His head shook. "He feels slighted that no one took notice of him. He felt he was above us, we who came here to guide and teach, to find their soul mate and live in peace."

"What does he want," Robert asked through gritted teeth as the young one began to slump, already knowing the answer.

"Becca," He wishes Becca." Leonard whispered. "Their souls do not mate though he does not care. He wishes her for breeding. "The growl slipped from Robert's lips causing Leonardo pause. "He believes he will make a superior breed, one with both siren call and wanderer."

"No" Robert shouted the word. "Name, we must have a name and a location, Leonard."

A mocking laugh filled Leonard's head before the young one closed his eyes for the last time. The scent of the Elder slipped away along with that of the young one, leaving the room a little less cluttered than it had been.

"Benjamin." Leonard sat, feeling very weak after encountering something almost as powerful as he and straining to overcome the resistance. "His name is Benjamin and mark or not, soon he shall come for her.

His eyes turned to meet Robert's. "Time is short. You have only days to make her yours completely. To join your souls within dream and reality or there will be a battle for her. Right now your mark confuses him. He doesn't quite know how to get passed it though he is working on reasoning it out.

"We will watch over Becca" Markus, Giles and Jerard spoke at once. "She will be safe with us until she becomes yours in all ways."

Robert nodded, having already dismissed the young one whose soul was lost, turning his attention to Becca. As he closed his eyes to enter her dream he saw her resting comfortably. His mark was prominently displayed, the perfect symmetrical circle, binding her to him just as the kiss had. Now he had to find a way for her to see him in both worlds; waking and sleeping.

"What do you think we should do with the other two?" Jerard questioned.

"It matters little," Robert pulled himself from Becca's dream, just as she was beginning to stir, turning to his friends. "Let's keep them down there a few days. Perhaps then they will be more agreeable when questioned. Who knows, they may be willing to be guided by us."

"I'm not sure that is such a great idea, Robert" Markus interjected. He paused as Robert turned his eyes up.

"You're Becca; she projects so strongly, her call so powerful and potent, the young ones may have the ability to feed from her. The proximity is so close. "

"He is right, "Giles spoke. "It is going to be a battle to keep her safe without the added two we have here. We have had eons to learn to control our hunger, the need to feed off of others dreams. These ones have never been trained. They are virtually wild, slipping from dream to dream each night, wreaking havoc for some." The frustration was clear.

"I don't take a life, free a soul without cause," Robert glanced towards the door leading below, "though I am sorely tempted to right now. He turned, watching the sun begin to rise over the stalks of corn, signalling the dawn of a new day. Rest would soon be needed, more so for the young ones than for themselves.

"Rest today," Robert smiled as he patted each on the shoulder. "Tonight we can assess. They will have no choice but to sleep, their minds closing… "He stopped mid-sentence. "That is why the young one was out, how he had been able to be out during daylight hours. The marks; "he paused again as he began to pace. "The marks have vastly accentuated their skill. He is allowing those he has marked to feed off of him." Robert turned towards the other elders, his eyes wide, the black again dotting the whites of his eyes as the anger swelled within. "What has this Benjamin done?"

"We will rest three at a time," Leonard offered the solution. Robert nodded his thanks.

"If anyone senses those two awake during the day, kill them. " Robert's voice was cold as he spoke. There was no room for forgiveness or redemption, not with Becca's life at stake. No, no one would harm her. She was his.

Chapter 5

The moments between slumber and dawning awakening seemed the most confusing. Becca rolled onto her side, drawing her legs up as she moved. Her hand rested beneath her cheek, refusing to open her eyes and face the day. A ragged moan spilled from her lips as she visualized the dream; it had felt so real, his breath warm against her skin, his lips moist and gentle. She shuddered, pressing her eyes firmly shut, willing herself to sleep just a little longer. Would he be there waiting for her? That voice-so sensual it caused the hair on her arms to stand up and goose bumps to spiral downwards to her feet. Her toes curled in response to her thoughts as she felt the heat begin to radiate through her curled form.

It was Felix who decided her fate this morning. Hopping on the bed as though he owned it and was simply allowing her to borrow it, he crept up from the side, staring at the miniscule motion of her toes. His tail swished back and forth as his muscles poised to spring. With the grace of a young kitten, he pounced, digging his claws into her toes.

"Shit!" she sat up, yelping at the sting. Brushing the hair from her face she glared down at Felix who in turn looked back at her with the perfect expression of innocence. With a sigh she reached down, gathering him into her arms after disengaging his claws from the blanket. "Bad kitty," her voice was sleepy, distracted- her mind focused on the dream.

Absently she scratched Felix beneath his chin, eliciting a deep contented purr from the cat that apparently ruled the house. With her free hand, she traced her fingers along first her lower, then upper lip. In perfect detail she recalled the crushing, dominating, and exquisitely sexual kiss he'd stolen from her last night. It consumed her with desire as it offered a taste of heaven- perhaps hell. It was a dream after all. She moaned softly knowing it was the type of kiss she had always envisioned. A kiss that was forceful as his tongue parted her lips and took what she so eagerly offered. She paused in her exploration, sleepy eyes opening widely as the swollen flesh tingled. "Strange," dropping her hand to trail her tongue along them, half expecting the dream man's taste to have lingered. A stab of disappointment swept through her as she tasted, well- nothing. A soft sigh escaped as she nudged Felix aside, earning a hiss in return. "Must have bitten them, Felix;" Becca licked her lips again. "That was one hell of a kiss."

Stretching as she made her way into the bathroom firmly closed the door on her much uncoordinated cat. Showering with Felix was not on the top ten lists of things she wanted to repeat-ever. She still bore the marks from the last encounter when he slipped into the tub while she showered. She paused midway in reaching for the faucets. "Marked," She thought, "marked." Mr. Dream Lover had mentioned marked. What was it, what the hell was it about?" She strained to remember while turning the water on, absently checking the temperature before stepping beneath the hot flowing water.

Enjoyment of a shower was something she had luxuriated in for years after growing up with two sisters as it often meant short, luke warm showers. Becca had never lost the love for the sensation of the hot water cascading over her body, the pin prickle sensations as she set the shower head to massage. Tilting her head back so the water would soak her unruly hair, she reached for the shampoo. Steam, along with the fresh scent of strawberries filled the bathroom. She inhaled, the water pulsing along her back loosening tense muscles as she rinsed her hair before applying conditioner. Blindly she reached for the loofa, turning to soak the front of her body as she began to briskly scrub; turning her pale flesh red, attempting to scrub away memories from last night.

A high pitched yelp escaped as the loofa scraped along her chest. Pain filtered through the haze of scents, steam, and relaxation to stab at her brain. The loofa slipped from her hand as she looked down.

Hell that had been a dream, Becca shook her head as she traced the outline. "What the hell," She sputtered as her eyes followed the circular indentation. The reddish marks felt like a tattoo. This was no hickey and certainly not something she could; or would have done herself. Pure, raw fear choked her, chasing away other thoughts. She began to shake, sinking to the bottom of the tub; drawing her knees up to rest her cheek upon them as she closed her eyes. As steaming water poured over her still form, she scanned her memory; forcing every detail from last night to present itself.

He had been with her; but he was always there- she dismissed that notion. He was last night, as he was each night; demanding, pushing-testing her limits. Never before had he touched her however. Always he had been nothing more than a sliver of light amongst her darkness. Trembling fingers rose to circle her lips again, realization dawning that she had not bitten them in her sleep- they were swollen from a kiss, a real kiss amidst her peaceful slumber. She fought the urge to run and ensure the doors were locked, inhaling sharply as she chastised herself. Of course they were locked. In the remote area she lived with just the one house up the hill she always locked the doors. It would be far too easy for something to happen to a woman who lived alone with just a cat that didn't have enough balance to stay along the edge of the tub.

Terrified, she reached for the loofa, adding a large amount of soap before scrubbing at her flesh until it was raw, attempting to rid her of the raised mark. "No, no," Becca growled as she scraped at it with her fingers, succeeding only in causing the fresh redness to send searing pain through her body. The water turned cold before she was willing to concede. Turning the faucets off, she crawled to the edge of the tub and reach for a towel. Fingers wrinkled from the water trembled; her entire body shook with fear, cold and the inability to comprehend what the hell had happened.

It was long moments before realizing her teeth were chattering. She wrapped a towel around her long hair before reaching for another to cover her goose bumped skin. She was afraid to look in the mirror as she moved to the sink; willing her hands to wipe away the steam marks. She had to see-she had to. The compulsion was stronger than the fear and revulsion that turned her stomach. Her image seemed the same with the exception of her eyes. Wide with fear and confusion, her cheeks flushed from the shower and heat. Hesitantly Becca dropped her eyes, alarmed to see her already pouty lips were indeed swollen and red-an almost raw quality to their texture. It just wasn't possible! It had been a dream-nothing more.

She scrambled back until her legs bumped into the tub, her eyes not leaving the image of the frightened woman in the mirror. Her hand raised, mesmerized as she watched the silhouette mimic each movement. Long nails with a freshly applied French manicure traced her bottom lip as she parted them. They tingled as if the kiss had happened mere moments ago. A kiss that had truly occurred within her dream; yet in her reality, not possible and yet... she not only felt, but witnessed the evidence. Willing her fingers to drop the towel she held in a white knuckled grip. There was no option, though frantically she searched for one. Becca had to know; to see for herself what was causing the stinging throbs of pain.

Steeling herself; closing her eyes as she forced her fingers to release their grip, feeling the wet towel slither downwards. Taking deep shuddering breathes she stood naked in front of the mirror

Seconds or perhaps moments, felt like a lifetime as she worked up the courage to open her eyes. Before her; looking back with the same wild eyes of fear, stood a woman that many would consider beautiful. Granted though small in stature, she was tall in determination. Long tendrils of russet hair draped tantalizing over her pale flesh, leaving water droplets to trail intricately down her chest before falling onto her belly. Slowly, achingly slowly, the drops weaved their way downwards. She fixated on each bead; focusing on the change of temperature, distancing herself from her real goal.

"Okay," She gave herself a pep talk. "You are no chicken shit." Yeah you are, her subconscious whispered, already cowering in a corner.

68

Becca snorted as she reached for the countertop, clasping her fingers around the edge with a death grip as her dark green eyes began the slow trek upwards. Each breath began to hurt as she warred with herself. Only sheer force of will kept her from running naked out of the house screaming.

Amidst the red, now raw flesh caused by scraping and rubbing; was indeed a mark. It was perfect, circular; darkish in color; not red as she had first imagined. She couldn't breathe. Panic closed her throat, causing her legs to give out. She sank to the floor clutching her breast, ignoring the stinging sensation from the scrubbing. Tears, thick and hot leaked from frantic eyes as she fought to breathe- to remember. She knew the mark had been given during her dream. He had been there night after night for months; watching over her, tormenting and teasing her. He had been attempting to guide her towards that which she had secretly fantasized about; wished about- hell dreamed about.

Impossible. Just impossible, Becca shook her head as she rose; turning from the mirror, refusing to bear witness to the truth once again. Something was wrong; very, very wrong. Her thoughts turned to Robert, the new neighbour, the tormentor in her waking hours. "Fucking great," she mumbled as she landed face down on the bed. She pulled the blankets loosely over her body feeling uncomfortable being naked in her own house. It was all she could do to fight the impulse to run from the house to the safety of; anywhere else. "Chicken shit" Becca called herself.

Anger began to filter through the debilitating fear that had claimed her. "Screw this." she forced herself to remember her strength and determination. All that she had used to become the number one journalist for the Toronto sun was rushing through her, adrenalin instead of fear, a mystery to be solved. "Ok who are you kidding," her ever present sub conscious mocked while peeking out from the blanket, "You are scared as hell."

"Screw you." she muttered as she reached for the phone.

"Hey Carol," Becca forced enthusiasm into her voice as she spoke to the front desk at the Sun once she had gone through the entire spiel. How could anyone enjoy doing that day in and day out? She shrugged the thought away.

"It's Becca, Can you tell the big guy I'm out of town for a few days. Something just dropped in my lap and I'm going to take a closer look to see if it's worth anything.

"Certainly," Carol cheerfully replied.

"Thanks," she responded, resisting the temptation to inject the woman with some life instead of being so damn robotic all the time.

The next call was more important to her. Rising, she dressed in casual clothes, a pair of tight jeans and her standard t-shirt, choosing flip flops instead of wearing socks in this heat. Thank goodness for air conditioning.

"Brian," Becca's smile was genuine as she heard her long-time friend's gruff sleepy voice. "Get out of bed," she teased.

"Hey Bec, what's up? " He glanced at the clock.

"Need a favor Brian." He sat up in bed, glancing over, not quite sure who he had taken home last night, blonde. Figured, he grinned as he rubbed the stubble on his chin.

"Not alone I'm guessing Brian? You are such a male slut!" Becca actually laughed as she listed to him moving to another room.

"Only because you always turn me down Bec," He chuckled. They had been back and forth like this from the time she arrived in town. Now they were inseparable friends. Sex was definitely off the table. "So whatcha need?"

"A new security system in my house." Becca did the best to hide the sound of fear from her voice as she spoke." Not even Brian could she tell this story to. How the hell did she explain when she couldn't yet explain it to herself? "Complete new system, Brian."

"Everything ok?" As much as she tried to hide it, Brian could hear the note of panic.

"Good as it's going to get, Brian," she smiled, feeling the protective instinct enter his words. "I want a complete system. Windows, doors, cameras outside, the works."

"Must be serious Bec," Brian was the only person she knew that could shorten her name further than Becca.

"Being cautious, that's all. Do me a favor though Brian. Keep an eye on my new neighbour when you come do the work please."

"Wait!!" His eyes opened wide. "Someone lives in that house beside you? Hell, that's creepy. You should never have bought that house."

"Don't dis my house. I love it. Felix and I are quite happy here thank you. "Or were, she didn't add. "How soon can you do it?"

Brian glanced back to the sleeping blond. "Um... Maybe a few hours or so?"

She laughed. "Dump the chick, Brian. I'm sure she will return. Ok. I'm out of town for a few days. Going to Norwich to visit my aunt and uncle, but I'll have the cell. I'll leave a cheque on the table for you. You still have the keys? And don't forget to feed Felix!"

"Uh huh, "Brian answered, totally distracted now as the blond sat up, letting the sheet fall from her. "Better make that more than a few hours, Becca."

"Perv." she laughed and hung up. Doing something made her feel marginally better. Taking control of the situation instead of being lost in the dark that was what she was accustomed to. She couldn't help but blush knowing as she let go in her dreams, it was the last thing she wanted. Truth was she ached to not be in control, but to be loved, cared for-wanted

"Yeah like that's going to happen," she had given up on that fantasy some time ago though she revisited it every night in her dreams. There was something missing in her heart, a melody, a song that was incomplete. It had yet to find release. It had become part of her make up to place her own needs last; especially when they had anything to do with finding that one person. She wasn't sure why but there was a compulsion to glance to the house next door. There was no movement she could see. There was something about him. "Robert," she let the name roll from her tongue.

With an effectiveness that was very unlike her, she packed an overnight case. She closed out thoughts of her dreams, of the man down the hill and focussed simply on the task at hand. She left the payment for Brian and cat food on the table. Quite sure the last few words she had spoken had gone in one ear and out the other with him. Finally she made herself a cup of instant coffee, her nose crinkled in disgust, but she didn't want to waste time brewing a pot. Grabbing her purse she closed and locked the door.

It would be good to see her Aunt Florence. Though they lived so close in comparison to the distance that had been between them when she was a child, it had been since her grandmother's funeral that she had visited. She knew her aunt would be happy to see her, even knowing Becca thought her a little eccentric. Voodoo and vampires and ghosts and all the things that went bump in the night. She would love this story, Becca thought as she made her way to the car.

Something tingled along the back of her neck. The feeling one got when they knew they were being watched. It was him. "Mr. I want to jump your bones" from next door. Though she wasn't sure how she knew, she just did. Her reaction to his presence was even stronger today than it had been yesterday "shit" she mumbled, wondering how to avoid him without appearing to be a complete bitch. Being a blathering idiot twice in a matter of days was not something Becca relished, but the alternative was to stand next to him, embark on small talk and try not to drool.

Bitch it is, she smirked as she studiously ignored him, continuing to her car, quickening her pace as she caught the sound of him closing in. More than that, she caught his scent.it was so purely masculine, purely addictive and purely him; and the exact scent that had filled her car yesterday. "Damn the man" she frowned, trying to make it to her car before being intercepted.

"Becca," The deadly sensual voice called out. Her heart skipped a beat before beginning to thump in double time. Redness crept into her cheeks at the girlish reaction she was having.

Humming off key to drown out the sound of his voice, Becca unlocked the car door before opening it, letting the first wave of sweltering heat filter out of the car before getting in. So far so good she thought, a smile of "ha I did it" sitting smugly on her puffy lips.

"Becca," He called again.

"Well damn," she paused. Becca glanced at the door then over her shoulder to him before looking back at the door, a perfect imitation of a bobble head doll. Chiding herself, she pasted a smile on her face before turning to face him. At least this time she remembered not to lean against the hot exterior of her car.

Her mouth parted and a surprised "Oh" escaped as she braved a glance at his face. Even with the sunglasses, the urge was stronger than it had ever been. Hopefully curling her fingers around the base of her cup would prevent them from reaching towards him. "Damn' she whispered. He wasn't alone. Flanking either side of him was two other very handsome, tall sexy, men. Vibrant sea green eyes moved from one to the other as she nibbled her lip trying desperately to figure out where to look. Finally she chose her cup. Safe; the cup was most definitely the safest of her options. Lifting it, she took a large drink, biting back the cry as the hot coffee seared her mouth.

Robert laughed, though Giles and Leonard did their best to disguise their amusement. The first mark gave Robert the ability to sense her more clearly in her daylight hours. To know the basics of her thoughts and her needs though it would take three further marks for him to know every secret she held so closely to her. He understood that were he to project right now, she would hear him in her mind. He also realized she was unnerved already, afraid after seeing the mark this morning. That she had decided to run was going to be a major complication for them. Definitely not something he had anticipated, but the thrust of her jaw told him she was not about to change her mind.

"Rebecca," Robert's sensual voice captivated her, "I would like to introduce Giles and Leonard. Giles, Leonard, meet Rebecca, my neighbour." He paused as she smiled towards them, transfixed. The complete transformation on her face was beyond exquisite. Her eyes glimmered with a free and joyous pleasure, cheeks slightly flushed and that little dimple on her left cheek. Oh to run his finger along that dimple. He swallowed back the desire, though barely. It was the snickers and comments his friends were making that helped cool the libido for now.

"It's a pleasure to meet you both." Becca offered sincerely. "And please, contrary to what he,' she pointed in Robert's direction, "says, it's Becca." She reached out to shake their hands, a gesture that had been instilled in her as a child. Both men looked slightly startled as she extended her hand. Touching her was not wise. With the power she projected and the growling ringing furiously in their head from Robert, they hesitated.

The blush grew as she remained with her arm extended in friendship, neither of the men accepting. Humiliated, Becca lowered her arm, ducking her head at the same time to hide the red stains she knew would be there. Giles reached forward, a forced smile hovering along his lips as he tensed every muscle in his body. Time seemed to slow for Robert as Giles closed his large chilled hand around Becca's much smaller one. She swallowed, feeling a slight tingle rising up her arm from the simple and innocent touch. There was a dry chill as his hand closed around hers. She looked down before shrugging it off, realizing she had most likely held the cup in that hand just before and had forgotten. As quickly as was polite Giles withdrew his hand.

He had felt her, strong and brilliant; like a beacon of light against an otherwise dark canvas. The power that emanated from her was equal to that of a feeding. Giles knew that beneath Robert's dark glasses his eyes would be black as midnight, anger turning them to a shimmering mass of ire. The incessant growling in his head was pure Robert, and it confirmed what he already knew. Leonard however smiled a delightful grin as he moved forward, clasping her tiny hand within both of his. He snickered at Robert as he held her hand longer than was necessary not only to annoy the hell out of him but to attempt to analyze and discover a way to block out the siren call that emanated from her even without her knowledge. "Christ," Giles resisted the urge to wipe his hand on his side, still feeling the power that had passed to him. "I wouldn't mess with Robert much longer if I were you, Leonard," Giles tilted his head towards Robert's hands, clenching and unclenching. Leonard coughed, hiding the laugh as he pulled back.

The same sense of chilled, dry flesh surrounded Becca as she drew back her hand to wrap it around the cup again. The electrical current was there, softer-less pronounced than with Robert but still palpable. Stepping back, more than just a little confused, her head tilted as she gazed openly at the trio. As beautiful as Robert's friends were- and boy were they sizzling, aside from the tingling awareness as their flesh met, there was no further draw. But the similarities were so pronounced she wondered if perhaps they were relatives of some sort, all so pale, pallid flesh, and the same muscular frames -odd. She felt calm and in control of her rampaging hormones and libido for the first time in days. Of course it would have to be the one she couldn't utter a coherent sentence around that would be the one she yearned for.

Robert smacked them both along the back in a friendly gesture, not bothering to temper the strength he used. "Giles and Leonard will be my guests for a couple of days. There are also two others you've yet to meet." Robert directed her attention back to him. His words, though friendly, were tinged with curtness. Robert's jaw tensed as he worked to control the baser instinct to throttle both of his so called friends. And if Leonard snickered one more time, Robert glared towards the man…. "I thought I would introduce you so you didn't worry about strangers wandering about. "

Becca nodded, biting her tongue as she tried to form words. "Damn it" She cursed. "Very kind of you Robert," she offered that million dollar smile again before turning her eyes from him. There was something so mesmerizing, she mused, frustrated with the constant need he instilled. It was almost painful to turn away.

Robert nodded and smiled. "I see you're heading out," he tried to act nonchalant as he questioned her. Though he had unashamedly listened to her phone conversations- and her mind, he wasn't quite sure where her final destination was. He didn't want her out of his sight. What if something happened to her?

Again she nodded. "Brilliant" she thought, nod again. She rolled her eyes. "The man is going to think you have the vocabulary of a gnat… "Um yes," Becca spoke, "going away for a few days. Oh, a friend of mine will be in and out of the house. Don't mind him."

Robert's brows rose above the top of the glasses. "A friend hmm" Though he tried to make the words sound teasing, he failed miserably. A man in her house, he growled. Perhaps I'll have to visit his dreams tonight, he thought.

"Well," she shivered, though the glaring sun beat mercilessly down upon them as she glanced towards Robert and then the others. They all wore the same dark glasses and all had the same pale flesh. Something was just not right, and she fully intended to find out what it was. "Have a good day," she moved backwards to her car, fumbling with the handle before slipping in. Summer in Southern Ontario could be exceptionally hot and it appeared the heat wave had just begun. Becca blew strands of hair from her face as she began to sweat.

His hand was on the window before she could pull out of the driveway. She turned confused eyes toward the outline of his hand against the glass. Frighteningly familiar, her brows furrowed as Images fluttered of that very hand caressing her, weaving through her hair night after night. She raised her eyebrows, giving her best 'I'm onto you look even though she was confused, tired, frustrated and afraid. Oh and did she mention frustrated? As she put the gear into reverse she glanced pointedly at his hand before looking back to him.

"She can't go searching, Robert. God what a mess that would create," Giles actually shuddered as he thought of every single young one finding their way to her.

Robert turned his eyes to her. He considered taking his glasses off but knew he did not yet have the energy to sustain life yet beneath the bright, glorious ball of light. It would, within moment's burn him from the inside, should the sun's direct light reflect into his eyes. "Don't go," he wanted to say. "You aren't safe. You are mine." All the things he wanted to tell her, share with her, he couldn't as he was held spellbound within her lost green eyes. They reminded him of the beautiful depths of the ocean. He was lost in them. Yes, he thought, they eyes were definitely the window to the soul; the soul that was meant to be his.

It was inevitable Robert supposed. He had gone too long without rest. Though he fed nightly from Becca's dreams, it was small amounts, far less than would normally be consumed during a feeding. The first mistake he could ever remember making. He projected towards her. Saying "be safe my Becca," in his mind to her instead of speaking the words.

Becca could feel an intense pull- a throbbing in the circular mark that rested above her breast. What began as almost erotic quickly began to twist into something far more painful... Words echoed in her head- "Be safe" and "my Becca." Hell of an imagination I have. Inside she felt raw, exposed and stunned. The desire to get away, to find answers propelled her into action. She couldn't help but glance back before backing out of the driveway, wanting to ask; no that would be foolish. His lips hadn't moved. He didn't speak. But fuck she was sure. "I'm going crazy, that's all." She refused to look back as she pulled onto the dirt road, though she could still feel his gaze following her.

Chapter 6

Fragile, Becca thought; fragile and completely overwhelmed by the events of the morning. She fought the fatigue even before reaching the ramp leading to the freeway. The weight of every fearful, painful and unexplained encounter descended causing her shoulders to slump, her entire body feeling the enormity of what she was facing The more miles- the more distance put between she and the house, the more conflicted Becca became. Although the fear never dissipated, not one iota, the mark dully throbbing, a constant reminder, there was something-an important piece of her that was missing. Studiously she ignored what that something was-him. She growled at the inexplicable compulsion that captured so much of her attention on Robert- returning her thoughts to him again and again. Tossing back long russet curls, Becca reached forward and cranked up the volume until it drowned out any thoughts in her head. Adele's 'rolling in the deep' filled the silence, and off key-disturbingly off key, Becca sang along until finally her muscles began to unwind.

Turning off onto route 59 brought the sting of tears to her eyes. Becca couldn't count the number of times her parents had taken this exact route to visit our grandparents. This turn had become her fantasy world as the trapping of city life with its stone and cement foundation; the increasingly tall structures designed, she was sure, just to block out the sun of life, into a world of breathtaking beauty and silence. Gone were the sounds of the multitude of vehicles; gone were the millions of flashing lights from billboards, factories and row after endless row of buildings scrunched together until there was no space for singular thought —the rush and hustle of normal life. Even now as she made the circular ramp that would lead her into Norwich, she felt it; that taking a leap into another time, another place-another sensation. Though their road was now paved nothing else had really changed. It was lush with vibrant green vegetation, and huge old weeping willows that bowed almost regally to those that passed beneath their limbs. Most of southern Ontario was at one time, covered by Carolinian forest, characterized by large, slow-growing hardwood trees, like Oak and Beech. Very few stands of old growth Carolinian forest remain. Between Delhi, Ontario and Lynedoch, Ontario, the creek passes through a 5 kilometres long incised valley that has stands of old growth. It was deep within that particular area that her great grandmother resided. A gypsy by birth; by skill and by training, she was more often than not considered the "one" that everyone had in their family that no one spoke of. She however, loved her and was intrigued with the ancient knowledge she practiced, even if part of it was just to annoy the hell of Becca's father. She pushed the button to unroll the windows to enjoy the clean air. Inhaling sharply as they slowly rolled downwards, Becca felt her eyes burn and she gagged, quickly rolling the window back up. Part of farm life she tended to forget. The scents left by the animals.

This section of the sleepy little street had just a few farms, some of them utilized for the farming of wheat, corn or tobacco. On windy days you could see the stalks of the long rows of crops flowing in an intricate dance with the wind that caressed the growing stems, matching rhythm, bending, flowing with the direction of the strong breeze that encircled it, commanded it.

That, Becca thought was the first time her errant thoughts had turned in the direction of creating visions with words. She still remembered the pounding in her chest, the quickening in her breathing and the need to find release. It was the last year she had visited. The following year she had gone to University and engrossed herself in thoughts other than the ones she had buried deep inside. They rained down on her now, one memory after another crashing into her like wild waves that slammed along the beach. As the water flowed back out with the tide it took with it little grains of sand, capturing them with its force, luring them into the depths. Her thoughts felt the same as they washed over her, leaving her more and more vulnerable as each one was greeted with the complete recollection of time, the complete emotional need. It felt as though a damn had broken as she had to slow the car until she could gain control.

The mark began to pulse again, painful in its intensity. She rubbed it, trying to assuage the pain though the more she attempted to dismiss the memories and the burning evidence, the stronger the aching became. It throbbed now, drawing her attention until finally she gave in and continued to rub gently enjoying the flooding warmth spreading inside the circular indentation. As the heat spread, the throbbing quieted as though finally assuaged with her attention. Now if she could just rid herself of the mini inferno in other places, she might be able to put it behind her. Clutching the wheel more tightly with her free hand she slowed the car even more. Somehow she was sure that showing up panting and writhing would not be the ideal greeting. Ignoring the heat outside, and the barnyard stench, she opened the window and inhaled. Clean air. Well, clean as in smog free but not farm free. Her aunt's neighbour had a milk farm. Many, many cows that did their business where they pleased which left an odor one never quite adjusted to, Becca included.

It did serve its purpose however. Pulling herself together she clicked the left signal. The wheels crunched on the gravel road as she drove up the long driveway. The same old trees stood tall and strong in their front yard, creating a canopy for the new deck that had just been built, and she revelled in the twinges of nostalgia at the familiarity. The house hadn't changed at all on the outside, still an older white siding with smaller windows. Becca smiled as she pulled into the parking area. Her aunt was waiting for her as she stepped out of the car and with great joy and need for comfort she accepted her hug.

"It seems like you have grown again, Becca" her Aunt Florence stepped back to eye her critically.

She laughed, a full throaty sound, realizing how much she missed her family. "I'm 25! I think I stopped growing some time ago." She laughed again while reaching for her overnight case before draping an arm around the much shorter woman. "Hmm," Becca looked at her, a teasing look in her eyes. "You shrinking?"

"Brat," The word was said with love.

"How is Dan these days? She questioned as they made their way towards the house.

Florence stopped and looked down the hill. "He took over Grandma's house after she passed." Becca could hear the note of tears and squeezed her arm.

"Well that's good. You get to keep your son close!"

"You will have to go down and visit him after you settle in, Becca. He's been looking forward to your visit. Some friend of his visiting him for a few days, showed up just after you called, in fact. Name is Benjamin something or other.

"No matchmaking" Becca warned.

Florence tsked as she led her into the house. "Course not. So tell me what is going on with you, how have you been, how are your parents.

She chuckled as she set the bag down and leaned in to hug her aunt again. This time she pressed against her, not the half hug they had exchanged out in the yard. It felt like being home. She sat and prepared to spend the next few hours catching her up on the family gossip.

Something was wrong. Becca could feel it. She turned to look at her Aunt who in turn was looking at her with wide eyes. "What? Becca looked curiously at her. "What's wrong?" She glanced down wondering if a bug had landed on her, making a quick but thorough inspection. There was nothing though she did notice heat still radiated from the strange protruding mark.

Florence swallowed, needing a moment to compose herself, turning to fuss around the already pristine kitchen. She had sensed it immediately, her dark eyes brimming with the shadows of what had passed and what was now to come.

"Aunt Florence?" Becca rose and walked to her, the question lingering unspoken in the air between them.

Closing off the legacy of emotions, she turned, offering half a smile. "You must tell me everything that has been going on child - everything. "

She shrugged as she sat again, accepting a coffee from her aunt. "Nothing unusual, work, sleep, more work,"

An older hand covered hers, squeezing it. "There is more, much more, Becca. Leave it to you to get into things you don't understand." Again she tsked as she puttered around the kitchen, looking for something.

"But," Becca protested. "I really haven't done anything this time. I mean not like the "it wasn't me that accidently let the cows out of the pasture by leaving the corral door open" anything. This time I really haven't."

Florence patted her hand as she had as a child. "Take your coffee and go visit your cousin. He is waiting anxiously. It has been, "she paused, "a while since you have visited. I need a few moments to search for something essential; something that you will soon require."

She looked curiously at her aunt, intrigued, another piece to this puzzle perhaps? Waiting for more would only lead to further frustration she knew though she huffed with exasperation at her aunt none the less.

Patting her on the cheek she shooed Becca out the door. Odd she thought her brows furrowing as she watched her aunt dart across the kitchen "Full moon maybe?" she shrugged before taking a drink of the coffee, choking back a gag. "Well nice to know some things haven't changed. She had seriously considered seeking guidance from her aunt about what had transpired, forgoing the notion; quite sure her aunt would be on the phone to her parents, whispering words such as overworked, stressed out and nice long vacation. She tucked back errant strands of hair that tickled the side of her face before yelling through the closed door, "Alright, I won't be long. And just so you know, I don't care who is down with Dan, I am not interested."

The screen door closed behind her and she blushed while glancing down to her grandparent's old home. Her sub conscious snickered. Ok so maybe if he was drop dead gorgeous he might be able to satisfy an itch that was becoming more unbearable by the hour. Pausing she turned her head, looking around for an animal as she heard a deep warning growl. "Weird." Finding nothing she walked down the well-worn path to see her cousin.

As she drew closer she slowed her pace, enjoying the cooling evening air, the gentle breeze that billowed beneath her t-shirt. Discreetly she poured the coffee out as she walked, giggling softly. Her aunt had never been able to make drinkable coffee. Holding the mug, she passed the corner of the house and moved to the front entrance, having to swallow back tears. She didn't bother to knock; their doors were always open and welcoming.

"Dan," Becca called out. "Come greet your cousin." She walked up the five stairs to the upper level of the house, stepping into the storage area. Or washing area, she'd never been able to figure out what it was. Except as a kid it was the place where they could steal popsicles from the freezer. Now a little of everything was in this area.

A smile formed when she heard the other door open and she turned. Funny how it smelled so much the same as when her grandparents were alive, yet another scent lingered. Before realizing it she was wrapped up in a huge bear hug. Her slender arms wrapped around her cousin.

"Missed you too Dan," pulling back to look him over. "Amazing how we grew up isn't it?" She couldn't help but laugh. "There were a few times we weren't sure that we would. Remember the dare to see who could climb the highest in the silo?" Becca had lost that bet quickly. Turned out she didn't have the stomach for heights. Who knew?

"Come on in. "Dan motioned. " I see you dumped mom's coffee out on the way down. You'll kill the grass you know. He laughed and motioned Becca to the table she had spent 18 summers eating at. She ran her fingers over the polished top as he made her a coffee that wouldn't burn a hole through her gut.

She shrugged innocently. "I'm not the one that needs the hair on my chest- has her coffee helped you yet?" She snickered as Dan scowled.

"Mom coming down?" he asked as he took out cups.

"Don't think so," She answered, distracted as she looked around, marvelling that so much had changed and yet, nothing had changed. "She said she had to look for something. Seemed to be having one of her, "she paused, "erhm, moments"

His smile was one of indulgence. "Yeah, she has been into this voodoo shit lately."

Both heads turned as the sound of someone climbing the steps, the creaking letting them know the person was far too heavy to be her tiny aunt.

"Oh, you will be able to meet Benjamin." He grinned like the little matchmaker he was. Like mother like son, she guessed while rolling her eyes at him.

"Don't even think about it buddy or we are going to go a few rounds like we did when we were kids."

His laugh filled the room. "Not sure you would win now though Becca."

"So this is the much talked about Becca," A deep sultry voice resonated from the entrance.

Her belly curled and she hadn't even turned to look at the man yet. "Damn it what the hell was wrong with her?" Inhaling to compose herself before turning, she slowly let her eyes travel up the strong masculine form. Her subconscious was doing back flips yelling wow, wow." She thought about doing the same thing but held back, offering a smile.

"Hello Miss Becca," the voice, she didn't particularly care what his name was; she was calling him "the voice," drawled as he stepped inside. He waved away the coffee Dan offered, his eyes remaining on her which at the moment suited her just fine as her eyes seemed to be glued to him.

Her legs trembled as she stood. "Yes, I'm Becca," she smiled, pleased that she found her voice and hadn't made a fool of herself like she did with Robert. The new abrasion made its presence known again as she thought of him. "And you are?" Her inner voice snickered knowing the question was asked simply to hear that beautiful rich sultry voice again.

"Ah, my manners are terrible today, do forgive me. I am Benjamin. And it is indeed a pleasure to meet you."

She was charmed with his manner. It seemed like what one would envision hearing hundreds of years ago. Offering her hand to his she again waited. What the hell was up today with people being rude by not shaking hands? , She took note of the pale flesh that covered his slender hand. And what was it lately with all these ghostly people? Did everyone stay completely out of the sun? Maybe she was in some sort of "Adam's Family rerun. Blushing with embarrassment as she began to lower her arm, her gaze locked on the light tanned coloring of her own flesh.

He reached out to grasp hers, his eyes, almost the same dark ebony as Robert's began to gleam, a smile curling his lips. She gasped as Benjamin hissed before taking a pace back."

Why do all the yummy ones have to be so freaking odd?" She wondered as she watched him withdraw though his eyes remained fixated on her.

"Again I must beg your forgiveness. Where I come from, erhm, my culture, it is impolite for a male to touch a female in any way before spending some time together."

Well there goes a night of hot dirty sex, she groused while pasting a false smile on her face...

Dan brought the coffee over to the table and sat by Becca, Benjamin settling in the seat furthest from her. She pondered discreetly sniffing to see if her underarm deodorant wasn't doing what it advertised but then she blushed. Perhaps he... "Oh god," she thought, "What if I read him all wrong. What if he is just not interested?" Crimson stained her cheeks. "Shoot me now please."

Benjamin brought his hand to his chin, scratching it gently as he recorded to memory each facet of the woman. She had a mark. This would definitely change the game. He had meant to take her tonight but could he get past an elder's mark to mark her himself? He fought the urge to break everything around him, his violent anger barely contained. She was the key to what he desired the most. His eyes narrowed as he tried to look within her, to probe her mind as she chatted with her cousin but was met with just brief images and blackness. "Fuck" he swore in his mind.

She jumped as her phone rang, knocking over her coffee in the process. She looked, apologetically towards her cousin. "Sorry Dan

I'll get it in a moment, it could be work." She reached into her purse and pulled out her phone.

"Hey Bec" Brian spoke, his voice not quite what it normally was.

"Brian?" Becca sounded surprised. She assumed he would have spent a few more hours in bed with the woman before even beginning the job.

"I think you should come home Bec," Brian spoke, his voice almost robotic.

"Is Felix ok?" She began to panic. "Brian what's wrong?"

There was a moment's hesitation before he continued. "New system installed. Yes, Felix is ok. Took a nap on your couch and um, met your new neighbours."

"All right," She strung the words out, confused and wary, struggling to understand the strange tone of voice. "The check is on the table for you Brian."

"Yes, I have it, could have waited." The monotone in his voice was unnerving. Brian was never like this. What's happened?

"So you will come home tonight. I don't think you are safe there, Bec, come home ok?"

"Uh huh," Becca looked around, shrugging off his words. "Everything seems fine. "

"Becca," His voice changed. It was deep, almost not his voice, though it rang familiar to her.

"Your neighbor just showed up, Bec. I invited him in, he was worried about who I was. He would like to say hi."

"Wait, what is Robert doing in my home?" She turned her back turned on the men seated at the table, missing the arch of brows from

Benjamin. "Brian, what the hell is he doing in my house?" Now she was getting angry.

"Good evening Rebecca," Robert's voice was calm as she greeted her.

"What are you doing in my house?" Hmm, ok, so being pissed off was the best way to remember how to speak around him. She could do that.

"I had forgotten you were having someone over and came to ensure all was well." The lie slipped out easily. After hundreds of years, it became second nature.

"Alright," she hesitated, hating the curling in her stomach, the hungry need to feel him, to be closer to him. "What...what can I do for you? I'm assuming Brian didn't destroy the house."

"No, Rebecca, the house is fine." How did he say that she wasn't? How did he say her life was in grave danger? Already he had woken the others from their slumber and sent them to her. He had to remain where he was so he could find her as she slept.

"I just," he paused, "just wondered if you were going to be home this evening. I was thinking we might go out for a drink or something" Shit I'm bad at this, he growled again.

A startled laugh escaped. "What?" She shook her head, quite sure she had misheard.

"A drink, coffee, something stronger perhaps?" Becca was stunned. She had absolutely no idea what to say. The man left her tongue tied even if the rest of her body went into overdrive. She swallowed audibly.

"I'm um. " Damn it she didn't' want to say no! "I'm at my aunts for the night at least, Robert. Well, actually I'm at my cousin's next door right now, having coffee with he and his friend," She looked over her shoulder towards the table, "Benjamin, right?" She smiled as he nodded, "with Dan's friend Benjamin."

Silence greeted her. Becca sighed. She either couldn't find her voice or couldn't shut up. Now she wondered if she had upset him by saying she was having coffee with another man. What business was it of his anyways? Her frown deepened as the silence continued.

"Well, if that was all, perhaps we can erhm" she blushed delicately, "discuss things when I return?"

"Did you say Benjamin?" Robert's voice was more of a croaking sound.

"Yes."

She held the phone away from her ear as Robert cursed. "Excuse me?" Her voice turned ominous while her sub conscious was preening at his paying attention and being upset.

"Rebecca," Robert started only to quiet once again. The pause seemed to last much longer than it actually was before he spoke again… "I will see you soon, Rebecca." He whispered before hanging up. It sounded like more than mere words to her. It sounded like a promise, one that had her breathing rate increasing, her heart stuttering before settling.

Robert knew there was no more time. His eyes closed as he conferred with the other Elders. "He is there, Benjamin, in the same house as Rebecca."

"We are on our way," Jerard responded, not even winded as they raced through the fields, shielding themselves in the shadows. It would be much easier once the sun set.

"You have got to complete the markings" Markus warned.

"No." Robert all but growled. "I will not take what she does not freely offer. It will leave her with half an existence. I would be no better than Benjamin."

"Keep her safe until I meet her tonight as she sleeps." Robert sighed, as he looked around her house. He had no further use for Brian, he supposed he should release him, though the dreams he'd about Rebecca left him tempted to do other things.

They raced through the darkening evening, listening for sounds of their kind. None had any idea of what to expect, how many, if any aside from Benjamin. They knew if they got the chance they would kill him tonight. It would at least give some time to try and tame the caller in her.

Impatience settled in Roberts gut. He was fed, thanks to Brian but he would not feel ok until he was with Rebecca. He was not entirely sure how this evening would go with her but soon he would find out.

Chapter 7

Benjamin did his best to hide the rage as she hung up the phone.

"Your new boyfriend?" Dan teased as she sat back down.

A look that would have shaken a lesser person simply made him laugh. Her cheeks took on the coloring of her red hair as she looked down and muttered, "no, not a boyfriend, a neighbour." The flush deepened speaking volumes on Becca's thoughts said new neighbour.

"So tell us about this new man, Becca." Dan was thoroughly enjoying seeing her squirm. She smiled sweetly while kicking him under the table.

"Sorry Dan," she smiled insincerely, "I'm just not one to discuss my personal life, besides there is nothing to tell this time. Her words sounded choked, she was busy trying to keep the dark flush from working its way down her neckline, though she couldn't prevent the rush of need that made her hand shake as she picked up the fresh cup he had gotten for her.

It was time for a change of topic. "So what are you two gentlemen, and I use the term loosely with you, Dan," Becca teased, "doing tonight?"

He had to see her eyes, Benjamin plotted. "I was hoping perhaps you might join us this evening for dinner?" He tried compelling her to look his way, testing his power through the mark. Frustrating he thought as he resisted the urge to growl.

Two offers of a date in one day. She was flattered. Her subconscious was doing more back flips chanting go, go, go. She coughed before taking a drink of the coffee.

"Very nice of you to offer, Benjamin," Becca responded though she didn't quite meet his eyes, instead looking just above the collar of his shirt, "but I'm going to spend the evening with my Aunt. Apparently she has something to show me." She glanced over at Dan and gave him the "I'm in for a long evening look" even knowing she would enjoy it.

He gripped the underside of the table, leaving indentations as he controlled the fury driving him. "It would be very disappointing if you were not to at least join us for dinner." Benjamin tried the smooth sensual voice that would normally attract a human towards him. Long ago he had learned how to remain out in the day; to command with his voice, those both asleep and awake.

She tilted her head and offered another half-smile. "Sorry to disappoint, but as much as I may tease about spending time with my Aunt, I am looking forward to it. Besides I've given her my word." She felt the smooth tone as well as his eyes boring into her. For some reason she chose to keep her gaze on the lower portion of his face.

"It's ok, Becca," Dan smiled as he patted her arm. "We can have breakfast or something before you leave."

Benjamin glared towards the boy, his nostrils flaring. It was quite possible he would not live through the night. The urge to feed from him right now was growing quickly and fatally. "Or perhaps, we could go up and visit with your family as well, Dan?" Again he used the persuasive tone of voice, the one that had gotten him invited into the house.

Before Dan could agree, Becca laughed. Benjamin felt the sound deep inside of him, stirring a passion he had only felt once before. A longing to consume her flooded him and his nostrils flared again, this time to inhale her scent. He would have her. Mark or not she would be his.

"Dan hasn't told you much about his Mother I'm guessing." She laughed again. "She would toss you both out on your ears or chase you down the hill with a frying pan. " She paused, a look of love and past happiness softening her features. "My Aunt is quite um, unique. No one she doesn't know quite well is permitted to step into her house."

"That's right, Becca," Dan sounded confused. "I almost said yes. I don't know how I could forget something like that. She would tear a strip off of me."

"Uh huh," she nodded firmly, her long curls bouncing against the white t-shirt. "And it wouldn't be the first time. We all felt the wrath of your mom, Dan." She touched his arm. "And the deep beautiful love she has for all of us. She is a very special woman and I admire her very much."

His hand covered hers as he smiled. "Yes, she is. She has been lonely since Grandma passed away. It will be good for you to spend time with her. Make sure to fill her in on you northerners. She really dislikes the weather in Timmins you know. "He leaned back, cup in hand. She swears she will never go back after that last snow storm."

She couldn't help but snort. "You mom and dad just have no luck when they came to visit." She glanced at the time before rising. "Thanks for the coffee, Dan. "She reached out to hug him tightly. "Love you. I'll try to stop by to see you in the morning before I head back, but no promises, ok?"

"I'll see you in a few weeks down by your place if you don't make it in the morning." Dan returned her hug. There was genuine affection between them. Both families had remained extremely close through time and distance.

"Deal," Becca grinned. "And I make better coffee than you do."

Benjamin coughed to draw her attention. Intriguing; no -more than intriguing, and more than irritating, no one had been able to simply brush him aside as though he didn't exist. His patience had worn thin.

"I'm so sorry Benjamin," she apologized. "I kind of got caught up in old times. It was a pleasure meeting you."

There was something about him she couldn't' quite put her finger on but she was almost glad to be going back up to her Aunt's.

"I do understand, Becca," Benjamin rose as she did. Her scent filled each part of him. He could taste her as he inhaled and his mouth watered with anticipation. "Is there any way we could convince you to spend some time with us this evening?" he cajoled, willing her to look up at him.

The bitchy 'I've had a miserable few days' woman was emerging though she was doing her best to suppress it. Her glimmering green eyes held a trace of impatience as she looked up. She gasped but managed to bite back the pain as the raw mark began to throb with a fiery intensity. Ignoring it for the moment as she held his gaze, "I've said no, I'm sorry but I've made plans I have no intention of breaking, thank you though, Benjamin."

The sharp pain she felt was on par with what he was feeling-scorched. Inside he was burning. She had definitely been marked, Benjamin swore beneath his breath. He could feel the searing of his flesh as he tried to command her when she finally met his gaze. He would have to find a way around this, perhaps as she slept.

A smile of contrition played along his lips as he acquiesced. Rage, bitter and vile filled his veins. He swallowed back the hatred as she nodded to him before hugging her cousin again. "Bitch," Benjamin thought. You will be mine. You will be mine and you shall regret each and every moment of debasement you have made me feel.

"I'll call you Dan," she called over her shoulder as she slipped out the first door, making her way down the stairs towards the outer door. She closed it before leaning back against the metal, pausing to rub the mark. It still stung like hell though less so than when she had been in the house.

Something was definitely not right; the reporter in her sensed it. Pushing away from the door she made her way back up the hill, "I will get to the bottom of this" she promised herself while dodging piles of horse manure. Forgetting everything else for the moment she moved to the dark brown horse. Her eyes twinkled and her face lit up with a glorious smile as she cradled his head, scratching behind his ears. "Pussyfoot, my old friend." Her grin widened as the horse nudged her, seeking more attention. Running her fingers through the long mane, marvelling at the thick coarse strands that she could tell had been well tended to. She let out a peaceful sigh. Moving to her flank, Becca rested her cheek along the horse's side, feeling the motions as she inhaled. Offering a last scratch she nuzzled him before whispering, "Promise to come back." Turning, she raced the rest of the way up the hill and into the house. "I'm back," she called, though the barking dogs had let her presence be known.

"Ah there you are," Florence brushed dust off of her grey sweater as she entered the kitchen. She stopped in her tracks, her eyes wide as they focused on Becca."

"Yes, made it back before I got smacked for being late for dinner again," she teased while slipping off her shoes.

"Um," Becca tilted her head before walking forward. "Are you ok? You look like you've seen a ghost, or two." She reached out to brush a cobweb out of her greying hair.

Fear tipped the scales for Florence as she looked at her beautiful niece. "Yes child, I am well. I'm not sure that you are however." She paused as she took Becca's hand, feeling the power flowing through her as their fingers intertwined. Though a gasp was escaped she made no other sound, leading her to the kitchen table before sitting. "We must talk."

She cast a worried look towards her Aunt. Of course it wasn't the first time she had looked oddly towards her. Through the years she'd heard many far-fetched tales of things that went bump in the night. After the last few days however, she was far less inclined to brush off the fables. "Alright," Becca looked with concern to her Aunt. "What's wrong? And what is that huge dirty book in your hands? Oh," she continued, "Dan has some creepy friends, especially the one down at his house. Pushy little bastard."

She tried not to chuckle as she got the stern look from her aunt for swearing but within the chocolate depths of her eyes there was something worrying. "Tell me everything that has been going on."

She blinked a few times, looking surprised. "Nothing really, Aunt Florence, age didn't matter when speaking with her. She would always be Aunt Florence. I just finished a rather long investigation for work, I'm sure you read it in the paper you now collect," She smiled and tilted her head to all the cut out articles. Becca didn't want to worry her Aunt by discussing the massive pain that had threatened her sanity yesterday, at least not until she had it checked by a physician.

"No, no, what else?" Florence looked up. "Have you met or are you involved with any new men, Becca?"

"Um," she stammered, working away the blush. "Are you asking about my sex life?" She squirmed having not enjoyed "the talk" with her mother, never mind her aunt. Geez this day just gets better and better.

"No child, but have you met any new men recently?

"You mean besides the one down at your son's house?"

Florence nodded as she opened the dusty book. It looked ancient to Becca, and full of spider webs. "Ick" She hated spiders. "What was his name by the way, the one down at Dan's?"

"Benjamin," Becca responded absently as she watched her aunt leaf gently through the faded and delicate pages. "He actually tried to invite himself up here."

Florence paused and looked up, eyes widening before she tsked. Her eyes travelled back to the hand-made protectors that hung above every room in the house. "Benjamin, yes ok, has there been anyone else?"

"Well, "she felt beads of perspiration as she concentrating on keeping the stain from her cheeks and her libido in check. "I do have a new neighbour. Can you believe someone actually bought that old house beside mine?" She missed the look of knowledge and sadness in her aunt's eyes as she thought about Robert. Just the name caused shivers.

"His name?" Florence's words were growing short.

"Robert," she paused, though he has a few friends there with him. "I can't really remember all their names though."

Finally Florence stopped rifling through the pages. "Take this book up to your room and read while I finish dinner, Becca. It's important. "

Gingerly she took the book, holding it at arms-length to avoid the disgusting spider webs.

"This book, "Florence began, "Well I will explain more when you have read but it has been passed down for many generations. It was found in the house next to yours." She watched Becca's eyes widen with uncertainty and fear. "Go, read. I promise your safety here tonight."

Like a child, Becca listened to her Aunt, climbing the stairs slowly, trepidation filling her with an anxious feeling. There was inkling, some kind of knowledge that something was happening.

"Robert" Jerard called to him. "Benjamin is here. I don't know if he can feel us as we feel him. I don't believe so. There is a sense of madness within him."

"Do you feel any others around aside from him?" The terseness in Robert's voice betrayed the worry.

"Yes," Giles responded. They wander through the farms though they are very weak. They smell, "he lifted his head and inhaled again, "they taste on the verge of the same madness." He sounded confused. "It is like he is having them feeding off of him instead of acquiring energy from dream sources. Is that possible?

"Our teachings before going through the portal said that to feed from one of our own kind leads to madness and destruction for both."

"We are by her aunt's house, Robert. Leonard spoke, slightly stunned. "The house is protected." He laughed. "Not well, but protected enough that young ones would hesitate."

"What is Benjamin doing? Can you capture him?" Robert's voice was brisk as he watched the clock, willing it to go faster, to meet her in sleep.

"No," Markus growled. "He left moments after Becca. I followed his trail. He is fast, Robert, as fast as we are though not able to shield quite as well, perhaps because he is alone."

"What did you feel?" Robert sat up placing his arms on his upper thighs, straining to hear the thoughts the others had heard.

"He is old. Maybe fifty years or so younger than we, and he is mad." Markus paused. "Madness has corrupted his mind, all he seeks now is power. " He would give anything to not say the next part. "What do you hide?"

"He believes two things." Markus sighed as he continued. "The first is that your Rebecca is the answer to the power he seeks. That combining his power with hers, he will complete a circle that will fill him with total control over everything."

The growl was loud, long and spoke of death as it vibrated through the Elder's heads. Robert was not taking the news well. They had expected nothing less. "What is the second?" Robert braced himself.

"To defeat us, to kill us one by one until he is the last and only living Elder, and he begins with you, Robert. His intentions are clear. Take Becca, mark her, over your mark should he find a way. Then give her the remaining marks, regardless of what it does to her mental stability. He craves her power, not her soul, not the purity of heart. He seeks to take her from you and use her before discarding her."

"You must reach her tonight," Leonard spoke softly. "You must meet her in her dreams. Touch her, feel her power and decide how strong or how fragile she is. If you wait longer, it may be too late."

"Robert," Giles interrupted.

"Yes?"

"Her aunt may have just either helped or hindered."

"Do not speak in riddles please." Frustration lent an edge to anger.

"She has given Becca the book of our history. I do not know how it was acquired. You must find that out tonight. But it appears that she will be reading before sleep."

"There is one other thing," Leonard paused, unsure of proceeding.

100

"What?" Robert snarled, feeling a touch of his own madness, tasting it on his tongue. He inhaled sharply, controlling himself as the years of life had taught him."

"Benjamin thinks that by acquiring her cousin, he will force a link with her. " He turned his attention towards the silent white stucco house. "I hear no noise from there. I am not sure it is possible to create a connection but should it be, then the entire family is in grave danger."

"Markus," Robert's voice had softened. It was almost weary now with the knowledge of what he must do. "Please check on her family. Ensure he is still whole."

"Already done," Markus responded. "The boy is weak. He is weak but still whole. He bears no marks on him, but it's a though he has been drained repeatedly, taken right to the edge. It's strange Robert."

"What is strange?" Please he thought to himself; please don't let him say what I think he is going to.

"There are no dreams. It is total darkness within his sleep. No memories, no fantasy, no imagination. What rare glimpses I do get are not his. They belong to Benjamin. Just fragments; nothing of real structure but it appears he is either turning him by draining him repeatedly or manipulating his mind to become one of his minions."

Gasps resounded in Robert's head from the others.

"He must be stopped." Jerard whispered.

"Giles," Robert spoke quietly. "Can you implant a dream into his mind?"

"I'm not sure, Robert. It is worth a try. What were you thinking?"

"A trip if possible," I think. "Something he will wake to within moments with the desire so deep it cannot wait. Something that will have him leaving tonight, before Benjamin returns for him. Choose far away, Giles, an extended vacation. Implant the dream and also a place that he has been saving money. Leave it there for him to find."

"I'll take Leonard with me and search the house as well. Perhaps as mad as Benjamin appears he will have left something behind. Markus and Jerard will remain outside of the other house. Night closes in quickly, Robert. Be prepared."

As uncomfortable as it felt at the moment, the Elders separated knowing they were mere seconds from reaching each other should it be needed. Leonard and Giles faded into the shadows as they moved around the side of the house. Leonard paused and gestured upwards, seeing the small deck on the second level of the house. Giles nodded and leaped up onto the deck, as silent as the night itself. Leonard followed Giles inside.

The house was rank with the scent of humans, neither awake nor asleep; neither living nor dead. Leonard paused and closed his eyes, sensing the number of humans in the basement. The other Elders shuddered as they felt the destruction through their minds. "There are no young ones here." Leonard choked. "Shit" He spat the word as he moved downstairs while Giles entered the house to find Dan."

Giles glided along the old floor that normally creaked beneath a human's feet, guided by the empty mind to his destination. He shook off the sadness that one of his kind could be as cruel as he sank into the shadows towards the boy. The moonlight filtered through the curtains, casting an eerie glow upon the face. He was pale, so very pale, Giles thought as he gently probed within Dan's mind. It felt so empty, a room with no color, no light and no memories. Now he had to swallow back the anger that welled inside. He cursed as he pledged to find Benjamin and any he maybe have created in his image and destroy them.

With a gentleness that was somewhat unlike Giles, he began to imprint memories. Fragments only as that was all he had. Slivers of

102

light entered the blackness and Giles smiled. The rest would return with time. He took a breath as he wondered where to send the boy. Far enough away that he could not be harmed again for some time. It had to be outside of the country. He didn't think Benjamin would take the time to make a long distance trip to return his prey. Giles began the dream. Sweeping palm trees cooled the boy as he lay beneath them on the warm sand. The echo of the tall waves crashing upon the beach became soothing, lulling Dan into a sense of restful quiet. Magnificent sunsets filled with all the colors of the rainbow greeted him at nightfall, luring him to peaceful and safe sleep.

He waited with baited breath to see if the dream would take, hearing the ticking of the bedside clock as he watched. Light and life began to slowly return to his dreams and a smile of longing passed across the boy's lips. Giles nodded to himself before completing the task. Within the next hour he would wake, retrieve the money, make the first flight available and drive to the airport to wait. Excitement would fuel him, sustain him. He would leave a voice mail to his family saying he had decided to take a vacation.

Giles inhaled. The scent of relaxation filled his senses as he left the room and went in search of Leonard. It wasn't difficult to find him. He simply had to follow the distinct scent of near death.

Three bodies lay at Leonard's feet. Barely alive, their memories erased, filled with thoughts from Benjamin. He could sense the beginning of power flow within their veins as they crossed from the human world. Left without guidance, without concise thoughts that prepared the soul for change had permanently damaged these three. They were hopelessly lost within the change. Should they rise again, they would be soulless. They would be nothing more than mindless puppets for Benjamin to control, feeding on whatever pleased them with no thought to harm or life.

"They cannot remain this way." Leonard whispered to Giles though he knew the rest listened with a quiet sadness.

They could feel the souls that had been trapped. Feel the struggle as they strived to make the journey from one to the other with no guidance; with no knowledge and no destination. Leonard did the best he could do. He freed them from their agony. The light that had been so dim within them was slowly extinguished until there was nothing left within them except peace. They would have to rid the house of the bodies but first to see if they could find anything Benjamin may have left.

Nothing remained. No trace except the scent of the madness that lay within him. Anger leant speed to their goal as they retrieved the bodies and carried them from the house, running swiftly and with ease despite the added weight to the town nearby. They would leave them to be found and buried appropriately. Judging from their attire and the filth on them, they were drifters. Both doubted that any family would recognize them, none from this area anyway.

Once they completed their task the raced back to the farm, settling beneath the large oak tree in the yard.

Now it was Roberts turn. They hoped he could reach Becca tonight.

Chapter 8

She opened the book whilst climbing the stairs. Having climbed and fallen down these stairs more times than she cared to admit, there was no need to watch, she knew them intimately... Already fascinated, she became fully immersed in the strange script flowing on each faded page. The writing appeared so antiquated, she thought while staring at the flow and style of writing. This most assuredly did not come from pen, she was sure of it.

The bed creaked as she settled, placing the book down only long enough to turn on the lights before resuming from where she had left off. Trailing delicate fingers over the script, feeling the indentation from whatever had been used to pen the journal gave her a sense of foreboding- but there was more. There was a sense of answers, of finally understanding some of the questions that had recently plagued her. All of these strange occurrences, perhaps within these faded pages would be the answers she so fervently hoped for... "It must be hundreds of years old." She murmured as she carefully began to turn the pages.

The year: 1313

Our world slowly dies. With war and hatred now burning in the souls of those once chosen to lead, we've come to a time no world should face. Destruction. All things once valued now lay in ruins as two main forces vie for control. Little time remains now as revenge and retaliation becomes the focus instead of loyalty, kindness and growth. I am Vespera, the Creator of all those within my vast reach. My name, meaning Evening Star, was gifted to me as a child when the foundation of my calling was realized.

Each of my children I have gifted within their hearts a part of me. I weep with knowledge and pain as so many succumb or surrender to hatred and violence. Their souls; irreplaceable souls lost to the night. As each releases their light, so goes with them that piece of myself. My love was gifted to each that I bore. As the battles rage forth, death and decay surrounds me. Each piece of love given so freely to mine slowly dies. With the fading of their essence a piece of me also dies.

For many years I have taught those borne from me, imparted the knowledge passed down from generations. All so alike in many forms yet so different. Joined with the same values and intellect, each showed, as I had during childhood, their unique calling spill forth. Only then was a name assigned to them.

Becca paused before turning the page. Again her fingers travelled over the deep indentation of scrawl. The writing, so faded made it difficult to read, the words so poignant her heart broke for the one whose eyes she was seeing through

Absently she touched her face, warm tears clinging to the soft flesh. She hadn't realized that she had been crying. The pain, the slow death of something that held so much love was tragic. There felt like such a connection to this person writing. Not because of the depth of the journal that had captured her heart and not because of the familiarity of loss of life over wars and battles. It was something more. It was as though she knew the person- a kindred spirit, someone she was meant to know. Sitting up she pushed the book aside, unsure that she could read any further. Though as misty saddened eyes turned back towards the pages, drawn to what she didn't know but could feel she knew there would be no choice but to continue. Becca knew that love that devotion and the true commitment contained within the ancient pages. It was her deepest devotion. Maybe that was why her aunt had given it to her? Becca could feel the beauty, the wealth of love, the great humanity within the pages. She reached up to tuck an errant strand of hair behind her ear before continuing to read.

There is precious little time left my children. She gasped, feeling the pain that accompanied those words. It was as though she was there, encompassed within the person that writing them.

Our time on this world ends. Five of you, my beautiful children have been chosen to seek out a new home. For hundreds of years your training and loyalty has been

noted. Your desires documented. My time is gone but my children shall live on. As you stand before me tonight I shall name you. Names most deserving of the best I have borne witness to. Your names shall reflect that which is inside of you. Once you are named, I will spend what is left of my energy to open a portal for you. Doing so will seal my fate. Death will take me but I leave this world knowing that those most special will have life among another world and another people.

I ask that this journal, along with our heritage go with you if at all possible. This must be done with utmost haste. It will be expected that a few others will also follow through the portal-Young ones. It is my wish that you attempt to train them should they contact you. Let us hope that those riddled with madness for control do not find their way through.

Becca jumped as she heard her aunt calling her for dinner. The journal was so engrossing that it was all she could do to tear herself away. What happened, she wondered? Who had come through, how many and why did my aunt have this book? The reporter within her was running in overdrive as she glanced back at the book before pressing it against her chest, unable to be parted from it. It seemed safer this way, more comforting to hold onto it. To continue to feel the closeness from the words engraved inside.

Placing the book beside her, she settled at the table. "Ugh more coffee," Becca groaned, quickly forgetting the gruesome connotation as she looked with great curiosity towards her aunt.

Florence sat with her at the table after setting plates of food in front of them. Becca picked up her fork after thanking her. She played with the food, moving it around the plate, her mind unsettled.

"The book," Becca started.

"Has been handed down through our family," Florence interrupted. "Many, many generations have held the book, kept it safe, we have, I suppose you can say, been its guardian. "

"I don't understand," She shook her head.

"Eat." Florence commanded waiting until her all too curious niece popped a mouthful of food into her mouth before continuing.

"The house that you live beside has been there a very long time." Florence took a bite of her food, chewing as she thought. "It was so long ago." She sighed.

Becca tried to swallow the food finding it difficult to get past the lump in her throat. "So," she prompted her aunt.

"My great, great, great grandmother, which would be your," she paused, counting. "Well anyway. She was always into what you kids have always called the crazy voodoo stuff in regards to me."

She laughed as Becca blushed. "I'm sorry, we were only teasing."

"I did the same to my grandmother." Tears filled her eyes as she looked towards the house. "It's not the same without her around." Florence smiled sadly.

"I know," she responded, feeling the same sadness.

Florence turned back towards Becca but it didn't feel as though she were here. The glazed look that shadowed her aunt's chocolate eyes told her she was very far away

"Some years ago, when we found out Grandma had cancer for the first time; she called me into the room and told me a story." Florence looked at Becca.

"The book came into our possession because our great, great, great ... well whatever, grandmother was the first caller. Something had compelled her to go to that house. It was empty, barren of anything. Something, I don't know what as the story changes as the book is handed over, compelled her search." Florence paused. "Curiosity runs in our family, I'm sure you have noticed." She glanced towards the clippings of Becca's work that she had saved.

"I'm not so much curious as I am interested in finding the truth." She defended herself before shrugging her shoulders at the look from her Aunt. "Alright, so maybe there is some curiosity in me."

Florence nodded. "That curious nature is how we ended up being the keeper of this book, Becca"

"Five were chosen to come through the, gate or the portal or whatever it was." She paused to take a bite of her meal. Becca had already pushed uneaten meal aside, growing impatient, wanting to hear the rest of the story.

"Your great – well however many generations back, she was there; outside. She had been on an errand when she heard a strange noise coming from a house that was supposed to be empty. It was something unlike anything that had been heard by her before." Florence offered a rueful smile. "Curious remember?"

"She went to the house and glanced in the old window along the back. There was a glow. It wasn't a light she said, but something eerie and strange." Florence took a bite of food as she paused.

"I remember being told the story, Becca. She was still alive, though apparently until the moment she passed away, her eyes, so much like yours, remained touched. The haunted glow to her eyes never left." Florence stopped and glanced towards the charms she had placed around the home. "I hope in her sleep she has finally found peace." Her wrinkled hand wiped across her face before continuing.

"As they appeared through this entry, it was told to me that she shoved her hands across her mouth to stop the screams. Her intuition was to run yet her body wouldn't move. The fear held her immobile."

"Did they see her?" Becca enquired? "I mean obviously she got away, we are here right."

"Not exactly, Becca." "She was never the same, a ghost of the woman she was.

She told those around her that the ones who emerged from the portal stared lifelessly for a moment before collapsing. They appeared disoriented, weakened and though exceptionally different, they seemed gloriously beautiful."

"They were dead?" Becca glanced at the book before turning back to her aunt. "I. Don't. Understand." She accentuated each word.

"No, not dead Becca, well not exactly dead at least," Aunt Florence responded as her fingers played with the now cold coffee as she thought. "You will understand more as you read the book, dear. In essence the transfer from their world to yours completely drained their essence, hovering on the brink of death."

"All that came through were more like entities. Not human, but the first five that came through seemed the most robust." Florence tapped her chin as she tried to think of words that would describe the story. "The others collapsed immediately. It was as though the five were ensuring security before succumbing to the same fate."

Irritation swept through Becca. Bitch mode was setting in; she clutched her fingers to remain patient with her quirky aunt-a trait that apparently ran in the family. "Aunt Florence?" Becca kept her tone neutral.

"Oh, yes dear," She smiled to her. "Where was I?" mm right, let's see now. First five seemed though not human, almost immense in stature-regal, to Caroline," she paused and patted Becca's hand. "As you can imagine it was quite a shock to see or experience something so surreal. Nothing seemed real to her. As they sank to the ground it was as though they absorbed the essence of this world. Almost immediately they began forming bodies. Well perhaps it is shells of bodies. I really don't know." She glanced to her niece, withholding the sigh as she drank in the pallor of her flesh. Florence nodded. She was sure Becca was beginning to put together the fragmented pieces.

"Was it," she hesitated, not sure she wanted to know the question about to be asked to her aunt. Was it hideous? Did they seem to be in pain? How? "All of these questions floated from her brain past her lips, one after the other without her taking a breath.

Florence patted her hand. "According to what we have learned the transformation on the outside was stunningly extraordinary." She shrugged and rose to refill their cups before sitting again. "I mean naturally this story was so unbelievable that to even discuss it would have put her in a mental home for the rest of her life. Not even I believed what I heard... until I was given the journal." She held up her had as Becca's lips began to move to ask more; she needed more. "They entered through the portal more like luminescent shells of humans, ravaged by something that had ripped away the entirety of their outer skeletal figure, leaving just the inside. As they adjusted, inhaled the air around them, flesh, pale, very pale flesh began to form around bones that had been protruding.

"Well, like you would have been, Caroline was also mesmerized. The five she described as beyond beautiful. Not simply in looks for there was an oddity about all of them. Their eyes opened only once but it shook her to the very core."

Please Becca begged, please, please don't say they were black. She closed her eyes and braced herself for the words she were coming, words she did not want to hear.

"I believe I don't need to tell you the color, dear, for I fear you have already seen it for yourself.

It felt as though the bottom had been slipped from beneath her. Becca sank back into the seat, her heart thundering as she looked quizzically at her aunt. Somehow she was shaking her head no; it couldn't be though her aunt's eyes spoke the truth. Her fingers clutched the book and she pressed it against her chest causing the pulsing of the mark to increase in intensity.

Her voice sounded devoid of emotion as she finally spoke "And then…." She prompted.

Florence looked with pure exasperation at the impatient girl before continuing. "More began to almost- fight their way through, the glowing entry was dissipating, time quickly ticking by. Frantically they clawed their way over and around those that had already made the journey, breathless, almost lifeless as the glimmering light of the portal faded, taking with it endless screams of those trapped within. One of the first men through clutched the book fiercely against his chest. Florence shook her head. The rest, Caroline wrote in the book, child. You will find the answers there."

"Thank You Aunt Florence," Becca leaned forward to press a kiss to her wizened cheek. She dearly loved her, especially when she wasn't considering choking her beloved aunt. "I am going to read."

"Yes, I thought you might. Goodnight Becca dear."

The hallway was dimly lit, preventing her from delving back into the heart of the creator. The need was tangible, beyond that it bordered on desperation as she took the steps two at a time. She had to know. The sinking feeling in the pit of her stomach was something she relied on daily for work. It had never steered her wrong before. This was monumental, it was creepy and it was – she believed, very. She understood the reasons now that she had become enthralled. It was him. Instantly Robert fluttered through her mind. She didn't even bother to force the thoughts away. And the man on the street, the dark sunglasses he and his friends wore. The pieces were coming together and she wasn't sure she was ready for the puzzle to be complete.

Having left the light on in the bedroom, Becca flopped onto the bed, her attention fixated on faded yellow pages as she delicately opened the journal again. Skipping pages, the need to seek the finality of the story compelled her to forgo reading the middle section, moving instead to the ending. Nothing really goes well she chuckled softly when you read the final pages first, she had learned this the hard way more than once, but she desperately wanted to know what her ancestor witnessed. .

"At the very last moment," Caroline wrote, another emerged, perhaps half a heartbeat away from having his fate sealed along with the portal. I hoped he would make it, the others seemed so gentle; there was an air of peacefulness that surrounded them. In hindsight I should have prayed he had been one that was sucked back through the hole, never to arrive here. Destiny I suppose does not work this way however. He shimmied through, thoughtlessly pushing others back through the gate as he used them to propel himself forward... There was an air of supposed superiority to this one that didn't exist within the others. It felt cold as he, without thought or care discarded others for his own benefit. But perhaps it was fear that had lent itself wings for his actions and not the...being itself. He came through as the others had. It was akin to seeing the inner workings of a body without the organs humans needed to survive. As he stood and gazed downward to the others I realized this one was far different.

I watched through the corner of the window as he arched his lithe gaunt frame and inhaled deeply of the fresh clean air, drinking in the scents of summer, the hay being rolled and the morning dew that glistened upon the grass. It was as though he tasted life here on earth, absorbing it, drawing it inside to create his outer layering. I had seen his original form, what rested beneath but when he was complete it was breathtaking. Held mesmerized by hair the color of sunlight, eyes as back as the deepest part of the ocean; he was a god perhaps. An Adonis sent here to earth to seek refuge or perhaps simply live amongst us. . I held my breath as my heart fluttered like the wings of a humming bird, so beautiful, I thought. In me at the onset, was a gratefulness that this particular man had survived... Something so brilliantly stunning deserved their place here among us, even if there was something almost —feral about him. I could sense anger, hatred and a lust for power as he struggled to remain upright whilst the others remained in a comatose state. Yet like a moth drawn to the flickering dancing flames I was struck immobile and breathless by his beauty and his strength. I urged myself to leave, to run now before being seen as it was the safest and logical choice to make and yet I could not make my extremities work. Instead I stared, transfixed until my Adonis displayed the true evil nature that either he controlled-or it controlled him. I will never know the answer.

I watched in horror as he callously kicked those sprawled along the floor out of his way. T 'was a feat of strength no human should have. The bodies flew and landed with sickening thuds before laying strewn about the small house. I was sickened, not only that this stunning creature could be so deliberately cruel but to do so to those defenseless kindred beings was frightening. I made myself as small as I was able, now desperately frightened to move after being unintentionally offered a glimpse of his intentional cruelty.

Fate had played its hand, leaving me there just mere moments too long. I could sense it deep inside as I chanced another glance at the object of my former desire; now my nightmare. The man- I shall call him that as I never learned what they were, though the personification of perfection, was vastly different than the others. He seemed alive, complete and almost joyful at the hatred that fueled his blood. A deep rich tone, a victorious cry spilled from his full lips as he backhanded the man who clutched the journal; this journal out of the way so he could retrieve it.

Becca shook disbelief evident on her face as she reached up to wipe away the beads of sweat that glistened along her forehead. Rubbing the palms of her hands together before turning the page she continued...

My body shook with fear as I saw him begin to tremble as the others had. I suspected whatever he was; no matter the seemingly endless strength he seemed to exhibit, he couldn't escape the same fate as the others who lay on the floor in some sort of comatose slumber. For just a moment, a glimmer of hope sparked within me. Perhaps-a sliver of a chance if I were able to summon the courage and wait just a few moments for him to succumb to whatever ailed the others; I could steal away safely and quietly. The man however tilted his head upwards once again and inhaled. For some reason I shook as his nostrils flared. His face, already the ashen color turned deathly pale. My body began to shake. I knew I had waited just a moment too long.

A smile touched his lips. More a sneer- or perhaps a victorious smirk, one a hunter might use once their prey was in sight. Yes, that was the look. Blue eyes glittered, narrowing in recognition as he inhaled again. He had caught the scent of his prey-and was savoring the flavor. The black, the beautiful color dissipated as blackness stole the white coloring from his eyes. I bit back the gasp of horror as the entirety of his eyes turned the color of nightfall. The hunter had zeroed in on its prey. Cold lifeless eyes slowly rolled in the direction of the window.

Terror made my motions jerky; uncoordinated as I crept back, praying and begging that he would collapse as the others had before reaching me. But alas, my fate was sealed. It took not even seconds before he was beside me, over me, hovering as a large feline would as it perused its meal before its final attack. A strange scent emanated from him. It was pleasant, as familiar to me as my own scent-one I'll not likely ever forget. It smelled of my dreams. Every dream I have ever had rolled inside of him and projected towards me.

Muscles poised and clenched to run, I turned but his strength overpowered mine as easily as a spider would capture a fly. It is how I felt at this moment; caught in a web of my own making. I should have left- I didn't.

As though I weighed nothing, his large hands propelled me to the ground to kneel before him. I felt the pain as my knees were crushed into the dirt, the confusion as I fell downwards. Had he asked I knew deep inside I would instantly have surrendered but that was not his goal. Domination and fear were. I trembled, breathing at a frantic pace as I cowered at his feet, hoping against hope that this humiliation would satiate what appeared to be an intense desire for the driving lust within him; ultimate control. Tears rolled unheeded down my ashen face as I begged him to leave, my voice soft, quivering with fright. The once majestic smile twisted into an ugly semblance of a sneer, lips parting- a savage snarl of power echoing through the barren clearing. With perfect fluidity, he lunged, landing with his entire weight on top of me, shoving me back into the dried blades of grass. I could feel them pricking my flesh though I am unsure as to why I was focused on that.

Again Becca paused. The abject terror in Caroline's words caused goose bumps to rise on her flesh. Absently she rubbed them as she visualized her distant relative kneeling before some…super being. She inhaled sharply, taking a moment to collect her wayward thoughts before immersing herself in the story once again. Brushing aside her own pangs of fear and sadness for her relative she rubbed weary eyes before turning them back to the pages. She knew if she gave in to the emotions now, she would never finish and she had to know. Now more than ever she was driven to know.

She was right she realized... Nothing good happens when you read the ending first. She couldn't prevent the shudder that ripped through her.

He leaned forward, his fingers ripping the upper bodice of my dress and I began to scream. The sounds fueled his fury and he bit me, barely breaking the flesh. Instead as he did so, he invaded my mind. My thoughts were no longer my own. Slowly my mind was becoming a black abyss, holding nothing, no memories, no life, no love and no hope. He was draining me- draining my life through my mind, through my soul.

My body was of no use for him though the image of myself on my knees flashed continuously through his mind. He liked it. Liked the way he rose above me. My strength was waning. There was not much time left. I felt emptiness inside as his face grew flush with color, black eyes beginning to glow with the life he stole from me.

And then he spoke with a strange tongue I somehow understood. My only guess as to why I understood was his unwavering gaze as he imprinted his words on my mind, in my heart; on my soul.

"I shall steal into your mind and into your dreams," he began, his voice sultry and sensual. Designed I was sure to capture the attention of those with whom he spoke. I watched his face redden more, discomfort beginning to edge the once smooth lines into something almost gruesome. The sunlight! It had to be the light that was distorting his once flawless flesh. He had to be quick, he realized, I could see it in his eyes. His pain; I was glad for his pain as he drained my life, my soul, my dreams. He continued- his voice harder. "I will steal into all of your kind most shameful thoughts. You will feel me the rest of your life. In every shiver your pitiful world will feel me. I will be in ever spasm of souls and I will steal the beating of your hearts force. I will learn your most fundamental beliefs and turn them against you. Oh I shall create an army to feed on your irrational impulses and give voice to all unspeakable emotions. I will breed from you and from others until there is only my kind; until only I am supreme. "

116

"Oh God" Becca whispered, clutching her stomach as nausea rose. Shades of disgust so vile festered inside, causing acidic bile to rise. Her eyes hardened as she swallowed back the urge to empty the contents of her stomach. Anger was a useful tool and she used it now. He would not claim her fear, not like he had to Caroline. Drawing on any reserves of strength she could find, she turned back to the journal.

Fear lent me wings perhaps, or he grew weaker beneath the sun and was still feeling the effects of the entry. My lungs filled with air as I screamed as loud as humanly possible- until my voice was nothing more than a hoarse whisper. I pushed, kicked and scratched as he probed my mind again. I knew I was about to be lost forever-my strength leaving my by minute inclement. I barely felt my arms as they dropped lifelessly to the ground. With little left, I waited for the inevitable, hoping against hope he would take pity and the end would be quick.

Miracles happen. I prayed. I prayed for salvation, for release of this emptiness inside. Shadows began to cross my vision. Sunset perhaps, I no longer knew- it no longer mattered. My eyes began to flutter closed, no tears; no thoughts- emptiness, just a black cavernous hole. And then I was free. Free to breath in air. Free to feel life again. Dizzying relief warred with disbelief. Was he playing with his prey- allowing hope just to savor the sensation of his victim drowning once again in the black abyss of obscurity? Overwhelmed with horror, with indecision, I lay there panicked and overwrought, squeezing my eyes tightly closed. For moments- or a lifetime I remained there, quivering with tears falling down my dust covered face, leaving dirty streaks.

Sense began to return, the urge to run so compelling I could not fight it. I slowly opened my eyes, emotionally drained; utterly terrified I would see him hovering above me, that sadistic smile curling his upper lip.

Standing before me were five, strong and muscular- the most beautiful saviors that one could ever imagine. I was either dreaming- or I had died. The pain was too great to be the latter. Again my lashes fluttered. The same pallor to their flesh- the same black haunting eyes as the other had. I was sure my heart would beat from my chest. It was obvious they were still very weak, but together they pulled the- thing off of me. I scrambled to my hands and knees, looking frantically for a place to hide.

The one- the one that had bitten me and touched my soul had left a mark that would never fade Indeed I was now condemned and damaged for life. He had not the power to fight the five. He granted me a look of loathing; of regret for not completing what he had intended before shifting into the shadows. The book lay strewn on the grass, forgotten, survival his only priority.

The men, if that is what they are, urged me to rise. I looked fearfully at them, my hand covering the bite mark as though attempting to rid myself of it. I felt their weakness. Saving me had apparently waned what little was left of their strength. Wanting nothing more than to run, I resisted as I saw one begin to sway. I helped them inside, out of the light, laying them with the others.

They bid me leave. To go and hide before others awoke. I turned on my heel, more than happy to oblige. One reached an arm upwards as I passed. I danced out of reach and screamed, until I saw he was simply holding the journal out for me. The words spoken were soft and strained. Protect this-please. This is the same journal that I now write in. The man whispered something that sounded like;" I was the one- The caller." I didn't understand, nor at that time was I sure I wanted to, but he entrusted me with this precious work. It was all that remained of his world. It is to be passed down in our family. Because of the bite, we have in our genetics, the chance to become a siren caller. I asked what that meant, becoming more afraid. Would it bring that thing back? I did not understand. He said we will carry in our minds, in our hearts and in our blood deeper thoughts; stronger dreams that would through different lifetimes' call to them"

Again I was confused though I no longer cared. The desire to be away grew with each passing second. Clutching the journal I gave my word to keep it safe.

Trembling fingers brushed back her long hair. Incredulous was a good word to use, Becca thought. Could that have really happened? She thought back to her time as a child, wracking her brain to remember Caroline.

She had been recluse, giving birth to several children. From what she could recall, Caroline never attended any functions, nor was her

118

children allowed. They had been home schooled and kept virtual prisoners on their family farm. People would talk of course, whispered words about Caroline. That she had become unstable, that she filled her home with ancient ritualistic items designed to keep them safe.

It was Florence's great, great grandmother that had finally left. Others began to trickle away slowly until Caroline, the matriarch of her family was left alone.

"So that is why," Becca spoke to as she turned to the last page. There was just a short message.

The bite mark never healed. It burned the remainder of my life. Dreams and images were not forgotten. Death approaches me and I must now decide whether to keep my promise and burden the next generation. Had it not been for them, I would not be here. I would never have had love or children or grandchildren. I owe them this at least, though at what cost to the next that carries this weight. It is time to share the haunting story to the next keeper of the journal.

Becca's fingers traced along the last passage, feeling the much softer scrawl from a woman that had carried so much more than she should have.

Night cast its eerie glow into the room as she shifted. "Well," she spoke her thoughts allowed. "If this is true, then I'm guessing Florence is passing it down to me, but why? Why now?" Her fingers tapped her chin as she thought. Weariness consumed, but the reporter in her knew she wouldn't stop until she had all the answers.

Taking a deep breath she turned back to the beginning, flipping through until she found where she had originally left off.

I welcome you my children, the Creator spoke. Five of you stand before me, the best of all of my children in the last centuries, the last of my kind that I shall witness being named. Each name has been chosen after much careful consideration. Each name is a gift given to you from me. The final thing I am able to bestow upon you aside from escape. It is my belief that you all will, in time find your mate and rebuild our race. Find your path, your destiny and protect what is left within you. Please come forth.

I bestow upon you the name Robert. The meaning of the name is bright with glory. You shall be instrumental in guiding the young ones, and in helping the other Elders achieve their desires. Keep what you have been taught alive in your heart.

Through each of the remaining four the same ceremony and words were said. The nausea she had held at bay now came back with a ferocity that could not be ignored. She was thankful the bathroom was right next to her room as she sank to her knees and vomited.

Jerard which means strength of the spear

Giles which means shield bearer

Markus which means Warrior

Leonard which means brave

The names continued to run over and over in her mind as she retched. There were such things as coincidences and then there was the truth staring straight at you. This was bad, she groaned as she curled up, pressing her cheek to the ceramic floor-very bad.

Chapter 9

"Robert!!" she spat the name, infusing enough venom for the word to become an epithet. Robert, her neighbour, the man who starred in a number of her recent dreams, the… "Oh God", she gasped, leaning over the toilet emptying the remainder of her stomach contents. "If he is one of those…things- then he would have seen my dreams… Oh God!" The words trailed off as she placed her cheek back onto the cool floor. Hot salty tears splashed onto the tile as she imagined him invading her thoughts nightly. An aching pulse rose steadily from the mark on her chest. "THE MARK!" she shrieked while scampering up onto her hands and knees, clutching the reignited fiery anger that radiated from every shaking inch of her body. "That low down good for nothing sneaky little bastard, she fumed while rising from the floor. "I'll kill him!" she growled as she reached for her toothbrush. Brushing her teeth made her feel marginally better; not as much as a few sharp words with him would, but it would have to be enough for tonight. She stomped back into the bedroom, cursing him five ways to Sunday.

She lay on the bed curling around the book, curiously wondering how long a person could go without sleeping. "I'm going to kill him," was her last conscious thought as her body succumbed and her eyes closed.

Finally, Robert thought as he inhaled sharply. Hours he had been waiting for her to drift. His mark granted him the power to feel her emotions and anger-to put it mildly,{his ears still stung from her choice of adjectives for him} was on the forefront of this one. A smile curved his lips upwards. A little hell fire his Rebecca was. He heard his so called friends- a wry look crossed his features, cackling with laughter at each word they caught through his thoughts. "May you all find one just like her," he growled before laughing with them.

Anxiousness had filled him while being away from her. His senses were heightened as he raced towards his destiny. There was no further need to follow her by scent; his mark bound them enough that he was able to find her, but the flavor of her- so intoxicating- he couldn't resist inhaling the night air that filled itself with her. His friends caught the emotion as he allowed himself to be guided by the aroma, the passion, it was difficult even for them to resist when faced with the excruciatingly beautiful and profound sensations. He chuckled as he turned back towards the house, feeling his body relax for the first time in what seemed like forever. Now that she was close, he felt reassured of her safety.

He closely examined the strategically placed charms around the entrances. They were very good, he noticed. Whoever created these was exceptionally skilled in the ancient voodoo rituals. It really was quite impressive. There were few who could pass it, vampires especially, though his kind as well. He supposed that as both came to life after the sun set and darkness blanketed the world they were grouped together in one genre though nothing could be further from the truth.

As an Elder his skills were far more advanced. It would be quite easy to work around the charms though he did not want to invade the woman's house. It was obvious she understood the ritualistic ways of the gypsies, and Robert respected, even admired every form of human life and their skill sets. Closing shimmering black eyes he used the mark to reach to his soul mate. "Allow me entrance, my Rebecca." He whispered the words softly, soothingly and enticingly. "Say it Rebecca, allow me in."

A deep stirring began in the pit of her belly, spreading a need that at once encompassed the totality of her body. She moaned deeply in her sleep, shuddering and, whimpering, knowing for some reason she should resist, to say no; parting lush full lips to do just that. Apparently her mind and coiled needs had a brief difference of opinion as she softly cooed, "come in. "

"Thank you," was softly spoken as he played along the shadows of the wall. He inhaled her scent. It carried odors unfamiliar to him, things she would never notice, but it left him with a blazing anger that enriched the shimmering in his eyes until they glowed in the darkness. Death would be the result of this intrusion on his Rebecca, there was no longer any question about this. Calming himself before daring to venture further inside, he vowed revenge, images playing through his mind of times to come without fear for her safety. Casting a rueful glance in her direction and shook his head. That was not likely to ever happen-to strong, too beautiful, too powerful; and completely his.

Need filled her as it always did when around him. This time however she felt the capability to cling to a small vestige of resistance to him. This confused her-upset her as well as pleased her. Her subconscious was throwing a tantrum as she had flung herself onto the bed, awaiting the purely sensual riotous emotions he filled her with. She shifted and frowned, wanting those feelings. Damn the man.

He didn't even attempt to resist her call. He doubted anyone could, aside from the Elders. Closing the distance he settled on the side of the small bed. The paleness of his hand was enhanced by the blackness of the shirt that circled his wrist. He reached forward gently tracing cold fingers across the silky smoothness of her skin. So warm, he thought as he brushed back her hair. Rebecca's responding throaty purring noises propelled his fingers to retrace their path. Just once more. To hear that sound, to know it was meant for him. His gut twisted as she cooed. His entire demeanor softened as she parted her lips, a delicate sigh whispering forth as she shifted slightly, leaning into the touch. Robert couldn't resist. He captured her lips, invading her mouth with a deep lingering kiss.

Her fingers gripped the sheets as she felt her head begin to swim. Good Lord the man could kiss, she whimpered as he stole her breath now as easily as he had captured her heart. From the very first time he had invaded her dreams, she knew he was the one- the man she had searched a lifetime for, wished for on every falling star and every coin tossed into a wishing well. God help her, Becca's head swirled as she responded with equal fervor, knowing that tomorrow; or tonight if she woke from this heaven, everything was going to change. She sighed hungrily against his lips, releasing the death grip on the sheets. The ache to feel him was overwhelming. One hand swept upwards to weave through his tangled dark hair. It felt like touching heaven as her they danced to the back of his head, seeking to draw him closer. Becca moaned against his lips, knowing he swallowed her sounds as the kiss deepened. Wait, she thought, wait-she struggled, trying to weave through her passion filled mind, and I'm not supposed to be able to touch him!! "Bastard!"

Her eyes flew open as she wriggled from beneath his hovering form. "What the hell!" Her voice was more than livid; her body shaking from fear and the out of control spiralling need that one kiss had created. Reaching for the blanket she dragged it to cover herself with as her brows furrowed and redness stole into her cheeks. Confusion however was the first emotion to deal with. "How the fu... How the hell did you get in here? What are you? Why are you here? The questions spewed from her mouth faster than she could stop them.

Ah the shadows were always so much simpler, Robert braced himself as she all but charged at him. Might be nice if she did, he tried not to grin. He would most definitely enjoy feeling her against him. In a peaceful gesture, he held up his hands, gesturing for her to relax. She was coiled as tightly as a panther ready to spring. "I shall tell you all that you need and want to know, Rebecca, but believe; please believe I am not here to hurt you."

"I know," she responded though her teeth snapped together. She was tired and bitchy and ready to smack the man upside his head. "Answers! I want answers Robert. What the hell is going on? What are you? And stop calling me Rebecca!" She inhaled, feeling slightly better after her rant.

"I promise to answer every question Rebecca, but right now, you are not safe. We need to get you away from here."

"I think my Aunt's house is very safe." she rolled her eyes as she pointed out the dozens of charms.

"Only for a short time Rebecca," Robert cautioned. "Charms only work on those that do not seek to harm. And your name is beautiful, it deserves to be said." She snarled as he swallowed the laugh though his friend's chortles and chuckles were clearly heard in his head.

"You said you don't intend to harm me," she countered. "Yet you steal into my dreams nightly," she blushed furiously recalling some of the more memorable ones. "But not hurt me?"

"What the hell do you think that is?" Blinking; willing the tears to remain at bay. Crap she was definitely wired wrong. "Invading my mind?" She rose from the bed and paced, building up a full steam of anger. "Making me want you? Care about you? "She turned, the fury building to a rising crescendo. "What do you call that if not a complete invasion of my privacy as well as outright manipulation? "She paused, stammering, "Not that I care that is…" Liar, liar, her subconscious whispered, still savoring the kiss they had shared.

"No. I give you my word, it was not done with any intention of harming you or forcing you to feel anything you did not already feel, but there are others that do wish-he paused, more of you than you can imagine. It's why I had to place one of my marks on you." Oh hell. He regretted the words the moment they slipped from his lips.

"You!!" furious eyes narrowed as she spat the word at him, moving forward before stopping inches from him. "What is a mark? What. Have. You. Done? "Each world grew in volume, in intensity and each was filled with venom.

She hides the fear well, Robert thought proudly as he ran his fingers through already tousled hair.

"You have your hands full," Markus laughed loudly.

Robert offered a growl in response.

"I need you to trust me, Rebecca," He pleaded. "Please." He stood, cautiously closing the distance, not wanting to startle her further. "We will answer every question you have. " Robert included the other Elders, hearing them chuckle in his head as he pleaded with the girl.

"Stop calling me that!" Oh so brilliant a comeback Becca, she frowned.

"Right now both of our lives are at risk, Becca, Robert conceded on the name for the moment. Your family, your friends as well as mine are in grave danger. He turned his full gaze towards her. The effect was almost immediate.

"Wow." Becca was lost in the ebony depths. Her heart yearned to trust the man she knew in her dreams, but the rest of her was more than a little pissed. The mention of her family brought her up short. Her teeth chewed her lower lip. Her family was her life. They meant everything to her. Could she risk putting them in danger? It was quite obvious the man that stood before her was not, well-a man.

"If we leave now, my aunt and my cousin will be safe?" she queried, having to turn away from those eyes before she jumped the man-or wanderer... or whatever the hell he was.

He paused before speaking, debating whether to tell her about her cousin; the desire to shield Rebecca from any further pain warred with the knowledge of the mistrust she would feel. He hesitated before capturing her eyes with his. "Your cousin was found near death, Becca. My friends healed him the best they could." He sighed. "They restored some memories of his family, happiness in his life," he waited, judging the pallor of her skin, the trembling he could see as the blanket shook against her.

"What are you not saying?"

"They... inserted a thought; a dream, a desire." He did his best to explain something almost unexplainable.

126

"They… who, I don't understand?" Sinking back onto the bed she gripped her head as it began to throb, fighting back tears, frantically concerned for her cousin.

"Not all of us are evil, Rebecca. My friends; the other elders, shared a thought of peace and of safety with your cousin- of love and family and hope. Right now he should be on a plane, smiling as he dreams of the warm, beautiful location he heads to; far from here, Rebecca- far from harm."

He took her silence as a good sign, continuing before she could speak. "Your aunt," He motioned downstairs where she slept, "will be of no use to the others once you are away from here, though we will of course monitor her and the rest of your family." His tone darkened causing Rebecca to shiver. "They will not get anywhere near you again, none of them." His tone spoke volumes of the seriousness of his claim, growing deep-holding within each word a depth pain for what she had already suffered.

"Others? What others, Robert?"

"The most dangerous at the moment is a wanderer named Benjamin." Again he watched her face turn ashen.

"I…I met a Benjamin today." Becca shivered, remembering the intense dislike she had felt. "He was very," she paused, "different. Insistent that I remain there-or he, accompany me here to my Aunts. He seemed less than pleased to be… turned down."

Robert nodded. "That was him. You are in danger; grave danger. We need to take you away. It is the only way to ensure you and your aunt will remain safe."

Her arms crossed over her chest as she hung her head, fighting back the tears. She thought of her quirky but totally loveable Aunt that was at this moment downstairs sleeping.

"Tell me where to go, I'll drive there. " Taking a breath, resolving in her mind what must be done, she rose, tossing things into her overnight bag. Finally she was ready, the pack over her shoulder, her fingers clutching the book tightly to her. "But don't you for one minute think that I have forgotten one single question or one moment of the anger, Robert." She dared a look at him, willing her heart not to stutter.

He shook his head as he reached out to touch her hand. "There is no time, Rebecca. His hand fell to his side as she drew back from his touch.

"Don't. Touch. Me." The words were forced through tightly closed lips as she held precariously onto what was left of her sanity.

"Outside are many of my kind, and they are here for you. That, along with Benjamin means we have no more time remaining."

"How then?" Frankly she was curious now. Her Aunt had said she was far too curious. What was the expression "curiosity killed the cat', that was it. Well let's hope it won't be in this case she prayed.

"We shall run you in the shadows." He carefully scrutinized each feature and motion she made, marvelling at the strength and will that lay within her. Robert couldn't help but smile.

"Huh? You are going to what? It was her turn to hold up her hand as he began to speak.

The swallow was far too loud in the suddenly quiet room. Finally she looked up at him, allowing him to see the wariness inside while shielding the utter turmoil dancing within; straightening her back she composed her face into smooth lines of undefinable thoughts though she couldn't resist the next question. "You don't like... turn into anything creepy right? No bats, slimy things? Because I'm not going anywhere if you do." She held her stance as Robert sent a warning growl to the Elders in his head. They were roaring with laughter.

"She is a keeper, Robert," Leonard gasped between laughs.

"Why would we do that?" He was desperately trying not to laugh. "You have read one too many horror stories, Rebecca. Safety first, then answers," He promised.

She inhaled. "Fine, but you keep your mind far from mine! She paused, "And stop calling me Rebecca!" She shot him a warning look.

"I cannot remain out of your mind, Rebecca, we are now connected by my mark. " He growled softly as she backed up.

"The young ones are moving in closer, Robert. Move her now before it's too late. "The laughter was gone from Giles voice.

Robert nodded before gliding towards her. With motions so fast she completely missed them, Becca found herself over his shoulder heading towards the window.

"Don't look down Rebecca," he warned as she stiffened.

"Are you crazy?" she was terrified. "Try using the dam door! I am not going out the window, Robert!

Of course she looked down- didn't she always do the exact opposite of what she had been told. She blanched watching nothing but blackness, the rush of air against her skin, and then the ground racing to meet her much too quickly. Her stomach heaved. It would serve him right if she got sick all over him. Bastard. "Put me down!"

The words were swallowed as the wind screamed past her. She hung on for dear life as shadows and shapes blurred. Even familiar scents swept past too quickly for her to judge where they were.

"Oh shit," she blushed as her hand moved, gripping the closest thing she could find. It took a moment to, finally realizing she was groping his gorgeous ass. "Well," her subconscious was doing more back flips, "being tossed over his shoulder did indeed have its advantages.

His movements were so smooth Becca didn't feel the jostling and jarring one would expect. There would however be a few bruises as his shoulder dug into her ribcage, and a few along her chest from the book pressed between them. She grunted, trying to shift again. If he thought she was angry before he was going to be in for a huge surprise when she got down. There was nothing that captured anger more than feeling like a sack of potatoes.

Pounding on his back with the book had absolutely no effect, except to tire her. Blowing hair from her face she settled, seethed; and waited. Oh was he going to get a mouthful when she got down. Becca ran the words through her mind as he totally ignored her and quickened his pace. Chills ran up and down her body and she shivered. Maybe "Mr. hard as stone body" didn't feel the cold but she was downright freezing. "Ass," she muttered as she shivered again.

"Get her out of here now!" Jerard yelled as his fist connected to a young one's face.

"It's like a feeding frenzy here Robert," Markus grunted as one slammed into him. His large hands gripped the young one's body. He lifted him, taking aim before tossing him in the air. A cruel smile tugged on his lips as he watched the young one collapse, knocking three others down as he landed.

"What the hell?" Robert questioned as he increased his speed, ignoring Rebecca who at this point was again pounding on his back with the book she held, demanding to be put down.

"Nothing I've ever seen before," Leonard's voice held the ring of battle, the excitement. "These are not normal young ones, Robert. They smell of Benjamin and of death."

"That's not possible," Robert slowed as he shifted Rebecca into his arms. Gently he cradled her against his powerful chest. "Not unless…" he paused. "No, no."

"Unless he has been killing them and bringing them back to life with his blood." Giles completed Robert's thought.

He stopped running, frozen in place. His eyes began to turn black, slowly, so very slowly the whites disappeared until all that remained was the images of death and night. Even Becca's scream as she witnessed the change didn't register. His grip tightened as she tried to writhe from his arms. "Hold still" Robert's voice was gruff; filled with apprehension.

"They are much stronger than normal young ones, Robert," Markus sounded breathless, pausing for a moment as he shoved two off of him. "Get that next mark on her before it's too late. With this many of his minions they will kill her."

"We need to regroup." Jerard spoke as he grabbed two by the neck applying pressure while lifting them off the ground, squeezing until they stopped moving.

"They're leaving, Robert, they know she has gone." Leonard waited for a response. Hearing none he began to race towards them. "Robert!!" he yelled, finally jarring the Elder into action.

"Benjamin has to be one of the Other's," Robert cursed, "the ones that caused the destruction of our planet with their taste for control; their ruthless attitude towards others. " He began running again. "I thought…all these years I thought it had been another of our Elders that had made it through the gateway-and that he had died." He held Rebecca more closely to him, needing to feel her, to know she was safe. Fury raged inside. No one would harm her. "I promise my little Rebecca," he whispered into the night, "I promise to keep you safe."

He could feel the others moving to him, finding comfort in the knowledge they would flank and protect her. "They thought it better to kill rather than simply feed gently. Bring those that were useful to the brink of death, force them to drink from them." Anger rolled from his tongue, he could taste it; feel it as blood lust surged through him. "They were content to leave them neither human nor a wanderer; just death.

"I smell him, Robert. I can smell Benjamin." Gilles increased his pace, bringing Robert back from his thoughts of the chaos, the madness that had overcome his world.

He gazed at his Rebecca, knowing there was little time left. "There is so much to explain, Rebecca. So much I have to tell you. Things that you deserve to know. I know the manner in which we met was not," he searched for a word. "Ideal." "I knew from the moment I saw you; met you that we were meant to be. I have…" he wanted to tell her he loved her. More than his next breath it was what he wanted. Now was not the time. "Benjamin closes in on us."

He looked down at her, seeing her beauty as she gazed up at him, her cheeks red from the wind, the cold and anger, her fathomless green eyes snapping with unsaid words. Her hair was a tangled mass of curls that fluttered aimlessly around her angelic face, and there was nothing more beautiful in this world than her. "One mark is not enough to bind you to me, Rebecca. It is strong, very powerful and would stop any normal young one of our kind from attempting to enter your mind. Prevent them from feeding from you.

"I don't understand marks…feeding?" The nausea was working its way up again and she was exhausted. She rested her head on his chest, barely listening. He shook her.

"Rebecca, you must listen."

"Promising herself she wouldn't scream again at the sight of his pure black eyes, she looked up. All the emotion within him poured from the shimmering depths. It was almost an eerie glow but the shine was filled with truth. "Damn the man," she mumbled only half serious. "He is killing my hate buzz."

"They tie us together, Rebecca. Marking begins the process of uniting our souls. With the second mark, it will be much more difficult for him to access your mind." He paused, choosing his words carefully. "I cannot say with certainty that with only two marks he won't find a way to break our bind; force his will on you, but I am convinced that it will be a deterrent. To do so would leave him very vulnerable."

"Wh..," she cleared her throat, trying desperately to hide the fear that threatened to choke her. "What will the second mark do?

"It will bind our souls more closely." He thought for a moment. "Think of a string, Rebecca. One tied tightly to you, the other end tied to me. Each motion would be felt. If the string were to be tugged hard we would both would feel the pain, but if broken; if someone were to cut the string, we would both lose parts of ourselves. It will also allow you to hear my thoughts and with the completion of marks; the thoughts of the Elders if they so desire."

"So you will hear me call you a bastard." Snappy comeback Becca, she chided herself, but at this moment she was afraid- very afraid. Her body was shaking, her mind a whirlwind of questions, thoughts and accusations.

"It will also increase your strength exponentially, Rebecca. It will open the doorway to your skills."

She let out an ear piercing scream as a shadow emerged beside them.

"Now Robert," Leonard spoke out loud. "He does not come alone." He pointed towards an old barn.

She peered over his shoulder, seeing nothing but dark. She was beginning to despise darkness. What had she gotten involved in and more to the point-how the hell did she get out of it?

"I cannot mark her again without her consent," Robert gazed down at the woman he held so effortlessly in his arms. "I will not make her mine without her willingness."

"Mark her now and hide her in the barn; not that they won't smell her or hear her calls. This will take all of our skills, as well as hers." Leonard turned towards Becca. "Trust us," it is your only hope now."

Again she leaned into Robert as the others moved in front and behind of him. "I have no skills." She turned to look at Robert, seeking the truth on his face. He did not want to do this to her. He would sacrifice himself before forcing a mark on her. The very essence of him; the very truth was etched on every feature.

Tears trickled down her face. As much as she hated him for what he had done; how he had done it, she knew deep inside she loved him. She always had. "Mark me. It's only the second mark, right, there are still more, you said?"

Robert had never felt so torn. The scent of Benjamin was growing stronger. The young ones also carried his scent. "Go the barn," He whispered to his friends. "I will bring Rebecca there." His attention turned back towards her as he made his way at a slightly slower pace to the barn.

"Yes my Rebecca. There are four. With two you will have more power to resist me," he smiled ruefully at her as he started to run.

"The book you carry. Once marked, read the passages. No skipping to the end this time. You will learn what you are." He paused, realizing the slip he had just made, letting her know that he had felt her reading the ending. There was no doubt he would pay for that later. He took a few seconds to glance around before bending and jumping up into the hayloft. The others were just outside, protecting; waiting, a hunger growing within them for battle. A thirst for battle pierced the night air. It flowed through them all.

Gently he settled on the bales of hay, holding her closely to him. "I must do this now if you allow."

All she could do was nod. The circular mark on the one side of her chest throbbed in response as he leaned forward. With careful and gentle fingers Robert lifted her shirt, his fingers splaying along her thin stomach before moving upwards.

His lips closed over her belly, working their way upwards. As much as she tried to prevent the cries of pleasure she couldn't. There was a fiery trail followed the path of his tongue as he slowly drew it up between the valley of her breasts. Her fingers dug helplessly into his back as she arched. Robert could feel her body trembling, desire sweeping through her as he began to suck above the swollen globe of beautiful flesh. He wanted nothing more than to draw this out but the urgency was felt from the other Elders. Privacy and time were two things he appeared to be very short on at the moment.

Closing his lips more tightly he bit down, releasing a heat that seared a circular formation around the flesh. She couldn't prevent the scream from spilling passed her lips... Releasing the skin, Robert captured her lips in a hungry kiss, mating her tongue with his as he swallowed each scream.

She felt faint. The mark, the kiss, her senses were overwhelmed. "Please Robert," Becca whimpered. She drew back as his voice filled her mind.

"Later my Rebecca, later should you desire, we will complete the marks."

Her fingers gripped him, not wanting to let him go. "Please, please you could get hurt."

"You will be safe Rebecca. I must go. He is almost here." He kissed her again before effortlessly dropping down and leaving the barn.

Chapter 10

She thought it painful to be in his arms as angry as she was-it was nothing in comparison to the hurt that ripped her apart while she watched him go. It hurt to breathe-hurt to feel the danger that crawled towards them. Tears streaked down her face and she brushed them angrily away. Taking stock of her feelings, she rose, looking down at the mark before pulling down the shirt. She didn't feel any different, just another sore mark. "Humph," she snorted. "Could have just asked for a taste if that was all that was about!" She cringed as she massaged the area.

"Rebecca," Robert warned, the sound of his voice echoing through her mind along with the others laughter.

She froze as the words-his thick smoky erotic voice came from inside her head. "Damn it, don't do that!" She ran her fingers through her tangled hair, drawing it back from her face, muttering, oh crap, this was going to take some time getting used to. "And why do I hear an echo of laughter?" She growled, pausing as all noises stopped, leaving her mind completely empty. Now she wasn't sure if the silence was welcomed. There was nothing-an aching emptiness that didn't ease the worry growing by not hearing them.

The air suddenly grew thick, heavy and pungent. She could feel it descend upon her, wrapping around her like a blanket. Cautiously turning, her eyes scanned the interior of the barn but she could see nothing that could be the culprit of the vicious scent permeating the air. Blushing, she raised her arm, brows furrowing as she tentatively sniffed at her arm pits, breathing a sigh of relief. "Ok, so it's not me...what then. Them...the others. My God, she thought, I can smell them through Robert and the others, their senses so far more heightened than hers. "Gross," she shuddered. "You never said this was part of the marks." She tried to breathe through her mouth to avoid the putrid scent that approached.

"Read, Rebecca," Robert ordered.

She bit back the retort at being ordered, forgetting he could hear it anyway. She shrugged. "And just how would you like me to that Mr. I have all the answers? I can't see and I left my flashlight in my other pocket."

He closed his eyes and counted to ten. "I thought these marks were supposed make her less sassy, more….gentle," Robert turned towards the other Elders. Their humor at his expense was beginning to gnaw at his nerves.

"Just open the book, Rebecca," Robert urged. "See the words through my eyes. Feel the darkness; embrace it as though it were light."

"Fine but if I go blind it's entirely your fault!" She was only half kidding. She really was eager to read.

Moving quietly to the back edge of the loft trying, to hide herself as the disgusting odors became more obnoxious, the noises sounding so much closer than she was comfortable with, she felt her fingers tremble as she opened the book. A faint glow emanated from the pages. She found if she leaned forward enough she could read. Quickly she scanned the page trying to remember where she left off.

Tonight I have named my children. The knowledge that these five unique and very special ones will survive far outweighs the pain that rests deep within me. I cry for those already lost. Each death is nothing more than a foolish waste that should never have occurred. My body and my mind scream with agony as madness consumes some, death the others.

We wait until the fall of the sun before attempting the gateway. So little time left with my beloved family; enough perhaps to complete this journal for my children.

I am a special. It was noticed soon after my turning. Many nights I dreamed of a man, sightless as I was in the dark, in my sleep; I knew he was there with me. I had called to him.

My heart yearned for what most people sought. Love. Not the love someone felt because a body may be beautiful but a love that speaks to the spirit and the soul within the person.

I did not know that I cried out silently in my sleep, my thoughts, needs and desires so strong that it crossed time and distance to the one that would match my soul. The moment he entered my dreams I knew; I felt him there. He moved silently through the shadows, weaving between light and darkness to find his way to me.

How very beautiful it was to feel completion during sleep as the faceless man came to me, watched over me-kept me safe. Day after day I searched for him, knowing that somewhere, sometime I would find him. I began to ache with desperate need through the daylight hours, waiting eagerly for night to arrive so that I might meet him once again. Over and over I wondered if this would perhaps be the night that I would see his face, feel his touch, or perhaps learn his name. I knew he was not like me; not like my kind for he could so easily slip into my mind.

I felt his love; his need as strongly as I felt my own until finally I believe that I began to grow. I turned towards him and beckoned him to me, pleading for a touch, a look; to just gaze upon his face. He vanished. For weeks I wondered what I had done that had him leave. Sadness welled inside of me, pouring out through my dreams as I wept in them night after night.

My call grew in strength and in intensity. It was a call that few of his kind could resist, though this knowledge was not told to me until much later.

Becca began to shake as she read. She glanced from the book to the entrance of the barn, knowing he was there, feeling him as strongly as though he were right beside her. What the hell? She leaned against the cool wooden wall of the barn, drawing her legs up to her chest. As if her strength had waned, she slowly wrapped her arms around them before resting her cheek on her knees. Life as she understood it was a myth, a fallacy. Nothing was real-nothing.

138

She felt silent tears rolling down the side of her face but didn't have the energy to brush them away. There was no stopping the trembling as reality began to sink in. Reading more seemed impossible and yet something deep inside of her yearned to know the complete story. Somehow it was her story she was reading. Every word scrawled in the delicate script touched her in a manner that told her more than anything or anyone could. "I can't read anymore." she whispered.

"Finish it," Robert spoke gently as his eyes watched for movement in the night. "Rebecca, you must finish it. You must understand."

"I can't….please, I can't." Becca's voice caught on a hitch. She swallowed as she tried to clear her throat.

"You are not weak, Rebecca!" His words were spoken with a harsh tone. "You do not quit."

"You know nothing about me!" She all but screamed the words as she covered her ears.

"I know everything about you, Rebecca. I know every single dream; every desire- every love and pleasure that fills you." He paused and sniffed. They were closing in quickly. "I know your heart is pure and that you are beautiful. You are kind and gentle and you are mine. I believe you can do this, Rebecca."

"I hate you," she whispered as her body unfurled and she crawled back to the book.

I despaired I would never see my faceless love again. Hope began to wane. I lived for the moments I would sleep and perhaps find him again.

My calls wounded him with the level of excruciating need and love. He could not fight the calling any longer. Neither could others of his kind. I felt him the moment he returned to me. There was a peace that descended upon both of us. The calls quieted as he soothed me and protected me.

What I didn't realize was that he had been reorienting his body to be able to be with me through day and night. He stepped out of the shadows that night in my dreams, though he tried very hard to hide half of himself. As I reached for him, he drew back from me. A stabbing pain robbed me of breath and speech.

He felt the pain as though it were his own. Reluctantly he came forward. Finally I could see him. It was burned badly on the hidden side as though the flesh had melted away. My hand rose upwards to stroke his face in my dream and I smiled to him. I thought he the most beautiful person I had ever seen and I spoke those words to him through my dream

Time disappeared. It was only he and I. His name was Ettore, its meaning was defender. Others of his kind began to come to my call though it had quieted once he returned-it was too late by this time.

Becca moaned as she felt the love, the power within the words. She rubbed her eyes, trying to ease the burning. Sleep was approaching; she could feel it as much as she tried uselessly to fight against it. There were noises outside the barn. Grunts, slamming bodies; wake up call. Quickly she turned back to the journal still unsure of what was so important.

Ettore spoke of marks that would bind us. I begged for them, pleaded for them. He refused saying it would change me. He did not realize I was already changed.

Many nights he left my dreams as others tried to feed from my mind. His strength began to dissipate. It would not be long before he would be unable to protect me. I cared not about myself. I cared that he would be hurt.

Finally as he came to me through dream, I begged again for his marks. My heart was already his and should anything happen to him; I would also cease to exist. He granted me the four marks over four days. Each one drew us more closely together, deepened the union, so much so that the emotions and feelings moved from simply dreams to waking hours. Ettore was able to spend short periods of time with me in the daylight. We revelled in the beauty of togetherness.

The fourth mark would make me his forever. It would bring me close to death and allow me rebirth to live in his world-and he in mine. I would become his. I wanted nothing more in this entire world.

My strength grew with the marks. I was beginning to possess the qualities of him. My sight became far clearer at night, physically I was much stronger than I had ever been. He kissed me that final night and told me I was what his people called a siren caller. One with gifts of their own that lay dormant until their soul mate found them. I possessed the gift of fire, he told me though I did not realize the totality of it. It would glow from me; burn those around me.

Red rimmed eyes glanced up as she read the word fire. Becca arched a brow as she glanced down towards her hands. Is it possible? Fire; huh, ok, fire isn't so bad. Her head turned as she heard the commotion outside.

"They just keep coming, "Giles grunted as he grabbed a two by four, slamming it into one's gut.

She glanced between the slats of the barn, looking up towards the sky. Far off in the horizon was the pinkish glow of morning. Could they make it until then? She sensed so many of them.

There was just no more time to read. She had to do something. There was no way she could just leave them out there to perish without trying to help. "Ugh," she frowned. "Why doesn't the book come with an index so I can just look up how?" She placed the blame squarely on her own shoulders. It was her that had called out to him.

Grabbing the journal she clamored down the ladder, not wanting to attempt the jump. "Show offs, "she called out as she reached the bottom rung. There was no response. Panic filled her for a moment until she reached out to touch him.

"Ok... If I could blow up a barbeque, I'm sure I can find a way to light this flimsy wooden building." Becca spoke to herself as she frantically searched the small old wooden structure.

There wasn't much, unfortunately.

"You blew up a barbeque?" Jerard couldn't help but question.

She shrugged. "No one told me not to turn the propane on high while the lid was down before lighting it. She thought it better not to mention the can of evaporated milk she had exploded all over her ceiling.

"Whatever you are thinking of doing right now Rebecca, stop."

"Yeah, yeah." She continued, ignoring him. "So how fast could you get us out of here and um..?"

"NO," Robert growled.

"Look, apparently I have this fire gift. I always wanted to be a fire bug; now's my chance."

"I'm going to kill her," Robert snarled.

"She might have a good idea," Jerard spoke up.

"I am not putting her in danger."

"She is already in danger, Robert." Jerard retorted. "We need to get her and us out of here before light. We won't make the trip back to the house before the sun fully rises. And none of us are ready yet to be spending hours in the daylight."

"No," Robert swore as he threw a young one in the air.

"We aren't going to the house," Becca spoke calmly now that she had the support of the others. She shrugged hearing the snarling. Must be more tired than I thought, she mused. His snarl isn't doing anything right now; well aside from wanting to giggle. What was that expression, in for a dime, in for a dollar?

142

"What the hell do you mean? She could feel the frustration in his voice.

"Look there is no time. You know that. If you stop for one moment to think rationally, you will see that I am right. She smirked at the thought. We are going back to my aunt's house." She couldn't help but cringe knowing how much her aunt disliked guests. These ones would be even lower on the list; perhaps on par with a cockroach.

"Becca, can you do the fire? Without knowing that this is all mute," Markus shouted to be heard.

"I dunno? How does one turn into fire?" Shit, she swore. I never thought of that. She nibbled her lip, a nervous habit she had been meaning to quit. I don't suppose any of you smoke? "Probably should have read more of the journal huh? "She sounded sheepish as she yelled back.

"How the hell do I know? Feel hot?"

"Feel hot?" Great…just great."

Robert sighed. "Feel the danger, Rebecca. Feel it surrounding you. Benjamin is close enough that we can almost reach out and touch him. You need to close your eyes and feel that fear. Turn it in towards yourself."

"Right," She shook her head, not understanding one single word he had said. She was proud of herself for resisting the urge to stick her tongue out at him. Instead she stood in the middle of the barn, thinking about the danger while shaking her arms, loosening them up-as though it would help… "Ok I can do this, I can do this."

Her thoughts turned first to Dan, found near death which was caused by Benjamin; who was now after her. "Geez that sounded complicated."

"Focus Rebecca!" Robert yelled at her.

"Stop shouting then. You are making me nervous. It's not every day that a person tries to become one with fire." "Shit, shit, how do I do this?"

She closed her eyes focusing her energy, doing the best to close out the sounds from outside. Fire...Fire, think fire, she spoke to herself. Finally she snapped her fingers as she had seen done in a movie. Cautiously she opened one eye, hoping to see fire leaping from her fingers. Nothing. "Well shit. I don't know how to do this." Frustration began to grow. "Maybe there is a chant like Abra Cadabra, hmm maybe hocus pocus." Again she peeked and sighed. No sign of fire; not even a puff of smoke. Fatigue was making her a little punch drunk.

That was the moment she felt it. She bellowed, falling to her knees, her hands covering her face before moving them to her ears. Benjamin was near; she not only sensed him-she felt him. He kept the five occupied with his mindless minions while he lashed at Becca from within. She could feel the ripping sensations as he strove to find a way through Robert's marks.

Pain-there was nothing but pain as she fought to resist him. He was evil incarnate. No other words could describe him or the pain he was inflicting on her. She doubled over as she began to retch, hearing his laughter in the depths of her mind as he picked away at a corner. Eventually he would find a way in.

Robert screamed as he felt Rebecca's pain. The insanity within Benjamin was evident, but what also became crystal clear was his plan; his objective. Keep the five Elders occupied with his disposable minions at the front, while Benjamin crept closer towards the back of the barn. He could smell her; smell the marks of the Elder on her and it infuriated him. He would have her. With his mind he reached out towards Becca's mind, slamming into her with full force in hopes of breaking the bind.

He would kill Benjamin. There was no question; no doubt in his mind as he searched for the elusive man. A new pain erupted as one of Benjamin's followers lunged, his fist connecting with Robert's face.

"These distractions are growing tiresome," Giles growled frustration evident in his voice. He wanted Benjamin. They all wanted him, none more than Robert however. His thoughts were pulled towards Rebecca as he felt her pain. He turned to intervene.

"NO," Becca screamed. "Keep him focused; keep him safe." Slowly she rose as she fought the waves of nausea and pain. Every probe was like a needle being forced into her mind but she closed it out. He meant to have her; to use her, she could feel his intent.

She felt anger welling and she channeled it. Becca was weak in comparison to the Creator but that didn't matter. New or not, she would not let him win. Again she cursed herself for not reading the remainder of the journal as with sickening intensity Benjamin hammered away at her mind. Closing her eyes she focused once more, as much as she could with the around the depth of pain he was inflicting. In her mind she imagined a steel door slamming down. The pain began to dissipate and a sneer worked its way onto her face. She hoped he felt the victory that flooded her right now. Pin prickles still stabbed at her temples but she ignored it. Other things first, like fire. As she had imagined the door, she began to imagine fire. Hot, bright with its orange flames that danced, the motions mesmerizing as it weaved and licked at whatever was in its path.

She swayed to the entrance of the barn, searching for the men, having to lean against the door for support. Her eyes remained closed as she envisioned the flames stroking those whom sought to harm them. Her breathing grew shallow as she raised her arms. Only her fingers began to glow but it was enough to shoot a spark onto the dry grass beyond the barn. The wind would now become her best friend as it swirled about the burning ember, blowing almost lovingly on it until it began to grow. She opened her eyes to watch the flames create a barrier.

The waves of rage from Benjamin echoed in the air. Becca felt triumphant, she wanted to scream, to dance within the flames and mock him but she could feel the sunrise approach. Time was quickly ticking away. Fresh shouting was heard as the minions tried to move past the blaze that was quickly spreading. The scent of burning flesh was beyond nauseating. She gagged and retched, doing nothing more than aggravate her already upset stomach.

"Only seconds," Giles whispered the words, somewhat in awe. "We must leave now."

Gently Robert lifted her from the ground, cradling her still body against his.

"Take me to my aunt's," she mumbled. "Must learn."

"My Aunt's," she struggled to speak, to remain awake. "Can't make it home. "Oy is she going to be pissed at me; again."

She fought the overwhelming fatigue as they raced with incomprehensible speed to her aunt's house... It was also easier not to think of the reception they were going to get when they arrived. Visions of her aunt holding a huge cleaver or perhaps a machete popped into her mind and she giggled.

The Elders kept their thoughts quiet as followed alongside Robert. They needed shelter; quickly. They could always bunk down at Dan's place but it did not have the safety that her aunt's had.

Becca struggled from Robert's arms, straightening her smoke scented and thoroughly ruined clothing before turning towards the door. The Elders glanced at one another, then to the sky knowing for a short time they would be safe but not for long. What seemed most curious what the abject fear that had Becca's hand held motionless in mid-air. She just faced dead people. How could one little woman cause such a reaction?

They were about to find out.

Chapter 11

A terrified screech spilled from her mouth as the door swung open before she could knock. The most frightening portion of the entire evening was now standing before Becca, her legs parted, hands on her hips and she was giving her niece "the look". All five foot two and one half inches-thank you very much for not forgetting that, Florence would say.

"Mmm" this isn't good; Becca cringed as she tried not to sway. Forget the machete, forget the butcher knife; Aunt Florence had her cast iron frying pan, and if anyone knew how to swing one of those-it was her.

"Morning Aunt Florence," Becca spoke though the words sounded muffled to her own ears. The pain that had been inflicted by Benjamin still radiated through her head, leaving a pounding sensation much like... well getting hit on the head with her aunts frying pan.

The Elders remained stationary as Becca fumbled her way through getting them into the house. It was still very curious to them. Short and stocky with fiery red hair was the best way to describe her aunt, but really... how bad could she be?

The look Florence cast towards Becca would have shrivelled a less tired person but Becca was beyond much of anything right now. "What have you done this time young lady?" Florence enunciated each word, giving weight and strength behind them...

"Um, can we come in please Aunt Florence? I promise to explain everything."

"One night! One night you have that book and you bring home not one but five!"

Oh God Becca thought as she listened to the shrill tone in her Aunt's voice. It was going to be a big one. She took two steps back, keeping out of frying pan range as her aunt built up a full head of steam.

"Five!!! Girl what were you thinking? Do you have...? Oh, don't you give me that look young lady. And you five," she held the pan up threateningly as she continued. "What makes you even think I would let the likes of you in? Think I'm crazy do you? Ha. .I know what you are. I know you aren't human. What have you done to our Becca?" By now she was shouting. Florence moved forward, intimidating even with her short stature. "And just what do you think your Uncle is going to say about this, Becca?"

"Erhm, whiskey is in the freezer?" She regretted the words the moment they popped from her mouth. Fatigue had caused her filter to short circuit though she giggled. "Uncle Ed is the most generous, laid back Uncle-ever, Aunt Florence, and he loves me. He would want me; want all of us safe."

The five tried not to laugh. Under different circumstances they would adore this woman, look forward to seeing what her dreams were. Strength just radiated from her. Oh this was going to be good.

Robert turned burning eyes towards Jerard as he listened to him snicker in his head.

"Quite the family you are inheriting there, Robert," he choked back a laugh. "I almost envy you."

The resounding ringing sound caught Jerard off guard. He glanced down to see that the older woman had maneuvered close enough to whack him along-side his arm; only because she couldn't reach his head, Jerard was sure. He blinked as his gaze turned towards the woman.

"I'm not done speaking. You all listen up."

"Aunt Florence, please," Becca looked up to the rising sun, feeling the heat of the day beginning. I promise you can yell at us all day but we really need to come in first. Please."

Florence cast Becca a withering look that would have shook a lesser person; or a less tired person.

"I love you Aunt Florence, and you know I would never bring trouble to you unless there was no other choice. She coughed at the look she received. These men; no these friends," Becca qualified, "saved me tonight and they saved your son. You owe them. I can get Uncle Ed from the garage if it's better?" She knew the moment her beloved uncle discovered these men had saved their son, nothing else would matter.

Becca said the magic words. Florence would never be indebted to anyone; human or not. It was just not in her nature.

"Fine, you come in," she paused to give the men the 'I'm watching you look' as she moved from the entry. One toe out of turn Mister and your ass is mine."

Becca staggered in, settling herself at the table as she listened to her aunt. "Oh shit," she mumbled as she rested her head on the table, making note to speak to her in regards to threatening five extremely powerful Elders- she was just too tired now though.

Florence slammed the door behind the Elders, grinning as the charms began their gentle rhythmic swaying. The noise was high pitched and utterly annoying to Becca but the Elders seemed amused rather than daunted by it.

"They are beautiful, Ma'am." Robert decided politeness might be their best recourse at the moment. "Well made, the skill shown within each intricate piece could only be done by one very adept and knowledgeable.

"Oh don't be blowing sunshine up my skirts." Florence tilted her head back to stare directly at him. Becca simply moaned again as she turned her head to the side. There was no stopping her aunt now.

"These are the right design," Robert continued, "They are only designed to keep out those that intend harm. Even then it will only work for a short time. "

Florence tilted her head as she inspected the lot of them. Robert continued, confident now that he hadn't been on the receiving end of the frying pan. "They need to be stronger, Mrs. Williams. If you wish to keep them out permanently, then you will need to add a dried bone from the head of a cow. He reached up to touch the beautifully designed charm, hearing Florence gasp behind him. "The horn of a bull that has been soaked in a mixture of blood from the cow the bone came from and the venom of a rattle snake. Soak them for five days and on the sixth night take it out and dry it in the cauldron over the fire. He turned to face the smaller woman.

"Grind it into fine powder and sprinkle it over the completed charm and those wishing harm will never be able to enter."

He moved around her so he could reach Rebecca." Right now however, she needs sleep. Do you have anything that will give her a restful sleep; one without dreams? "

Becca blinked as Florence nodded and almost smiled. "What the hell?" She pinched herself to see if she was dreaming but felt the pain. He actually schmoozed her aunt! "Bastard," she mumbled as she laid her head back down, yelping as she felt the cuff along the back of her head.

"Ow!" Becca rubbed her head as she looked at her aunt.

"Watch your language young lady." Florence turned towards Robert. I can make her something that will allow her to sleep in a dreamless state." She moved past the men, shooing them out of her way. "Be of some use, boys," Florence was growing frustrated from having to weave between the large men. "Get out of my way, shoo. Through the living room is a door. It will take you down to the basement.

"For a little woman, she is very bossy," Markus surmised as he moved into the living room. Florence finished the drink and handed it to Becca. "Drink it honey." Her tone softened, filled with the love she carried within her for her niece-the worry.

Becca was just too tired to argue. Couldn't be worse than the coffee her aunt always made for her. She was wrong. She choked and gagged at the taste as she pushed it aside. "Are you trying to kill me?"

"Drink it all, quickly." Florence held the cup to her lips. Becca sighed as she drank the remainder of the foul liquid. Within moments her body began to sag. Robert reached to gather her in his arms stopping only when Florence wrapped her small hand around his arm.

"Have one of your friends take her downstairs with them. You and I need to talk; then you may rest as well. You have my word that you will all be safe.

He didn't want to let her out of his sight, glancing towards Rebecca as her body fell limp with sleep. "Leonard, can you take Rebecca please?"

Robert chose him for one simple reason. He had been the one that had snickered the least. He was beginning to understand why Rebecca said "Bastard" all the time. It was tempted to say it now as the others laughed.

"I'll meet you downstairs shortly," Robert turned his attention back to the small woman though his thoughts were clearly on retaliation to each and every one of his friends. They just laughed more loudly in his head.

"Sit," Florence gestured to the chair. She waited until he settled his large frame in the too small chair. She had the same freckles along her nose that Rebecca has, he noted. "So," Florence paused; do I offer you something to eat-or drink?"

Robert shook his head. "No, thank you though for asking. We don't eat the same", he hesitated over the words, "foods as you do." He laughed outright as he saw the look of disgust that crossed her face.

"Blood suckers?" Never one to beat around the bush, Robert noticed. Part of him was fascinated by her, but the larger part was downstairs watching over Rebecca.

"I'm sorry?" Robert looked confused.

"You know what I mean," Florence rolled her eyes. "Big fangs, black cape and the "I want to suck your blood, line."

He blinked as he tried to figure out if the woman was serious.

"Well? Are you?"

The laughter in his head was so loud that he could barely think. He thought of a hundred different means in which to torture his so called friends once this conversation was done.

"No, we don't have fangs and we don't drink blood," Robert responded before growling a warning in his head to his friends- who happily ignored him.

"What then? What happened to our relative way back; the one that had the journal?" She looked over to the book and traced the cover with her fingers, much as Becca had done.

"Something that should never have happened," Robert started as he looked to the woman.

"We feed on dreams; on energy, Florence-if I may call you that." He smiled as she nodded. "We don't intentionally harm anyone. Do we have the power to? Absolutely, but as Elders we have learned to control what and who we are; something others of our kind were not able, or willing to do."

Florence settled back to listen. Her instincts had always been good and right now they were telling her that this man spoke the truth. They also told her that he was meant to be with Becca, though; her very independent niece may have some things to say about it.

"The energy from dreams is our source of food, Florence. It fuels us; sustains us as food does for you. We are always very careful and only feed from those that have cried out to us in their dreams. "He watched carefully to see how she was doing before continuing. "At the point that they begin to cry out is the time they have too much energy within them. It builds up; we ease that for them."

"What happened to our relative then?"

"As we came through the gateway, a few 'youngers' did as well. We had expected some would. We didn't however expect another Elder to come through. It was him that attacked your relative." he paused, remembering that moment as clearly as though it were yesterday. "There are two kinds of wanderers now, our kind which is controlled and the others who are not."

Leaning forward so he didn't' tower over the woman but could look directly at her, he placed his forearms on his knees as he spoke. "Though we have the same power, if not more, we do not use it simply to harm or control. The other Elder and his kind; think nothing of it. They have madness within them, Florence. One we don't know that can ever be cured. The other Elder, the one with the insanity is the one that attacked your relative."

"He bit her. He has-we all have venom…" Robert paused to stare into her eyes, "and he ensured she was never the same afterwards." Florence held his gaze, staring into the black abyss as she tried not to shudder. "Is that what happened to my son?"

"I am sorry to hear that she never recovered. We do all have venom in us though it is very rare that we would use it. That however, is not what happened to your son." He was hedging, not quite sure how much to tell her. Something told him however, that anything less than the truth would earn him a whap with the pan. "The Elder, Benjamin is his name," Robert tried to find a way to explain what happened. "He drained your son; invaded his mind and began the process of wiping out his memories. He would have ceased to exist, Florence. Once the memories are gone; once you have drained a person too much, their soul will die."

"Is..." Florence hesitated, "is he ok? Where is he now?" She glanced from Robert towards the white stucco house down across the pasture.

"It will take some time for him to recover. He was found very close to death. My friends gave him back some memories as well as offering a new one, a trip that he had been meaning to take for some time. They left money for him and when he woke, he was happy. He called the airline and caught the next plane out to a sunny location to heal. You have my word he will be fine."

"Why wasn't our relative then?"

"He bit her. We don't have fangs; we don't drink blood or kill people unnecessarily but in many aspects we are much like the vampires you compare us to." Robert smiled as Florence blushed and coughed. "It's ok. There are so few that know of our existence that I suppose we would all be categorized the same. Benjamin bit her and even without fangs our bite, when we break the flesh will leave a permanent mark. He injected his venom into her."

"I don't understand why." Florence shook her head.

"Madness makes them want to control; to create others to do their work for them. They will drain the majority of their energy; enough that their heart stops and their soul begins to leave. They will then force their blood into the victim. That binds them to him until he is killed. They are lifeless; nothing more than puppets."

"Is that what is going to happen to Becca?"

Finally, Robert thought. The real reason she wanted to talk. He shook his head. "No, Florence. No, I would die before allowing that to happen to her. Our souls are meant to unite. Becca is a siren caller, coincidence perhaps or maybe because her relative was bitten and carried the venom. We may never know. Benjamin however wishes to have her. By having her, he believes that will give him the ultimate power."

"He doesn't know Becca very well if he thinks she will allow that." Florence scoffed as she rose.

"She may not have a choice, Florence. Right now, we are doing our best to keep her safe but Benjamin is relentless. Running with her is not an option. Her call is too great; he will simply follow it. The danger she is in right now is grave."

"Will you and your friends keep her safe?" Florence looked worried. You could see the love that she felt for Rebecca. He softened with that knowledge.

"We can promise to do our very best. I don't know though if there is anywhere in this world that we can hide her from him. She is…special; a rare."

"I know," Florence spoke softly for the first time. "It runs in the family now."

Robert shook his head. "Rebecca first and then we will find the rest of her family. He does not know about the others yet obviously."

"I know somewhere safe." Florence spoke quietly. It was difficult to trust this person; to trust anyone. She had sworn never to trust any of them and here she was, sitting in her house with five.

"Where? Robert stood, anxious to find a place to keep her safe.

"Rest now," Florence nodded. "Rest and tonight we shall make plans to take Becca where she will be safe."

Robert smiled as he leaned forward, pressing a kiss to her cheek. He felt her shiver, their temperature differences was great. He had forgotten. "You know," he smirked and winked at Florence. "For a grumpy old woman you aren't half bad."

For the first time in a long time, Florence laughed. "Get sleep. You will need it, and I must speak with my husband about being away a short time." Florence hesitated, her hand on the doorknob. "Um, you might want to stay in the basement. I'm not quite sure how Ed will respond seeing five huge strange males in the house."

Chapter 12

Robert closed the basement door before taking the stairs two at a time. The area was compact for a man his size, but it was a relief to have Rebecca someplace she would remain relatively safe. It also allowed the Elders the time needed to rest-more like meditate, their bodies. As he entered the room, he noticed her lying on the cot. She was deep in sleep, her muscles relaxed, and the tension lines removed from her beautiful face.

"She was asleep before we got down here," Markus glanced up at Robert before leaning back against the wall.

"Not the most comfortable of accommodations we've been in." Giles chuckled, knowing it wasn't the worst they had been in either.

Long fingers traced along Becca's face while gently pushing aside tendrils of hair that rested across her flawless features. He looked towards the other Elders as he sank to the ground beside the cot, needing to be near her. "I don't know what we are going to do." His gaze encompassed all of them.

"First we are going to reenergize," Leonard smiled, "and then we are going to end this."

"Becca's family may carry the gene." Robert paused as he heard the gasps. "That day we came here," his voice carried the weight of his words, "we didn't save her in time. It was so long ago- I hadn't thought about it for years, but it's an awfully huge coincidence that she is a siren caller. I suspect the reason Florence knows so much about it; aside from the book is because she had been told the story as it had been handed down through generations. His eyes glanced towards her before looking back to the men. Caroline; that was her name, wrote in the book. He inclined his head. It's all there.

Markus reached for the journal as he listened. Opening it he rifled through the pages until he found where she had begun her entries. "Shit, he is dangerous, Robert," he glanced up, "extremely dangerous."

"I know. I just don't know how to fix this; how to keep all of us safe."

"We fight," Jerard responded, always ready for battle. It was in his blood, the excitement; pitting oneself against another through strength and wit. He paused.

"You know…"He drew out his comment, taking the time to think it through carefully before speaking. "I got the impression that Benjamin doesn't like to do the dirty work. Did you notice how he stayed in the background watching and waiting until his minions closed in on us?"

Giles opened one eye to look at Jerard. "So we know he is spineless. He lets others die and then he swoops in for the kill." He closed his eye again. "What is he going to do; create hundreds; thousands of minions-enough that finally he attains his goal which we now believe is Rebecca? I don't understand his motives-just know he needs to be dead."

"Look, there are a few things we need to find out." Leonard straightened. "First; is he capable of turning them into more than mindless," he had to pause, searching for a word that would correctly describe what they had faced, "entities, neither alive nor dead," and secondly; how many has he created?"

Robert snarled with frustration. "We have no answers.' Right now Robert wanted to put his fist through a wall; anger was getting the best of him. "The three in the basement," he looked up. They could be the key to finding solutions. "If we can find out where he resides or how many of them he has created, we have a beginning."

"No, they won't have the answers, Robert," Markus interjected. "Those were early ones. Think like Benjamin does for a moment. He had to know we would capture or kill them. They were simply lambs being led to a slaughter."

"What then?" Leonard growled, wanting the answers; wanting to end this.

Robert glanced over to Rebecca. She still hadn't moved from the position she had been placed. His fingers weaved through the tangled mass of her hair. "We keep a new one alive." He turned to look at the Elders.

"Tonight we keep one alive." They watched as his eyes turned coal black. "I don't care how we get the information; just that we get it." He turned back to her. "We find out all that we can from him." A smile crossed his face. "I somehow suspect old Aunt Florence upstairs would be more than happy to help with it. And then we go after the source."

"What can the woman upstairs do?" Giles asked; genuinely curious.

"If we can't get answers from him then she can starve him." Robert leaned back. "She can discover the strength of Benjamin through his minion. How long will when surrounded by her charms; but one way or another- we will find him." he last? Especially

Sleep claimed them not long after. They remained almost in an almost deadened state when they slept. Not a muscle twitched and no sounds were emitted. Their eyes remained open though all that was seen was blackness. Their heartbeat; minimal at the best of times was non-existent. Any part of their body that was not absolutely necessary powered down, conserving energy for when they woke.

For a wanderer, the time between sleep and wake was one of their most vulnerable. Weakened by the slowing of their body's vital organs they generally chose somewhere extremely safe and well hidden. When they woke it was tantamount to having one's heart

160

restarted. Sharp intakes of breath would be heard as the blackness leeched from their eyes until it only remained in the centre.

As Robert's body began to relax he looked around a final time before tilting his head upwards. "Keep us safe Florence." It was rare to have five elders resting in the same place. The ease in which their entire life form; their entire race could be wiped out with one fell swoop was worrisome. Tomorrow they would make other arrangements.

Clouds covered the sun though it did nothing to diffuse the stifling heat wave. Perhaps the white fluffy balls of what looked like cotton would turn greyish, then dark, offering some relief with rain. Florence hoped that the white fluffy clouds that played hide and seek would have no bearing on the amount of time he needed to sleep; in fact she was counting on it. Reaching into the closet she took out a suitcase and began packing items. The journal rested on the top along with her frying pan and her cleaver. "Don't leave home without them is my motto," She spoke to herself. 'Not sure who started that but it is a very good habit."

"What's a good habit, Aunt Florence?" Becca drowsily asked. She leaned against the door frame, yawning though she did feel much better than she had several hours earlier.

"Hmm? Oh nothing dear," Florence responded. "Just an old lady's ramblings; nothing to concern yourself with," she turned and offered a smile. "You look like hell, dear. Why don't you take a shower while I make you some coffee and lunch?'

The thought of the shower prompted Becca to move. She had felt grimy for the last twelve hours. A hot shower would be just the thing; the coffee-not so much. "Sounds great," Becca leaned forward to kiss her cheek as she spoke. "Have I mentioned how much I love you lately?" The first real smile graced Becca's lips, lighting her beautiful features that were filled with uncertainty.

The shower felt wonderful on her sore and aching muscles. She lingered beneath the hot water for as long as possible, pushing aside the guilt as she wondered if the others needed to shower-or if they showered. "Pffts...they can use a hose. This is entirely their fault." Sighing, she turned the water off knowing that wasn't quite true. Apparently it was her dreams that had been the catalyst. Grabbing a towel she briskly dried off, pushing the thoughts of them; ok-of Robert aside. Her body tingled each time she thought his name which was extremely distracting.

Rifling through the overnight case, she threw on fresh clothes; shorts and a t-shirt before reaching for the brush. She took no care, ripping the brush through her hair as quickly as she could before tying it back in a ponytail. The inside of the house was already muggy; Aunt Florence didn't believe in air conditioners-modern day contraptions. "Cool contraptions," Becca countered smartly. That was one of the times her aunt had gone after her with the frying pan. "No wise mouth's around me, girl!" she smiled at the memory as she entered the kitchen.

Overcrowded was one word that fit what Becca walked into. Five huge men and one short woman filled the kitchen. Claustrophobia kicked in. She tried to step back, managing only to step on someone's toes before brushing up against strong muscular bodies. "Hell of a way to be closed in," Sucking in her breath she weaved around the men, moving to the table. Perhaps sitting would give her a little breathing room; and a few less muscles to consider groping.

Most didn't notice her enter. They were busy discussing strategies; their heads close together, their words nothing more than brisk whispers, almost too quick for her to catch. Perhaps the strangest and clearly the more surprising was Becca's aunt. Deep in the midst of five Elders; talking animatedly, looking as though nothing was amiss. It took a moment to realize she was staring with her mouth agape. Well will wonders never cease, she mumbled as she reached for an apple.

"Your aunt is delightful," Robert spoke the words in her mind. Becca choked on the piece of apple as his sensual voice rang in her head.

162

She could hear her aunt tsking through the spasms of coughing. "Wrong hole," Becca blushed. There was nothing worse than being the center of attention when you are red faced with your eyes shimmering with tears.

"Stay out of my head!" Becca threw Robert a warning look as she tossed the apple into the garbage and rose. Too much togetherness for her at the moment; finding the room's temperature elevate far more than she was comfortable with. Pushing between the bodies, using her elbows to push through the men, she made it to the other side. Gratefully she opened the door and stepped out. The fresh air, though hot, felt glorious after feeling caged in the kitchen.

Leaning forward to place her upper arms along the patio gate she glanced down to her grandparent's house- her cousin's place now. Childhood laughter still echoed along with the pain of losing both of them. Now with Dan gone-she could only pray he would be ok.

Robert watched as burnt auburn shades shimmered in her hair as it toyed with the breeze that flowed along the side of the patio. The rise and fall of it was almost mesmerizing; so many different colors. He was confident there would never come a time he would tire of watching as it billowed around her lovely face; confident there would never be a time he would tire of just gazing at her. Her face looked so serious-so sad; he wished he could comfort her. Truth was he really didn't know how. All of them at the moment were neck deep in trouble, and the odds of coming out of it alive were not as promising as he would like.

She tilted her head upwards, letting the sun beat down on her creamy flesh as it fought its way between clouds. She knew he was there, could feel his presence as strongly as she felt her own heartbeat. It was difficult to try and keep her mind blank; empty, so he had nothing to pick through. She wondered if he could tell she was still pissed at him. A grin formed on her lips as she imagined a flashing neon sign that said "pissed."

He choked back the laugh. She was just an enigma to him, all five foot seven inches of her. There was nothing ordinary about this incredible woman; though she believed she was plain. He let his gaze roam up and down her body. Not one single thing about her was anything less than extraordinary. The fact that she could feel his look and responded with tiny goose bumps running along her flesh had him smiling.

"You shouldn't be out here alone, Rebecca." Robert started...

"Told you, it's Becca." She didn't turn around. At the moment she was feeling a little too fragile. One look of sympathy from him and she would be crying and in his arms. The thought caused her heart rate to increase and her pulse to race. "Damn it." she swore before straightening.

"What do you want, Robert?" Finally she turned towards him, lost for words again as she saw the most beautiful creature she had ever seen. Had it just been a pretty face, she knew it would be much easier; but no- he had to go and be just as beautiful inside as he was on the outside. "Bastard."

"It's not safe for you out here, Becca." he acquiesced, knowing things were going to be hard enough.

"Well I'm not safe in my own home, or anywhere else for that matter right now, so what is the difference?"

"I'm sorry, Becca." His voice held the edge of sorrow which was the last thing she needed.

"What exactly are you sorry for, Robert? For invading my dreams, for buying the house next to me knowing what you had done?" She took a breath, fighting back the tears and failing. Angrily she brushed them away. "Or maybe you are sorry for marking me during a dream when I had no chance to agree? Which one, Robert? "Her arms came up as he stepped forward, holding him at bay. "Or maybe, just maybe, you are sorry because you couldn't tell me the truth about what I was. That it was just more fun to slide into my dreams; night after night, becoming part of them, an integrating presence into every nook and cranny," she paused as the sobs began." Making me love you before ever even knowing you!" "Crap, I didn't; I mean, oh god." She turned from him, her voice low, filled with pain and confusion. "Just leave me alone."

He felt her pain. Every single tear cut deeply inside. If he could take away what she was, he would. He loathed seeing her fall apart. His Rebecca was far too strong to not survive. Slowly he stepped closer to her.

"I am so sorry for all of the accusations; for all of the things I have done." His hand brushed aside her hair before resting on her shoulder. He could feel the heat of her skin against his cold flesh. It was so incredible to merge the two sensations into one. "I heard you call from across the world. Your soul called to mine." He paused, moving closer as he heard the quiet sobs, his hand vibrating along with her body as she shook.

"I'm sorry, Rebecca; I'm sorry I hurt you in the way that I found you." He began again as he wrapped his arms around her slender waist, drawing her back until her head rested on his chest. "I love you Rebecca. I have from the first moment you reached out to me in your dreams. He hesitated as she stiffened before relaxing into his embrace. "I am sorry that Benjamin attacked your ancestor and perhaps began this path that leads us to here. You must listen and understand now. Your call, though a match to my soul and hopefully to our two souls uniting, also reached out to many others like me. But I'm not sorry for knowing you, for loving you. In over six hundred years, you are the most beautiful experience, the most incredible person in my life."

She was torn-so torn. A part of her wanted nothing more than to shrug his hand from her shoulder but the comfort was tangible, and the coolness felt amazing against the scorching heat of the late afternoon. His words rang with the truth; with the pain he also felt inside. God she was tired. A few days ago everything had been normal and she was just dreaming about jumping the gorgeous neighbour next door. She felt the chill as his arms held her securely. Inhaling sharply as she debated with herself; he smelled like sunlight-his arms felt like heaven. Slowly her body succumbed to the need for his arms; his touch.

"I don't…" she paused as he slowly turned her body around until she faced him. His hands rose to brush the tears from her flushed cheeks before he leaned forward to kiss each eyelid.

A soft sigh spilled from her lips as she tilted her face upwards to him. She was at least honest with herself. She wanted him; needed him. Leaning into his touches as the pads of his thumbs dried her tears; absorbing the cold sensation of his lips as they pressed against her lids before slowly making their way downwards.

Their lips met. Hot against cold; heaven and hell. Shivering as his arms wrapped around her again, tugging her closer as his tongue traced along her lower lip before weaving its way inside. Just one taste, was her last coherent thought before heat flooded her body. Fire; she felt like she was on fire and he was the only thing keeping her from burning alive though it was him that was creating the inferno.

Her trembling fingers splayed along his perfectly toned chest, feeling each bump and ridge as she raised them, enjoying the trip upwards until they finally found their way into his hair. Tugging gently, pulling him closer as her lips parted completely for him.

He tasted like sunshine as well, she moaned against his lips as she shivered. He held her more tightly as his fingers tightened along her back before moving in slow rhythmic motions. The next breath was not nearly as important as the feel and taste of him; chilled like a cold winter's day and yet tasting like the heat of summer, of sunshine. It was like an overload of sensations as their tongues duelled; probing before drawing back only to return to attack again.

166

In six hundred years he had never felt anything so powerful or so perfect. The urge to consume her was damn near uncontrollable. The breathless moans he swallowed were going to be his undoing if he didn't stop-soon. Or soon-ish. His fingers travelled from her back to her tapered waist before climbing up to feel the slope of her breasts. It was his turn to shudder as the pads of his fingers grazed along her tight hard nipples. The marks sprang to life the moment they came in contact with his skin. He tightened his grip on her as she sagged with the sensations his touch was creating within her.

"Shit," she panted while stepped back; leaning against the railing again as she tried to remember how to breathe.

He released her; albeit reluctantly. It would take some time for his body to return to some sense of normalcy after that kiss. His eyes, shimmering with desire turned towards her. It was time for her to see what happened at times. Bracing his body for rejection, he reached and tilted her chin upwards until she had no choice but to look within the ebony depths.

She blinked and then blinked again. Her lips opened and closed as she tried to speak but no words spilled out. She felt like a mute as she gazed at his face. A touch of fear brushed aside a small part of the aching desire as she saw the blackness cover the whites along the irises. She had always known he was too beautiful to be real; this just proved her summation correct. And yet, for someone so perfect, with such power and beauty; she felt the fear of rejection within him as he remained an arms-length from her.

She wanted nothing more than to go to him and alleviate the worry but there was just so many questions left without answers. She did have to say something though; it caused an incredible aching sensation to know he felt as she had so many times. She found herself rubbing her chest as she stared openly at him. Her eyes closed as she shook her head.

"I understand," his voice was toneless; empty.

"You understand nothing," she countered as she lifted her eyes again. "You understand nothing; especially about me if you think for one moment your eyes would have any bearing on how I felt about you. Oh yes, anger was much easier for her to deal with.

In another six hundred years he was sure he would never understand the female species. Christ; they were worse than any other being he had ever encountered. "Then…" he left the question hanging as he heard the snickering in his head again.

"Be quiet!" She shouted in her head before gasping. She heard them all; was that supposed to happen? Judging by his face and the sudden stillness within her mind, she was going to lean towards no. Her lips pursed as she settled into the quiet, not at all sure how to break it. Her fingers began to tap along the railing and she rocked back on her heels. She had never done well with enforced or awkward silences and right now it was killing her. Finally she stuck her hands in the front pockets of her shorts as she began tapping her foot. "Ok; what the hell is with the silent treatment?"

Grabbing her by the elbow he led; rather pulled her into the house again before stopping. "What did you hear?"

"Your buddies," she pulled a hand out of her pocket and pointed towards the other four; her cheeks flushed with embarrassment, laughing and chuckling like a bunch of apes." There, she thought. Let them chew on that for a bit.

"Ow! "She yelped as she jumped forward, rubbing the back of her head. "What the hell?"

"You will be polite to those in my house young lady," Florence drew herself up to her full size as she looked threateningly towards Becca.

She arched an eyebrow as she reached for her cell phone. Ok; so I was only asleep for ten hours. Becca glanced from her aunt to the others and then back to her aunt, attempting to figure out what had changed in that short span. She just couldn't resist.

Leaning forward she poked her aunt before pressing a hand to her forehead. "You sure you are ok Aunt Florence?" The flush that stained her aunt's face was worth the next cuff upside her head.

"You should not be able to hear the others yet." Robert's voice held a hint of awe and wonder as he spoke.

Becca shrugged as she looked down before looking at four other identical looks. Ok so maybe it was more of a big deal than she thought. "um, sorry?' she mumbled as she scraped her toes along the floor.

For the first time Becca was glad of her aunt's interference. "She is more gifted than anyone realized," she spoke with conviction and knowledge. "Now however; we must leave here before night arrives."

"Where?" Markus questioned as he glanced out to see the sun reaching its peak before it would slowly begin to set.

"Where they will not expect us to go; where it will be us that is on the offensive, not the defensive."

Chapter 13

"Oh shit," Becca cursed, finally realizing where her aunt meant to take them. "You honestly believe they are going to accept us, Aunt Florence? Good lord it will be a lynching."

"I've already spoken to your grandmother," Florence offered a smug look. "She is willing to allow us there; for a short time. You are her grandchild you know."

"Uh huh, the grandchild of the grandmother everyone thought was kooky and we never got to visit." Becca ducked the smack this time as she continued. "You know it's true! Dad refused to let us go visit her. He used to say she was a few fries short of a happy meal."

The Elders glanced from one to the other as the women spoke. "What do you think is going on?" Markus asked.

"Stop doing that!" Becca protested having heard the question. Again she looked down when they all focused on her. "Ok so I'm not supposed to hear you yet but I do, I can't help that. And it's damn right frustrating suddenly hearing voices in my head." She sighed. "I'm sorry, this is all very... I feel very disjointed. It's not everyday someone can say they hear voices in their head without being locked up."

Having had this ability since conception it really didn't seem out of the ordinary to the Elders, but they felt her confusion. "We will do our best to speak aloud for you." Leonard offered a smile.

"Yes, yes, all very nice," Florence flitted around. "Are you able to travel yet? We have a ways to go and not much time to get there."

Becca blanched. "You are not driving Aunt Florence. I refuse to get in a vehicle with you again."

"Oh hush child, I drive just fine."

In her head Becca chanted; Danger, danger.

"If you would permit, Florence, I am sure that we can travel much more quickly without a vehicle. That is; if you would allow one of us to carry you."

Another groan escaped. "I changed my mind, I vote my aunt drives." Becca's stomach revolted as she remembered the last ride she had gotten.

"Grab what you need," Giles ordered as he glanced towards the sky. "We must leave now."

"With permission, I shall carry you, Florence," Jerard volunteered.

Becca blinked. Why that cagey woman. She is blushing and enjoying every moment of attention. She bit back the laugh as she watched.

"I'm packed and ready," Florence offered as she pointed towards the suitcase. "I also packed all that Becca will need; including the book."

Her mouth parted to make a smart retort but she quickly closed it as she saw the warning look from Robert.

With ease he picked Rebecca up, holding her against his chest while he waited for the others. It was all she could do to remain still and not kick and scream for him to let her go.

Jerard lifted Florence gently where she settled in his arms. "Now we are going to the south end of Norwich. It's about twenty-five miles along a dirt road. The entrance is near impossible to find. When we get close I'll tap on your shoulder so you know to slow."

Jerard nodded. He looked at the others. "Markus, Leonard; can you go slightly ahead to ensure we won't be ambushed and Giles follow a slight distance behind. This way we have all bases covered."

"If you happen to find a minion," Robert interjected, "please do bring him along. Perhaps the relatives would make peace more easily with us should we have something to... sacrifice." His smile was not one of pleasure. Robert wanted this over. The waif of a girl in his arms was his and he would be damned if anyone would get in his way.

Donning their sunglasses, Markus and Leonard slipped quietly out the door. It was so shockingly quick that even Florence gasped. Becca wanted to snicker and say I tried to warn you but thought better of it.

Robert and Jerard waited a few moments before leaving with their precious cargo, Giles shortly after that. They took the risk of burning and injuring themselves to run at this time of the day but there was no other option. Instead they raced towards the treeline, weaving between the shadows of the weeping willows, their long weaving branches billowing as they passed.

For her part, Becca kept her eyes tightly closed, her body held rigidly in Robert's arms. Though she could feel each sinew; each muscle move and caress her as he raced along the shadows, she just didn't care. All she wanted was to be off this nauseating ride before she got sick all over him. She wondered if her aunt was faring any better.

They heard Jerard's laughter ringing in their minds as he moved with effortless grace beside Robert. The wind was too loud against Becca's ears to hear anything but her own chattering teeth but apparently she learned; through Jerard speaking to Robert, that her dear cherished and somewhat elderly woman was yelling yeehaw and laughing with great joy.

Becca just shook her head, burying her cold face against Robert's chest. Not that it would warm her any but at least she could focus on

172

the smell of sunshine instead of the speed of light they seemed to be travelling at.

"We got one!" Markus shouted, his voice filled with pleasure.

"Is he still alive?" Robert's question was almost urgent. They needed him alive.

"Alive and scared shitless," Leonard snorted.

Becca shivered. She was beginning to realize just how intimidating and formidable these men were.

"I am never riding like this again," she groaned, not at all comforted as Robert drew her closer to his chest. Becca sniffed, her nose running as though she were in the midst of winter as she shivered again. "Keep your eyes closed; just keep them closed," she chanted. "You won't be ill; you won't be sick though it would serve him right if I did throw up on him."

There was no hiding the laughter that followed her last comment, or the growl that emerged from Robert. "Tough, that's what you get for climbing into my head."

Florence tapped Jerard on the shoulder. Instantly he slowed, calling out for the others to do the same. Becca opened one eye to see if the scenery was still all a blur or if she would be able to tolerate the image rate. "Thank God." She glanced over to her aunt, shocked to see the old woman looking ten years younger. Her hair standing up in all the places it wasn't shouldn't be; her face ruddy from the wind, and her eyes sparkling with a joy and life Becca had not seen in- forever. Tears sprang to her eyes but she quickly blinked them back. The ride was worth seeing her Aunt like she was.

Florence pointed to the clearing not far ahead and the men entered. They were sheltered amidst the clusters of trees; feeling much more comfortable than being out in the open. Night edged its way in, pushing aside the sun to cover the earth with a blanket of shadow.

They had slowed even more so Florence could direct them. More than once Becca insisted she be put down only to be studiously ignored. "Fine," she thought. "With luck my relatives will truss you up like a Christmas turkey and cook you for dinner."

Robert blinked as the other Elders howled. He glanced down to Rebecca as she rested in his arms and shook his head. With complete ease he reached for her ponytail, dragging her head back until her face was tipped upwards. Moonlight spilled across her features; her eyes wide as he pulled a little harder before lifting her until their lips met.

"You talk too damn much," Robert whispered before claiming her lips in a kiss that made her toes curl and her heart skip a beat-or three. Whew that man could kiss, she thought as her lips parted to accept his tongue.

Their tongues danced together; an ancient ritualistic bonding that had been done since the beginning of time. Forgotten was the captured minion; forgotten was her snickering aunt who had been sure no man would ever be able to take on Becca, and forgotten was the fear and worry. It was just Robert. She moaned against his lips as her chilled fingers caressed his face, trying to bring herself closer to him.

A cough finally drew their attention. Giles had caught up to them and had tried to discreetly cough a number of times to garner their attention. He wasn't sure an explosion would be noticed.

"What!!" Robert growled as he pulled his lips reluctantly from Rebecca's.

"Mmmm, not too much, Robert; just well, we are here and surrounded by little miniatures of Florence."

"Oh hell," Becca buried her head as she listened. Carefully so she wouldn't be noticed, she peered out and groaned again. He was right. They did have an audience. "Just freaking great."

"Put me down, Robert," Becca pushed at his chest only succeeding in having him tighten his arms around her. "That is not down."

"I don't think you want me to put you down right now, Rebecca." Robert leaned forward to whisper for her ears only. "I don't think your relatives would really want to meet and greet me sporting the um. " He lowered her enough that she hid the obvious desire racing through him.

"Wow," Becca had the decency to blush. "Could this day get any worse?" she wondered. Of course it could. She was now in the midst of the throw backs of the Beverly hillbillies san the millions of dollars. Benjamin might not be so bad after all right about now. Becca sighed.

Florence was just as gently put down as she had been when Jerard picked her up. As was her nature she turned and gently patted Jerard's cheek before moving to the fire that burned brightly just a short ways away. She had motioned for us to stay and Becca for one was quite content to remain as far away as possible.

"Put me down." She snapped. "I'm sure you can um, well you know…" Becca blushed, "return to normal without me in your arms."

Reluctantly Robert released her. She felt instantly better as her feet touched the ground. She pondered patting his cheek as her aunt had done except she would probably do it with a fist. Better not to chance it. God he confused her. She was head over heels in love with a man that she knew nothing about; especially his race and whether he was a man at all. It was all too much to take in at the moment; considering she was still livid at the manner in which he found her.

She roamed past him towards the edge of the treeline where Markus and Leonard stood with their captive. He looked a little worse for wear Becca noted.

Curiosity got the better of her –it normally did and she stepped a little closer to see what they referred to as a minion. She gasped as she saw him. There was no life within the depth of his eyes. They were dead; empty, devoid of any thought or emotion except that which was fed to him. Anger welled inside. How could anyone do this to a human being? There is just so much a person could withstand and whatever Benjamin was doing, was far beyond the point of no return.

Robert moved up behind her; a protective stance as he stared at the minion. He did not share the sympathy that Becca did for the young one. He grabbed her as she took a step forward.

"Let me go, Robert." Her voice was cold.

"He's not safe."

"That's not for you to decide. With five of you here, I'm sure I will be perfectly safe. "She didn't know how to explain that something drew her to him; a pull that ran more deeply than anything she had experienced.

She felt him as his eyes turned towards her. There was no anger; no rage, no feel of revenge. He called out to her for help. To be released from this horror he had been placed in. Fresh tears welled and trickled down her face as she stepped closer.

The young one made no move towards her though Markus and Leonard held him closely. She looked at them as she shook her head, knowing he was not a danger, inching forward until she was almost directly in front of him. Pain radiated from every cell in his captive frame. Did the Elders not see this; feel this? Carefully; so she didn't scare the young one or the Elders-she could feel them ready to swoop on her, she reached out to touch the tattered clothing he wore.

A visible shudder was seen at the gentle, innocent gesture. Turning her eyes up to his again, tilting her head as she felt the horror of what he had gone through. Pain unlike anything anyone should know or experience was his legacy now. Gently her fingers touched his arm, just above Markus's hand. The young one felt cold; much colder than the Elders were. She wondered why; making note to ask Robert about it afterwards.

His eyes watched the stroking of Becca's hand, heat; blessed heat coiling inside of him for the first time in- he couldn't remember when.

"Who are you?" She asked out of curiosity, not really expecting an answer.

"George," the answer was whispered in her head. She forced her muscles to remain still as fear ripped through her entire body. It was a battle to keep herself upright as the morbid voice echoed around and around inside her mind. It took every concentrated effort to control her breathing. Shock registered on her face as it blanched. She began to shake as she felt the complete emptiness within him.

"What the hell?" Giles moved forward as he saw the overwhelming panic flare in her eyes; the turmoil in her mind.

"No; please," Becca murmured aloud. "Please stay there, Giles. I don't know why; but I know I am safe."

"I heard him." Becca's voice was less than a whisper; containing all the pain that flowed from the young one.

"He should not have the power to speak with his mind," Jerard sounded very confused. The young one looked towards him before returning his deadened gaze to the small delicate hand as she resumed caressing his arm. She could feel the tension radiating from Robert who stood mere inches behind her. If she were to turn, Becca was quite sure she would see his arms waiting to clutch at her. "We need to get her away from him... now!" His voice was dangerous.

"Robert," she reached back to feel him. "This is not your decision right now. Please allow me to find out what I can."

A low; livid growl escaped. Robert's teeth snapped together as he fought his natural instincts. "Two minutes and you are moving far from him."

She rolled her eyes as she turned back to the young one. "How are you able to speak to me," she questioned, reluctantly looking up into his eyes again? What rested in the fathomless depths would torment and haunt her remaining days.

"I do not know?" George seemed to struggle to speak; as though so much time had passed he no longer understood how.

"Why do you hunt us, George?" She had to try to understand; for all of them.

Robert pulled her back. He had enough; the imminent danger to her was more than he was able to take.

She frowned as she was pressed back against Robert's chest even as delicious tingles spread through her. "Stop doing that!" It took a moment for her to remember that she didn't want to be pressed against him; savoring the feel of him surrounding her.

It became quiet; eerily so. George looked down to where she had gently touched him. He didn't fight to escape; didn't war for his freedom.

"Why do you hunt us?" Robert had difficulty controlling the venom in his words. They waited for him to respond. "Answer! It is an Elder that questions you."

Becca weakened as she felt the power flow from Robert. Her knees buckled, knocking her off balance. "Shit, what the hell was that?" She rubbed her arms as the flow of power rushed over her.

Robert tired of the games; of having her so close to this minion. His power radiated from him; almost crushing her beneath its weight.

178

"Control, Robert." Jerard spoke gently.

As he inhaled, Robert did his best to absorb a portion of the power that flowed through each pore. He nodded.

"I think we need to allow Rebecca to speak to him, Robert." Leonard turned towards Robert. "She hears him; we need answers, and this may be the only way to gain knowledge of what we are dealing with. Perhaps gain leverage."

"NO!" The venom was back in his voice. His fingers clutched Rebecca, pulling her tightly to him.

She felt the pain in her head beginning. Everything floating around her was beginning to weaken the strength within her. "Stop; all of you," she screamed in her head. "Robert this is NOT your choice. This man is in pain and we need answers. "Her voice softened as she turned to look up at him. "Please Robert, help me with this; guide me, but don't try to stop me. I need all of you to direct me right now."

His fingers cupped her chin; pure ebony eyes gazed down at her. She wondered if she would ever grow accustomed to that; probably not, she thought, but his touch was like- home. "Please, Robert. I will do this with or without you; I would rather have you with me."

"If I feel one hint of danger; anything that might harm you, I am taking you from him- no questions asked."

She rolled her eyes as she turned towards him. "Fine." She muttered

"Fine." He responded.

Chapter 14

"Ah; a match made in heaven-or hell," Markus chuckled as he listened to the continuous tug of war between the two of them. "Perhaps you two can meet on neutral ground so we might continue before Florence comes looking for us with her frying pan."

Becca ignored Markus for the moment, focusing on George. Tentatively she reached out to stroke his arm again. She felt the flow of pain again; torture and surprise at the tender, innocent touch.

"Why do you hunt us, George? " Becca spoke aloud so the Elders could hear the questions.

Bones creaked as George tilted his head. Each motion seemed to cause agony within him. "He will torture me further."

"Who will torture you more, George?"

"Benjamin." He spoke the name with great reluctance, terrified of the consequences.

"He isn't here, George. What happened to you? Tell me, please; tell me why you hunt us now." She continued to speak aloud for the benefit of the others though Becca's eyes and entire mind remained completely captivated on George.

"Bit me he did," Benjamin began. Markus could feel the tremors as George turned his eyes up to her wide almost haunted green ones. "It amused him. " Repeatedly he stopped as he tried to formulate thoughts. "My family as well; killed 'em in front of me he did. I begged to die; he laughed. Brought me to the edge of darkness many times; thought I would be free in death. 'He glanced down as she stopped stroking his arm, seeming to lose his voice as well. George's

180

eyes became devoid of thought or emotion. Mindless, more dead than any corpse she'd had the misfortune of seeing.

Again she rubbed her fingers over his arm, watching as he seemed to recover. "What happened, George? What did he do to you?" She clenched her stomach with her free hand, feverishly working to not vomit at the atrocities inflicted on this man.

"Bit me again he did. This time he was in my mind. I could feel him taking away my memories, leaving the ones of him destroying my family."

She gasped. Instantly the Elders were at her side. "No, No, it's ok; stop, he isn't hurting me. Benjamin inserted horrific memories;" Becca quickly explained what George had divulged thus far. She wouldn't admit it right now but she felt much more comforted with Robert pressed against her.

"Please, tell me the rest, George." She spoke in such gentle tones that all were captivated, not just George.

"Ripped away my mind until only pain was left; he said no more would I feel or think. It would be only horror; only terror." George looked down as he felt her small hand entwine with his. A spark of recognition flickered in his eyes before being smothered. "I am without a soul. He found a way to steal all but a little shard which is held captive within this dead body. One can't live or die without their soul. She didn't even try to hold back the tears as she listened, explaining to the Elders through her mind as George continued. With her free hand, she carefully touched his heart.

"We obey what he says and maybe he will give us death. " George spoke in his same monotone voice. There was no emotion left within him after so many years. "I am weakened; we all are, me more than the new ones. He does not allow feeding except from him. Nightmares; death, destruction-he has found a way to build their strength and skill by doing this." Finally he turned his eyes up to look at Becca. "Benjamin gave us images of you and the Elders; his conquests, and the promise of death." He bowed his head, drawn to the warmth against his chest.

"Why me, George?" She questioned. "Why me and the Elders and why can I hear you?" Massaging his heart seemed to bring him comfort so she continued. He felt so much colder than the Elders did; it was wrong, something was definitely wrong.

"The Elders because they were the best; he wants to be the best. Power infuses him, drives him and consumes him. He has created hundreds of my kind and that is the beginning. Each new one is built for a single purpose. To find you and the Elders; to prevent your souls from finding mates-to take from the five- what they took from him." Again he looked down at her, sorrow edging around the sides of his eyes. "He knows why you are what you are; why you are different. He will not stop until he has you. Nothing will prevent him owning you, mating your souls-wanted or not.

Finally she sagged against Robert. Fear drained her; terror held her in its deathly grip as she listened to him.

"You hear me because you are of both kinds now. You hear me because you wear an Elder's marks and also carry within you, the genes of your ancestors."

She sank to her knees and retched, empty of stomach contents it was more as though she were releasing the horror witnessed and felt. Robert bent over Rebecca as she continued to dry heave; gasping for air in between. "It can't be Robert, it can't be."

The Elders were quiet as they absorbed the enormity of the situation. Never before had they been faced with a complication such as this.

"Please end my suffering." George begged her.

She shook her head feeling the nausea overwhelm her again. "I can't; I don't know how, George." The words croaked from her as she leaned against Robert.

Robert looked to George then to Rebecca. Destruction surrounded them and there was not a thing he could do at the moment. Lovingly he picked her up and cradled her in his arms. She was weak. Talking to George had cost her far too much of her strength.

"He asks me to end his suffering," she whispered hesitantly to the Elders.

"Ask him if he can be killed by an Elder, Becca," Leonard prodded.

"Is there no other way? Can't we try to save him?"

"Sadly no." Giles answered. "There is too little left of him to be saved. Benjamin ensured that he would be neither alive nor dead."

"George, can you be…" She paused having to choke the words out. "Be killed by an Elder?"

His eyes closed; a sense of peace began to overtake the pain. "Yes. An elder may free what is left of my soul, but must destroy the body as well or I will simply return again. He captured portions, large portions. An Elder has the power and strength to grant me death and peace, but only by doing both."

Quietly she relayed the message. The Elders glanced to one another, shock and disgust evident on their faces. Leonard nodded and stepped forward.

"Wait; oh God wait!" Becca writhed until she was out of Robert's arms. She could feel her heart breaking as she moved to George. Reaching up, she gently stroked his face. "Is there no other way, George?"

"No, my fate is sealed. This night will see the end of my suffering. Be warned; others are stronger. They have his insanity as well and crave power-death."

"What is your last name, George? Is there anyone we can contact?"

"He destroyed my family. I am more than two hundred now I think, though I may have lost count. Scott was my last name. "

Becca shook as she nodded. "You will not be forgotten George Scott. A monument will be placed for you." She turned into Robert's arms, unable to witness the death of another human.

"I am going to bring Rebecca to the camp. "

"Wait." George whispered to Becca.

"Stop, Robert." She turned back to gaze sadly upon George.

"He has many places that he resides; quickly he named a few before pausing. The main one is your ancestor's home. You will find most of the others like me there. Be safe; find him and end the suffering of the others that wish it please."

"It will be done, George," she replied with a voice filled with the tears she now tried to hide but also the firm resolve within her. "Thank you George."

Robert strode towards the camp with Rebecca, slowing his pace only when he reached the clearing. He didn't want to frighten anyone here tonight. A cursory glance found Florence deep in conversation with a very old woman. She leaned on a cane, a slight hunch in her back preventing her from standing upright. There were traces of Becca in the wrinkled features however; and the same strength and determination emanated from her.

"Florence," Robert announced his presence as he walked with carefully controlled steps towards them.

The old woman looked up; fear evident though she held her position. She closed her eyes and spoke some chant or words that Robert didn't' understand but it seemed to make the old woman feel better.

"What's wrong with my grandchild?" She spoke with a heavy accent and a slight lisp. Robert noticed a few of her teeth had decayed leaving spaces yet beneath the outer exterior he saw the beautiful woman she once was.

"She is weary. It appears there is much more to this story than we expected. Some you may know or have anticipated" Robert turned his gaze directly on the old woman who had the decency to look away.

"Rebecca is now touched by both sides. She is in far more danger than we expected. I am not sure what to do,' He paused. "We could use your guidance and council please."

Florence smiled. Robert had done exactly what he should have to grant favor with Becca's grandmother. Tonight all of the story would be revealed and hopefully they would find a way to end this.

She gestured them into her home. Small and sparse was an apt description for how Loraine lived, the bare necessities and nothing more. Robert would be back he promised himself- should they live, with comforts for this woman. He laid Becca on the couch so she could recharge before moving to the kitchen area. The place was just one room, encompassing both the kitchen and living room. He assumed the bedroom was beyond the closed door, but he didn't' want to let Becca out of his sight.

"Where are the others?" Loraine was as curt as Florence. It seemed to run in the family.

"They are taking care of one of Benjamin's minions." The sadness that tinged his words was quickly picked up by the old woman.

"Why do you speak sadly? Do you not wish them dead?" she shot him a quizzical look as she asked Florence for a cup of tea.

He shook his head. "He was not responsible for his actions." Robert turned his eyes, fixing them directly on her as he continued. "Becca wears two of my marks, Loraine is it?" He continued as she chanted quickly while listening. "She also bears the gene from her ancestors. It has given her special gifts." Perhaps that would best describe it; Robert really wasn't sure. Softness crossed his face as he looked to Rebecca. She had curled up on the couch, clutching her stomach. He could still hear the hiccups from her crying.

Loraine followed his gaze before gesturing for Florence to take the tea to her grandchild. She had grown up to be a beautiful woman, Loraine almost smiled-almost. There was too much left to do for it to be genuine.

Robert looked questioningly towards Loraine as she sent the tea to Rebecca.

"It will soothe her nerves, nothing more. Tell me what happened."

"I don't quite know what happened," Robert started. He paused and looked up as his friends entered. Quickly he made introductions before continuing.

"Rebecca heard him in her head, Loraine; when none of us could."

"Told you; it's Becca," she mumbled from the couch, letting them know she was still listening.

"Hush child," Loraine ordered though her voice held a note of love for the grandchild she had not seen in so many years.

"He told her how he was tortured; he begged her for death." Robert continued. "George was his name; George Scott." A hint of recognition flickered in the old woman's sharp eyes.

"He also told us that even as Elders we did not have the ability to kill him without, um..." he leaned forward so Rebecca didn't have to hear, "without pulling apart the body."

"This is new," Loraine chewed on the words before speaking. "Why exactly is this?"

"He mentioned something about Benjamin having learned new abilities. That he takes out all memories brings them to the brink of death and implants his own horrific thoughts in the person. He also captures the large majority of the soul. If he were to be killed and not dismembered, a piece of his soul would find him-neither living nor dead; no existence at all."

"Did she find out where he rested?"

Robert nodded as he looked to Florence. He creates minions at your ancestor's home"

Loraine played with the few greying chin hairs she never bothered to rid herself of as she thought. "He will hunt tonight." Her eyes closed as she mumbled words to herself again. "Dangerous; he has become more dangerous than ever. He now fights those he created. A few he gifted with Elder status before they were ready." Again she closed her eyes and chanted. The Elders looked at one another before glancing back to the old woman.

Florence switched her gaze from Loraine to the others, amused by the expressions on their faces.

"They seek to overthrow him and gain his power. " Her head tilted as she opened her eyes. It looked like no one was home. She spoke sporadically, her words disjointed. "Still they will hunt for my grandchild and you. Hmmm. He will seek to find Rebecca's mind tonight; locate all of you via that connection he has learned."

Robert stood, knocking back the chair. "No; we can't let that happen. What do we do to stop this?"

"Your power is great between you five. He knows this and will send many after you. Most will be like George. Seek out those that hunger for battle; those are the ones that are his closest. The others seek an end to the torture. Should you succeed in killing those; he will be severely damaged. Much of himself has been gifted to these ones."

Robert could taste the bloodlust surging through the other Elders. He held his back as he looked towards Rebecca. "She wouldn't be safe there, Loraine. I can't bring her into a battle; and I can't leave her unprotected."

A dangerous smile lurked on the old woman's face. "She will not be unprotected. Look around where you are; stop and feel the overwhelming magic within these walls. Rebecca needs to hear the rest of the fable, from both the book and from us. We will ensure her safety."

"I'm not staying behind." Becca glared at them all. She growled as they studiously ignored her.

"She wears two of my marks that bind her to me; and me to her, Loraine. I do not know if it is enough to prevent Benjamin from finding a way into her mind. "

"Perhaps the third mark would benefit. Becca would grow exponentially in strength as well as you. "She tapped her fingers. "The danger is that should anything befall you, she would probably not survive completely."

"I wouldn't survive anyway, grandmamma." Becca rose from the couch. She turned to look at Robert before glancing back at her grandmother. "I love him. Marks or no marks as much as I hate him; I love him. We may have a few things to discuss; but I can't lose him. And I am not staying behind."

"Yes; you are Rebecca." Robert stood as he spoke.

"No. I. Am. Not." Each word enunciated in a manner that let him and everyone else know in no uncertain terms that she would not be told what to do.

"You are not coming with us, Rebecca and that is final."

"I will do as I damn well; oww, please!" Becca glared at her aunt before turning to her grandmamma. "Where do we find them?"

She smiled and patted Rebecca's cheek. "You are much like your mother and your aunt, child. I am proud of you."

"Tonight you shall all remain here; gather your strength and learn the truth. Rebecca shall learn what she can and tomorrow night you will all be prepared to end this part of the journey. Consider the third mark; it will bind you more permanently. "

Robert interrupted. "What do you mean this part of the journey?"

The old woman smiled, displaying the holes where her teeth once were. "This will not end until the five of you have found your siren callers. They will come to you soon. This power will awaken what lies dormant in them right now. Be ready. It shall not make your journeys any easier."

The Elders looked stunned, frozen in place at the words just spoken to them. More than one siren caller, protect more than one? Their soul mates? Fractured sentences rolled through their minds, jumping from one to the other until none of it made sense.

Slowly Loraine rose. It is time for the rest of the history. Rebecca; you must read the remainder of the journal" she turned her eyes towards the five. You shall follow me."

If you thought arguing with Florence was an error; try doing so with her grandmother. Not even Rebecca was that brave. She sighed as she grabbed the book, watching Robert and the others being led to the other room they had thought was a bedroom.

Becca opened the journal to finish reading.

He entered my body and my mind at the same time. I became overwhelmed with sensations and emotions. My body began to come alive even as it began to die. Our minds connected as he and I mated. The moment he poured his seed inside of me; the fourth mark, I felt death; I felt life and new powers that began to roar through me as I lay unmoving.

I was his. My conscious knew I had become his; that I had changed. Forever marked and not a moment too soon. They came. They converged, drawn to the power I now possessed.

Becca glanced out into the night. She knew she could see more clearly than she ever could at night before. Concentrating, she could hear him; feel him and taste the anger that cried out for battle that poured from him as he had defended the entrance to the barn. An ache began inside, spreading outwards. "Don't you get hurt," Becca spoke in her mind before finishing the journal.

My Ettore began to feed life into me from his blood. A few drops at a time but I felt life returning slowly. It is said that I glowed. I cannot speak whether I did nor not. It is said that I burned hotly, radiating it around my body. It is said that a siren caller has the ability to store within her all of the gifts that were poured into the body with the fourth mark. I carried within me all of him, including our children, to be born upon our time and choosing.

As life was restored the glow faded until I could see my Ettore's beautiful face. I reached to touch him, to trace the smile that played on his lips. To see the love glowing within the pure black eyes was worth everything.

And then I screamed. I screamed loudly. Behind my Ettore was another of his kind. He was different however. Where Ettore was light in my eyes, this one was blackness.

I could feel him probing my mind but easily I shut him out. His snarl was sinister. My body began to glow once again. It was a protective mechanism that surrounded me, preventing him from harming me. He could not touch me, not with Ettore's marks, not with my new powers, but he could touch Ettore.

Before my eyes he lunged for my love, his jaws open; hatred marring his perfect features. I did not comprehend what he meant to do until it was too late; until he had bitten Ettore, scarring him; adding venom into him.

"Nooooo," Becca screamed along with the woman in the journal. "Nooo." Tears ran unabashed down her face as she read.

I glowed more brightly, pouring heat from my body as I rose. I became fire to him. I watched as his face turned from victory to defeat before he fled into the shadows.

Though I would always be deemed a siren caller, with the four marks, our souls united, quieting the call. For a year we lived in complete bliss. Our children were given life, many of them. They were the image of my beautiful Ettore. We smiled as we watch them grow from seedling to fully grown in just weeks.

And then the unspeakable happened. Madness began within Ettore. What we did not know, could never have guessed was that being bitten by one of your kind, having their venom injected would make you mad.

The last night we came together, united our souls, bonded with both mind and body was the last time I saw my beloved Ettore. The disease consumed him. He became unstable, deteriorating until he was neither alive nor dead. His eyes were haunting for they knew what was lost. They begged for me to use my powers to end the madness within him, to end his life. I shook my head knowing I could not bear to live my life without him. That for him to go meant my soul would leave as well.

His final conscious thought was that he be locked away until we could find a cure. My heart broke as his children placed him gently in his resting place. I would carry on his life through his children that had been stored within me.

Many more were gifted with life. This was my fatal error. The madness that consumed Ettore also became part of the seed used to bring forth his children. It was not known until some years had passed that the disease could be spread in such a manner.

"Oh god," Becca moaned as she began to rock. "Oh god, oh god."

The one that originally changed my love returned. For the first time hatred filled me, an emotion unknown to a siren caller. He sneered as he saw the beginning of the destruction he purposely caused.

Hatred changes a caller. My eyes began to glow black like Ettore's would and I turned on him. Again I became fire though this time I had no intention of allowing him escape. He would pay with his life for what he had done. He was surrounded by fire, thick, hot, glowing embers red and slowly the circle grew smaller. There was no escape for him. I felt nothing as he burned, not even when he smiled a knowing smile.

I was drained. I would bear no further children as a result of the hatred. Night after night I would lie outside of Ettore's resting place and weep. During the day I would teach our children what he had not been able to complete.

Those that bore the madness had no desire to learn as the others did. Their choosing was to have others do things for them; minions.

A breach occurred, the diseased left to form their own lives. The pain ravaged me further as my children separated. The children that remained were the true children of Ettore, not the children of the one that had injected the venom.

War began. Each life lost was a part of my soul dying. Soon there would be nothing left but the ravages of death.

The time had come. Ettore and I would cease to exist and in turn, we would grant a new life for our finest. As they were named, as they grew into what they were always meant to be, I understood. These five; the elders, would go forth and with fortune on their side, find the path to fulfillment-to their own destiny. To teach those that would travel through the gateway with them, or were born of united souls the way life was meant to be.

I close these passages now and leave this journal with my children as I begin to open the gate. It will consume both Ettore and me. Together in life; we shall be together in death- finally at peace.

Becca closed the book and hugged it against her. The sadness and love written between these pages were unexplainable. She promised herself that she would read it again; more slowly to absorb each word that was so carefully transcribed for future generations.

Chapter 15

At least this time they didn't enter another damp basement; though perhaps, Markus thought-he might have preferred the damn underground.

They stopped in the doorway, not quite sure what to say or where to go for that matter. Loraine wandered in as though it was nothing unnatural; though considering it was a part of her house it probably wasn't.

Long tall candles rested in sconces that hung around the cement room. More candles littered the entire outer area of the room; flickering gently as they passed. Barren with the exception of a few cushions strewn across the floor in what Robert suspected was strategic places. A wood stove stood in the far corner, ancient and well maintained. The chute was haphazardly placed through a hole in the upper section of the wall with duct tape to hold it in place. Along the floor was an intricately hand painted set of circles and diamond shapes. All of the marks intertwined in just one section, leaving the very center of the design empty.

Vials, bottles and an assortment of; well for lack of a better word, Robert thought-voodoo implements sat along the one long wooden shelf that had been set into the wall.

"Well this is interesting," Giles spoke sardonically. "How long before we can do what we need to, Robert?"

"All in good time, lad," Loraine glanced towards Giles. A laugh erupted at the expression on his face before she started hacking.

Markus turned to the woman, his eyes wide with shock. "Explain."

"The one you seek is far more dangerous than you understand. Sometime after you saved Catherine; he found her again. She was like a magnet to him; because she escaped.

"What do you mean he found her again?" Robert felt an edge of fear; trying to stifle the urge to check on Rebecca.

"The child is fine upstairs," Loraine whispered. "Five different times the stranger visited Catherine. He never bit her again, he simply haunted her; making his way into her room night after night- each time on the anniversary of their first encounter."

"Why?" Giles was trying to understand.

"Are you saying he physically went to her, Loraine?" Leonard spat the words out; anger beginning to radiate through him.

"He went to her; not through her dreams; she no longer had any. He had stolen those from her at the first meeting. However, each night on the anniversary of her escape; something drew him back to her. No matter where he was; he returned to her."

Loraine paused and looked up, her eyes somewhat glazed. On the sixth year Catherine came to my great grandmother; some months before the anniversary. Her eyes held the note of one that had been tormented beyond what she could cope with. With her was the book which Rebecca now carries with her. After reading it my great grandmother took it to the old woman who was training her. There was so much no one knew or understood; and my ancestor was very young then."

"What did he do to her?" Robert's voice was low; threatening and filled with disgust for one of his kind.

"That no longer matters. They opened the front of her top and saw the mark that remained, as fresh as the day it had been placed there; though it was in fact six years old. When they swabbed the area she screamed as though she had just been bitten again.

"His venom is different. Months it took them to find some means of helping her. Understand that they knew virtually nothing about you, except what was read in the journal. But time had not been kind to Catherine. Each day she waited; wondered and feared. Finally they made the charms."

"On the night they knew he would return, the charms were placed along her windows and doors, originally they were of course made of lesser spiritual magic than they are made of now; but back then, he was not as strong as he is now. They sat with her while she waited; finally putting her to sleep with a very strong drought. He showed up. The most beautiful creature anyone had ever seen; until now-until you five. Even the burned face was easily overlooked. "Loraine looked to the men, sadness now reflected in her eyes.

"What happened?" Markus almost whispered.

"He came to the window and beckoned her. Of course she didn't respond; she had been properly drugged and was in a comatose sleep from it. With no response he approached the window, preparing to open it and enter. Instead he encountered their magic. His prey was not available to him; insanity turned his beautiful face to something beyond hideous. He inhaled and smiled; a smile so sinister it was remembered forever for the remainder of those that had born witness to it. And then he turned towards the others in the room. Though he could not enter; he was able to reach their minds. Within moments he had killed my great grandmother's mentor; stripping away all of her memories leaving her barren-broken. My ancestor was next. She claims to have seen pure madness within the blackness of his eyes. He tried; she said the pain was excruciating-unlike anything a person could endure. But she was a direct descendant of Catherine and combined with her own magic; she was able to absorb his. It is why I can hear you; why my granddaughter with only two marks can hear both you and them."

Robert swallowed. "I am so sorry we have caused this grief upon your family."

"Without you, none of us would be here. Catherine passed soon after. It was a blessing for her I believe. But you are right. Within us is a part of him. Now that Becca has your marks, she has both flowing through her veins. What this will mean I am not certain."

"The five of you; together will overwhelm his power but it will not be enough. Within our family is his gene. Now with Rebecca we carry both; or will should you convince her to agree to the next marks. I felt the siren call strike me at the age that Rebecca did. Behind the magic I was able to shield it. "She turned from them as she spoke. "We also shielded Florence; hers was not as strong. Four more will be coming to age shortly. "Loraine looked back at them.

"They will be siren callers. Each strong in their own right though none will be as powerful as Becca. The girls will call to you and you will respond. Now that I have met you; I do not fear their futures with you. But should you not defeat the other; none will have a life." Loraine paused before turning to look directly at each in turn. "But be warned, not one will be out of danger until they are all bound to the Elders. Each of my descendants will call more than just the five of you. Each will carry a battle to save her from the others."

"An entire family of callers?" Giles was stunned. "That is myth; fable. Finding Becca after so many years was." He paused before continuing. "Four more? It is not possible."

"Something in his venom and within our blood creates what is myth to you. Rebecca is proof of that."

"Shit," Markus rose and began to pace.

"He is creating others as strong as he is. I am afraid your problems are simply beginning, there will be war," Loraine again warned.

"We can leave," Robert stood and moved towards the door. "Take Rebecca and run."

"He will find you. I am afraid this is not something you can run from; not any of you."

"Who are the other four," Jerard asked. "We can at least hide them until they come of age."

"It is not known yet." Loraine glanced with an ominous expression. "It may be that they are here in this time, waiting for their caller to come to light. " She paused, hesitating before continuing. "It may be they are of age, the call remaining in slumber, awaiting Becca's awakening. Destiny is a more powerful magic than any we contain. I cannot say where they will come from or when, or even if they will be from our family tree for certainty, only that they will, and with each wakening will be a harsher more dangerous war waged." Her voice lowered ominously as she completed her thought. "Especially if a maddened Wanderer should find a caller and become one with her before she can be saved. Understand this, Elders, the others now possess the knowledge of the power that lies dormant within a siren, and they will not hesitate to take what they seek no matter the cost."

"Son of a bitch," Leonard punched the wall before leaving the room.

"Robert" Loraine's words now laced with fear, her warning forgotten, "find my grandchild. She has completed the journal and has gone in search of him."

He was gone before she finished the sentence. The door slammed as he pushed through, searching for Rebecca. The journal lay on the couch where she had been resting but she was gone.

"She's gone!" Robert yelled to the others before flying out the door.

Becca knew what she had to do; perhaps she had known it from the moment she created fire. She raced through the night; knowing she was not nearly as quick as the Elders but with luck her grandmother would keep them occupied long enough for her to do what she had to. Her thoughts turned to Robert; pain twisted inside, the need for him so strong it was tangible. No; she would not let him or the others be injured because of what she was. Wetness gathered on her face, her tears-cooling in the night air as she put as much distance between them as she could. Not tomorrow would it end; but tonight. No more waiting.

"Rebecca," Robert yelled in his head as he followed her scent.

"We will find her, Robert," Markus tried to comfort him as he sped alongside.

Becca tuned them out, searching instead for a different channel, the one that she had heard George from; that was the key. Her heart screamed for Robert; for his arms-his love. Brushing it aside was the most painful experience of her life but it would be nothing compared to losing him.

She had to stop, her side aching. Though she had travelled much faster than she ever thought possible, Becca realized she was not nearly on par with the Elders. "Shit," she turned, beginning to panic as she heard them approach. "Ok, now or never."

Raising her head to the night sky, Becca opened her mind; calling out to Benjamin, to his minions. "You want me," she whispered in her head. "You want me like you wanted Catherine. I know you listen, Benjamin; you are so pathetic. You will never have me either."

She screamed as pain resonated in her head, falling to her knees as she clutched her temples. Breathing became a chore as Benjamin delved into her mind.

"Pain." She tried to speak. "Is that the best you can do, Benjamin? Are you so weak that two members of the same family will defeat you-resist you?"

Agony ripped through her head again, stronger; longer and far more powerful. She clawed at the grass as he desperately tried to tear away the barriers within her mind. Each attempt was like a white hot branding iron being thrust inside.

"You can't win, Benjamin." She struggled to her knees, barely able to see through the pain and the tears. They surrounded her now; the Elders. Robert wrapped his arms around her as she writhed in pain. Not until he touched her did she open her mind to them.

"All you know is pain, Benjamin; all you have is fear." She began to mock him; screaming as he retaliated not with words but with blazing pain that would have knocked her off her feet again had Robert not held her. "I beat you, Benjamin. The Elders and I have beaten you. Soon all of those you have used will come to me because I can call them; yes-you know it is true. I am marked by an Elder, Benjamin. There is no way for you to have me now. How does it feel to lose?" Her words were mere whispered sounds as she writhed with agony.

Opening her mind helped spread the agony to the elders, though it was still more than she could bear. "Find him," she whispered to Robert. "Third mark now Robert, connect with me as I connect with him. Find him."

"They will never belong to you." Benjamin spat before attempting to rip another layer from her mind.

"They already do, you bastard. They are mine. They will come to my call."

"NO." He screamed. Madness hung in the air, they could all taste it.

Robert held Rebecca gently as the other four surrounded them. "Now Robert, now the mark, it has to be now! " She screamed and bucked wildly as another wave of pain ripped through her.

Brushing the hair from the side of her neck, Robert leaned forward. He licked the perspiration that lingered from the pain as he traced a path from the lobe of her ear downwards to her shoulder.

She shuddered in response; suddenly consumed with fire; with a desperate need for him, angling her head she offered her neck. "Please Robert; please."

Bringing his large hand upwards he stroked her beautiful face. Whispering "I love you," before biting her neck. This time she screamed in sheer bliss as the mark began to form, creating a circular formation along the top of her collar bone. She opened her mind completely and thrust the pleasure outwards; directing it towards Benjamin and his minions.

Her fingers clung to Robert as he marked her. His tongue traced along the circle, soothing it as well as inciting fresh waves of need to rush through every vein; fill every thought.

"They come," Giles shouted, "dozens of young ones."

"You lose Benjamin," her voice was soft; gentle, she had given all she had tonight.

They could all hear Benjamin's scream as many of his lifeless minions lumbered towards her call. The promise of rest and peace was far more than they could resist.

"Come to me, my friends, come-find peace." She almost cooed as Robert continued to lick the wound. She arched into his touches, her fingers weaving into his hair, tugging him closer.

"Not all will come," Benjamin laughed as he tried to claw inside her again. The pain was less extensive than it had been before the mark; though she felt it clearly.

"Not yet," Becca's voice was soft as she drew back slightly from Robert. "But enough that you will be easily available, Benjamin, that is what matters. "Already the Elders can track you through me; there is nowhere for you to hide any longer. You are now one of the walking dead men that you so callously created. We come for you, Benjamin; be prepared."

His scream of rage echoed long after she shut down her mind to cut him off. She was panting with exertion, sweating and nauseated. "Did you find where he resides?"

Leonard nodded, not quite sure what to make of the brave woman resting within the circle of Robert's arms.

"They come;" Giles motioned towards the distant horizon. At least two dozen emerged from the treeline.

"How many are friendly and how many aren't?" Markus looked to Rebecca.

She shook her head, afraid to open the channel again to find out. Robert reached out to pull her against him. "One more time, open one more time so we know what we deal with. And you and I will be having a serious discussion afterwards."

"Shit," she mumbled as she leaned against him, feeling and using his strength as she opened her mind to those that approached. Dozens of voices clamoured in her head, cries for peace-all but two.

"Two, there are two that do not wish peace. She closed her eyes; focusing on the ones that approached. "In the back; they are hiding in the back of the others."

"Stay here," Robert ordered. Leaning forward he kissed her before moving to stand with the other Elders.

"Stay here; no problem," she began to shake and sunk to her knees; curling up as tightly as she could hoping to be invisible.

Fear began to gnaw at her insides as the group descended upon them. It was quiet; eerily so, something didn't feel right. "Crap," she thought as she opened her mind again. Slowly she began to crawl away as the elders braced themselves for battle. "Talk to me," she whispered as she began to rock. "Talk; please."

"They are not all safe," the voice was so quiet Rebecca could barely hear it.

"Where, where are they; you have to trust me-please."

"Long black hair; mid…" was all she heard before a grunt. Silence followed.

"Robert; look for a few with long black hair. Those are the ones. They just killed the one that spoke to me."

She bowed her head in concentration though it thundered and fear ravaged the better part of her thoughts. Becca did her best to close that channel as she raised her hands upwards to the skies, her fingers parting, her face ashen and tear streaked. Heat began to radiate in her fingers. She opened her eyes as they edged closer.

Frantically she looked for those with the long hair; "Where-where are they; where, where?" Panic was beginning to set in the center of her core. It was taking all of her concentration to block it out. Straining her eyes she saw a slight break in the rows of minions that approached. It had to be there she thought; god please let me be right. Raising her arms she focused; imagining the fire circling those where the break existed.

She bounced like a kid at Christmas when a ring of flames surrounded a half a dozen men. "Oops, focus-focus" she chided herself as she raised the flames higher, completely closing them within it. The others continued to come, paying no attention to the fire. It was obvious there was nothing left within them.

"Get them," she hissed as she tried to remain focused. "Come back in one piece. I will lower the flames when you say so you can all enter then I'll raise it again.

And then they were gone. She was quite convinced there would never be a time she would grow accustomed to the speed in which they travelled. Yuck.

"Now Becca," Leonard shouted.

She lowered the flames so the five could enter before raising them once again to an unbelievable height. Finally with the last of her energy she expanded the wall, allowing no one entrance-or exit. Her focus remained on the men; she couldn't help the minions yet. "You are safe," Becca tried to comfort them though her voice was strained; her body shaking badly. She wasn't sure how much longer she could keep the wall up.

They made short work of those not seeking refuge though Robert chose to keep one alive. He would with luck prove to be useful.

"Lower the flames, Rebecca." Robert's voice held a note of battle; the glory of winning.

"Told you; it's Becca," she managed to say before collapsing.

Chapter 16

Markus and Giles held the one remaining minion, allowing Leonard to deal with the final one. Once Robert knew that his friends were safe, he disappeared back to Rebecca, having to push his way through the mob of young ones to find her.

"Here's hoping Loraine is wrong about there being more callers," Jerard snickered. "Look what it's done to Robert."

The others laughed while Robert snarled. "Watch it or I'll have to show you what it has done." He was never going to hear the end of this; at least not until the others found their soul mates.

He found Becca in a heap on the ground, the fear only leaving when he felt her pulse. It was a good thing she was alive because when she came to; he was going to kill her. How dare she pull a stupid stunt like that-ugh. Lovingly he lifted her and held her against his body.

"So what are we supposed to do with all of these young ones?" Giles grumbled as he walked around them to check on Rebecca. "Is she ok?"

"Yes," Robert's voice was filled with relief, "at least until I kill her."

"What she did was very brave, Robert. She drew him out and weeded out the young ones." Markus was really quite impressed with her at the moment.

"She could have been hurt," Robert growled.

"Robert, think rationally for a moment. She found him; she taunted him and she pissed him off; though-she does seem to be good at doing that, at least to you." Leonard snorted.

He glanced down at Rebecca, gently brushing his cold hand against her face. She felt so hot to him. "Wake up Rebecca; wake up."

Nothing but silence followed his words. "Bring her to Loraine." Jerard nodded.

"What about all of these young ones?" Robert waved his arm. "They followed her. We can't bring them to the clan, shit; Florence would be after us with that frying pan of hers."

"Alright, you have a point," Markus laughed. "Stay here and Jerard and I will go get them and bring them here."

He looked down at her as she lay unconscious in his arms. "Be ok, please be alright." Pain was racing through him as their connection waivered. In sleep it was different but this; she lay limp and unmoving-there was no thought and no connection. "Hang on, Rebecca. They will be right back."

Leonard kept a close watch on the young ones while Giles strong armed the last remaining hold out. There was something very different about him in comparison to the others. Stronger; with an edge of anger that radiated from him, Leonard was sure he would be very difficult to break. He smiled at the thought.

Robert finally looked from Rebecca to those that hovered around her. He saw no flicker of life in them; no emotion at all. How the hell did she call this many to her and what did she plan on doing with them now. Christ she was impulsive. He shook his head. The thought of locking her away somewhere for her own safety was mighty tempting right about now.

Markus and Jerard burst through the shadows clearing the crossing in mere seconds. Florence as per usual looked like a kid with a new toy but Loraine; well, tolerated would be somewhat overstating things. Very carefully Markus lowered Loraine beside Rebecca so she wouldn't have to move far in the dark. He hadn't thought of bringing her cane.

"Place her down." When he continued to hold her she looked up at him. "I can't find what ails her until you put her down."

Reluctantly he settled Rebecca in the cool grass; hovering over her as Loraine began to check.

"She called these to her didn't she?" Loraine knew the answer before asking.

"Yes." Robert nodded as he watched her closely.

"They will have to be put to rest before Rebecca will waken. It is too much for her to bear. The sorrow and pain they have experienced will be too much for her."

"How the hell are we supposed to do that?" Giles rubbed his face as she stepped on the squirming minion.

"That one we will keep, "Loraine showed no emotion. "I suspect we can get more than just information from him.

"Great, we will keep him, but what about the others?" Markus eyed Florence's frying pan before dismissing it.

"In my pouch there is a flask, Florence." Loraine didn't bother to look up. "It's what they used on my relative's mentor when he killed what was her essence. It won't hurt them; merely put them at peace."

Florence shuddered as she reached into the flask. Even to her this seemed a bit too much. After finding it, she passed it to Jerard.

"One drink; that is all they will need." Loraine turned her attention back to her grandchild.

"Robert, carry her back to the camp. There is too much power here for her. When we are finished, we will return. She should waken by then."

Gladly he lifted her back into his arms, looking towards his friends, ensuring they would be alright before turning.

He set her down on the sofa, wanting to hold her; knowing he was too cold to do so for long periods. Each mark lowered her skin temperature enough that she would be able to withstand longer periods of time but tonight with all that had happened; she was shivering. Finding a blanket he draped it over her before brushing back her hair. "Come back to me Rebecca; please come back. I can't live without you."

With gentle touches Robert pushed back her hair before tracing the dark shadows beneath her eyes. She had been through so much in such a short period of time. He ached for all that he put her through. Perhaps she would be better off without him in her life; though he knew living without her would make him one of the walking dead. He shook his head; no, they had to make it work.

Loraine looked into the eyes of each of the young ones, hoping to find some form of life within them. Those the Elders could work with; guide them, help them become what they should be-not what they are now. A pattern seemed to follow. She would look; touch their hand and hold it until the drought took effect. She wanted nothing more than for their final moments to be filled with a sense of warmth.

The four Elders watched closely as they held the captive young one. They felt him shudder knowing soon the gypsy woman would stand before him.

"She is amazing," Jerard spoke to the other Elders as they watched the loving care Loraine took with each one.

"We can see where Rebecca gets it from." Giles responded. None of them saw Loraine smile. Her grandchild, like her- yes; yes she was.

She stood before the second to last young one. So many tired souls that cried out; exhaustion crept slowly into her limbs as she worked.

Loraine looked up at this one and paused before reaching out to touch him. Her eyes closed as she wrapped her hand around his. There was a jolt; a sensation of life. Her face lit up with hope as she motioned to Jerard.

"He has life within his soul," Loraine laughed; a joyous sound that filled the clearing that lay littered with the dead. "He can be saved." Her eyes turned to Jerard. "Your word of honor; the four of you, that you will help this one-save him. You can do no less after what has been done to all of these..." her arm swept across the carnage."

"You have our word, Loraine." Jerard spoke for all of them as he moved to stand before the one young one. "Should he desire, we will take him under our wing and teach him the ways of the Wanderer." He turned to gaze upon the young one.

"Do you have a name?" Though he tried to keep his voice gentle it was naturally a deep gravel tone that caused many to be wary of him.

The young one stood tall as he hung on Jerard's words. Slowly his head nodded; a look of fear crept into his eyes as they turned towards the one still being held.

"Get him out of here," Jerard felt the instant relief from the young one.

"Where would you like to... discuss things with him?" Markus turned towards Leonard.

"Bring him to the circle of blood," Loraine hobbled over to the one they were speaking of. "Yes; you know what I mean don't you? The place where piece by piece your mind will be prodded; your body dismembered, where all ancient rituals against a gypsy's enemy has taken place."

Loraine saw the fear in his eyes. Before Benjamin he had been different. There had been no anger within him; no hatred for those he did not know or understand. But he understood this; he was about to die a very painful death.

Markus lifted Loraine as Leonard and Giles dragged the man; kicking and screaming behind them. Jerard and Florence remained in the clearing.

"What is your name?" Jerard questioned. "We had no desire to harm you unless you are committed to Benjamin.

"John." It was just one word but it took a momentous effort for the young one. And he was young, not just as a Wanderer; but as a male.

"John, thank you," Jerard offered a short smile. "Can you tell us what happened?"

They watched his throat working as he tried to formulate thought to word. It had been so long since he'd spoken. "Benjamin-creating many..." he paused, "I was overlooked. The man you took-he. He supervises."

"I am going to touch you, John," Jerard moved closer. "As my hand touches yours, you will feel an exchange of power. It will help regain strength and return some memories. I don't know how many as I do not understand the exact extent of what he has done."

Ensuring his movements were slow and not meant to be in any way a symbol of fear, Jerard wrapped his hand around John's. Pain filled Jerard as he absorbed some of the memories from him while peace filled John. The power flowed between them, Master and student; alive and dead. Finally Jerard drew back.

Florence watched carefully; her assessment of the Wanderers substantially changing by the hour. They were; like humans both good and bad. Unlike humans however they had the power to destroy. She brushed aside a tear before anyone saw her being anything less than the cranky old aunt.

"Will you accept our guidance, John?" Jerard began to walk to the dead, knowing they had to be separated-mind from body. "Rebecca's right! You are all bastards, leaving me here to do this."

"Yes," John spoke clearly. Still very pale in comparison to other Wanderers he seemed to try to smile. Jerard nodded. "These men; they were your friends?"

He didn't look down as he shook his head. "There were no friends; there was only fear."

"Their bodies must be taken apart so Benjamin cannot call them again." Jerard tried to explain. "If it is too difficult for you to see, I understand. Just remain over there for me."

"We shared pain; we shall share peace." John moved to the first of what seemed like so many. He made quick work of the job that needed to be done. Between the two of them it was over quickly. Florence said a prayer for them before turning. She couldn't watch.

Jerard wiped his hands on the grass before approaching Florence. "Are you ready to go back to the clan?

She nodded, unable to speak. Jerard hugged her as he pulled her into his arms. What was witnessed tonight was not what even the strongest of persons should have to witness.

A hand on his shoulder stopped Jerard mid stride. He turned to look at John, a quizzical expression on his face.

"Thank you, Elder," John stuttered, still trying to find his voice. "I will not disappoint you or the others. I am grateful."

Jerard smiled as he listened before nodding. "Come; let us return to the others. We haven't finished teasing Robert." He watched the young one hesitate.

"To be among people; to belong to the Elders now. . . "John looked up. "I don't know how; my memories of that part of life are gone."

Florence reached out to take his hand, offering a rare but beautiful smile. "Then we shall create new ones."

Jerard led them into Loraine's house before setting Florence down. His gaze turned towards Rebecca who lay almost peacefully on the couch. "How is she Robert?"

"She begins to stir, thankfully," relief was evident within each word he spoke."

Jerard slapped him on the back. "Good job, Robert. I would like you to meet, John."

Robert stood, towering over the young one; his presence alone lent a tone of authority. He was not one to be disobeyed; except by Rebecca apparently.

"John is our new fledging, Robert," Jerard began. "Loraine found signs of life within him. He wishes to be guided by us and we have granted him this."

He nodded. Somehow he knew that eventually it would come to this point. They would save all they could; guide them towards the right path, share new memories and hope they will be able to work passed the history of their entry into Wanderer status.

John looked to the couch; his head canting. "She is the one that called?" His eyes fixated on the waif of a woman that rested beneath the blanket.

"Yes," Robert knelt beside her again; a protective stance, one designed to display who she belonged to.

"Felt her love; her pure heart." John remarked, his eyes soft; knowing that forever, he would be bound to this woman. "She called many; both dead and those like me."

Robert shook his head. "Yes, she did it without our knowledge or consent. We shall be having words about this." His voice was still angry though he attempted to control it.

"You don't understand, Elder," John moved closer before kneeling beside Rebecca. 'May I touch her hand please, Elder?"

A confused look passed between Jerard and Robert. Jerard shrugged his shoulders 'in his favorite I have no clue what is happening motion'. "You harm her in any way and I will kill you where you stand." Robert spoke the words slowly, clearly; and without any inflection within them; he meant each and every one.

"There is no desire to harm her, Elder," John gazed openly at Robert, displaying the truth in his words. "She is our caller; our … mother now so to speak. She gave us life with her thoughts. Many more shall come and those that do not will attempt to kill Benjamin."

Robert was stunned. He glanced at the journal and shook his head. She saw what none of the others had seen. 'You may touch her hand."

He watched carefully as John reached forward to coil his cold fingers with Becca's. Magic became tangible at the touch, a sharing of life.

"Just remember, John; she is my Rebecca."

"Told ya; it's Becca," her voice was raspy and drained, but it was there and she was here.

Robert folded her into his arms and held her tightly.

"Hi, you," Becca turned her head upwards.

"Hi, you," Robert responded; a grateful smile tugging on the corners of his lips.

Weakly she moved in his arms until she could reach his lips. She traced her tongue along the bottom one first and then the upper, moaning huskily as she finally pressed her lips against his.

Robert crushed her against him as he returned the kiss. She melted into his arms, her lips parting even more as she drank in the love and offered her own to him. She could feel her head swimming with the emotions that flowed through her; heady and more powerful than anything she had ever experienced.

His fingers traced along her arms; up to her shoulders before cradling her neck. He angled her head to deepen the kiss. Their hearts matched in rhythm, blood flowing thickly and hotly through their bodies as they melded together as one.

Jerard coughed loudly, receiving a hand waving from Robert-shooing him out the door. Again he coughed; a little more loudly this time.

Becca blushed furiously as she heard the cough, having forgotten anyone was around them. For her there was only Robert; in her eyes- in her heart and always in her soul.

"Sorry to disturb," Jerard offered.

"Like hell you are," Robert growled as he covered Becca.

"Ok so I'm not really but we have unfinished business to attend to." He motioned with his head to the one outside.

"Damn it," Robert cursed as he glanced at Rebecca. Unable to resist he kissed her again, hard and fast; filled with a passionate promise of things to come before morning. He smiled when he felt her shudder.

"I will join you, Elders; if you would allow." John offered. "I may have information that could potentially be useful."

214

Jerard nodded. "Yes come."

"Me too," Becca tried to climb from Robert's lap only to be quickly drawn back against him."

"You are staying here, Rebecca."

"Like hell I am, Robert."

He growled. "You are not going to involve yourself in any more dangerous shit tonight. "

"I would offer to protect her with my life, Elder." John bowed.

"See!" Becca cooed. "I'm perfectly safe." Reaching up she stroked his face. "Robert, we share three marks. I feel you like I feel myself. I understand your fear. Please look inside of me and feel what I need. This is important."

Robert turned to John. You will protect her while we guide you through your passage."

"Rebecca; Becca, he rested his forehead against hers. I feel your need to help, to see if any are salvageable. Promise me; no more calling tonight or without our knowledge."

She rolled her eyes before kissing him. "Fine; I promise."

He lifted her into his arms. "Let's go see what is happening outside then."

Chapter 17

She should have listened to Robert; not that she would ever tell him that, she would never hear the end of it. Along the back of the camp there was a trail that led them into a cavernous area. Inside was lined with flickering flames from lanterns that hung along the walls. It felt cool in here to Becca and she slid closer to Robert; finding him just as cold. The opening widened the deeper they walked until ahead she could see a well lit room. Acrid smoke filtered towards them as they neared along with some kind of an incense odor. Together they were very nearly overpowering. Her fatigued eyes began to water and she took to breathing through her mouth. Her steps began to slow as her heart rate quickened. Some instinct warned her that within that circular formation was far more dangerous than anything she had faced tonight.

"I don't think I should go in there, Robert." Her voice held a slight tremor as she felt the power beginning to crawl along the ground towards her.

"What's wrong, Rebecca?" Robert stopped; listening to the tone in her voice, the sense of urgency he felt within her.

"I don't know, "she whispered as her steps took her back towards the entrance. "When was the last time any of you fed?" she looked up at him.

"Some days ago, why," he responded quizzically?

"You need to feed, all of you; now." Rebecca's eyes began to glaze over and she swayed into his arms. "Call your friends, Robert; go feed now." A strangled cry escaped her slightly swollen lips and her head jerked back. It felt as though someone had taken a whip and began to strike her mind with vicious blows; one landing directly after another.

"He grabbed her before she collapsed; holding her to him as she screamed and writhed in agony until finally the sounds quieted. The further he took her from the cave the less ferocious the pain became. "Come to me, my friends." Robert called to the Elders. "Bring Loraine and Florence, but have them ensure the one in the circle of blood can do no damage. Be quick."

He knew Rebecca was suffering when she didn't protest being carried into the house. "John, get her some water," he tossed orders out like a drill sergeant without glancing back to see if they had been followed. She looked weakly up at him; a little wide eyed as he released the potency of his true strength.

Her fingers clutched at his arm before he could rise. "Please don't go yet, the one in the circle is not under control. You need to shield me." The words had barely fluttered from her lips when another wave of excruciating agony ripped through her body. Her body arched as the pain grew so intense she didn't know where to release it.

"How, Rebecca; what do you need?"

"Help!!!," She screamed as she bent like a bow again.

Robert could hear the others approaching; his eyes not leaving Rebecca.

"Kiss me," the words were jumbled as she struggled to remember how to speak.

"What?" Robert looked at her; more than a little confused.

Digging her fingers into the crisp linen of his shirt, dragging him to her until their lips met in a fiery kiss that left them both breathless.

Their marks began to embrace one another as she and Robert did, mimicking each motion in perfect symmetry.

His tongue entered her mouth, circling hers, warring with it as he deepened the kiss. His fingers gripped her hair, tugging on it until her neck angled, her head tipped back for easier access. He swallowed each moan, licked each tear from her face before roughly claiming her lips one more.

Her fingers climbed from his shirt to wrap around his neck, holding him as close to her as she could. Each place their bodies touched; each moment of their souls intertwining lessened the pain that had been purposely inflicted upon her. Spasms of need ripped through her trembling body as Robert rested his weight on her; covering the entirety of her body with his cool flesh, raising the aching desire and heat within her until she was arching and panting with need. Her screams turned to screams of pure bliss as his fingers began to roam over her body; lower and lower until he found the base of her t-shirt. Uncaring at the moment who was witness; he buried his fingers beneath the shirt, splaying them on her flat stomach upwards until his calloused fingers brushed over the marks on her breasts.

There was fire; nothing but an incredible heat claiming every nerve ending within her writhing body. Eagerly she returned each kiss with equal fervor using their connection; the marks and the merging of their souls to break from the lashes of pain she had been experiencing.

Finally he pulled his lips reluctantly from hers, kissing down along her chin to her neck, slowly; so slowly, inflicting a new torturous sensation to flood within her as he made his way to the third mark. His tongue felt like fire and ice; his lips brushing over the circular mark were like falling over the edge into an abyss of unending pleasure.

She moaned softly as he pulled back enough to plant a gentle kiss on her lips before stroking her cherry red cheeks. Energy flowed between them; around them, filling the room with what could only be considered as two people uniting as one entity. She felt exhausted and exhilarated at the same time. The blush staining her cheeks grew hotter as she realized they were surrounded by other people. She refused to move her eyes from his until she could at least control herself. His touches soothed her body even as they closed her mind from further pain.

Something unique had just occurred. There was not a person in the room that didn't feel the charges of electricity. Robert smiled; a smile that held the promise of a lifetime of moments such as these.

Rebecca reached up to trace the contoured lines of his face; no longer afraid of the blackness that filled the irises of his eyes. "Oh shit," she barely had time to speak before Robert jumped.

Rubbing the back of his neck he slowly turned; quite sure he knew exactly what had just smacked him. The chortling from his friends confirmed what he would see.

Florence; all five foot two and a half thank you very much stood there with her frying pan; her toes tapping and a look of supressed amusement deep in her eyes though her face maintained the firm angry look.

"Must I teach you manners young man?" She spoke briskly as she continued to tap her foot.

Robert did he best to tune out the howls from his friends that revolved inside his head as he did his best to answer her. "No, Florence, I assure you I am generally quite well-mannered." He was very glad his kind didn't blush because as sure as he was standing here; his face would match Rebecca's.

She linked her fingers with his as she spoke. "It was my fault Aunt Florence," she paused waiting for the smack. When none happened she continued. "What you have in the circle of blood is a leader. He and three others were raping my mind; trying to destroy it. Benjamin is slowly being drained as we speak."

Becca paused hearing the gasps from the Elders. It was just not possible. She looked curiously up at them, not quite understanding the significance. Offering a shrug she continued.

"He gave too much of himself to those he thought would be valuable allies. My call seemed to ignite their decision to rob him of his status and control. He will die tonight; his powers drained and shared between the four new ones." Rebecca leaned back on the couch, her body suddenly completely exhausted. From extreme pain to exquisite pleasure, her senses were in overload.

"Our connection; the three marks we share shielded my mind and body from the four of them attempting to empty it. Grandmamma; I'm not sure if there is something you can give to the one in the circle. Something that will weaken him enough that he cannot reach the other four; if not," Becca looked to the Elders, "he must be killed now."

Robert's eyes gleamed black; fire fuelled him. He could taste the desire to kill the one that tortured her as she spoke, "He will die."

Loraine nodded. "I can bind him within a wall of charms. Attempting to use his powers will drain him. However; each time he uses his power it will diminish the strength of one charm. Should he continue; he will break the binding and enable contact with the others. The circle of blood is special" she looked to the five Elders. It holds ancient powers that may well exceed your own. It's legend; its legacy speaks of a piece of all evil extinguished within the circle to have remained. It is what makes it so powerful. Let's pray the legend is true and it is stronger than the one trapped within it."

Becca nodded as she tried to sit up. "You will have to go feed now; all of you. Without the strength and energy; you will not be able to defend nor defeat the new powers. They have powers now; very strong powers that they are able to combine as they did tonight.

220

"I'm not leaving you," Robert sat on the edge of the couch, not breaking contact with her.

"You are, Robert." She touched his face as she spoke. Grandmamma can give me a sleeping drought that will last a few hours; at least until your return. With the fourth bound securely within the circle, distanced with whatever she will do to him; you will be able to feed. You will have to be quick but thorough." Her eyes turned to the others. She could see the shadows beneath their eyes; the paleness of their flesh. As strong as they were; they would have no hope without this.

Loraine turned to the stove, quickly making a drought for Rebecca. She handed it to Robert before going into the back room, emerging moments later with her arms filled with charms that dripped fresh blood. Rebecca didn't want to know where it came from.

She took the cup as Robert stroked her hair. What had he caused her with these marks? He had no understanding of the gene being carried and made note to speak to both Loraine and Florence about it after this was over. His precious Rebecca, he thought, trying not to laugh at the look of pure disgust on her face.

Within moments her eyes began to flutter closed. Robert leaned forward to kiss the top of her head; whispering, sleep my Rebecca. "

"Told ya; it's..." Was as far as she got before sleep claimed her.

Florence moved to the couch and covered Becca before rising. "All right, all of you; shoo out of here now and find food or..." she paused, "whatever it is you do."

The men rose to leave, already reaching out to listen for the calls; hunger rising with each whispered murmur of dreams.

"Oh and just to be clear," Florence stopped them as they were about to leave. "Outside of Norwich, not in my town," she nodded firmly before crinkling her nose in thought. "Though were you to visit the old coot straight down at the end of my road on your way out of town; I probably wouldn't be too upset."

Giles blinked as he looked at Florence; his head shaking, lips curling into a grin. How could you not adore this feisty woman, he whispered in his head? They could all understand why Becca was so completely devoted and loved her so much.

"What?" Florence gave him her best get out now stare. "He has been a thorn in my side for some odd years now, boys. It would serve him right." She snorted. "Now shoo; the lot of you so you can get back."

Hunger drove them out the door and into the shadowy night. Their thoughts were all similar however as they followed the breathless whimpers of those who called to them. None enjoyed leaving the camp unattended; unless you counted Florence and her pan. With Rebecca in deep sleep she would be unable to call and they were positive Loraine would do all she could to contain the fourth riser of power.

"John; have you fed before?" Robert asked as they moved with lightning speed; becoming nothing more than a fading streaks of shadow along the country side.

"No, Elder," John's voice was quiet; nervous and a little afraid. "We were not permitted. He feared it would give us too much strength to rise up against him. To regain who and what we were. Instead Benjamin reversed the cycle; supplying us with memories; dreams of sort. Horrific, despicable thoughts and memories implanted. With each feeding, he would carve out a section of our soul; drawing it within himself. It appeared to make him far stronger; his control was unbroken until your Rebecca called."

Robert nodded. "Tonight you will remain with Leonard. Allow him to guide you through a feeding. Learn well from him; feel the beauty and the joy of shared thoughts with the one you feed from. Remember to never drain; simply regain your energy." He offered a short smile to John before increasing his speed. His thoughts were on Rebecca; on getting back to the camp.

"Why did he take part of your soul and the others?" Markus curiously asked. "I mean what did he do aside from absorb it or release it?"

"He did neither," John responded as he looked to Markus. He absorbed them into himself..." He paused, attempting to formulate his thoughts into words. "I am not exactly sure how to express this, Elders; perhaps this way. Imagine if you would; a squirrel that forages throughout the summer, storing the nuts it collects in holes and finally in their cheeks. They are contained there for a time that the animal will find use for them." John hesitated seeing the look of horror spread along the Elder's faces.

"Have I said something wrong, Elders?"

"No, no," Jerard could barely force the words out. "Please continue."

"Benjamin contained the shards of souls within himself until such time that he would find it useful. Finally he found four and began to share those pieces. They grew in strength; in control and in age with great rapidness. They also seemed to have become somewhat...hmm; diseased perhaps is the word. Anger; lust, desire to control and consume everything in their path was all they longed for. Many times as Benjamin attempted to teach him what he himself had been taught; the young elders simply absorbed all of the soul."

"So they began killing those that Benjamin had turned into his minions." Giles was fascinated.

"Repeatedly; Elders. Benjamin would grow furious and reprimand them. At the time on an individual basis he was still far stronger than the four; but together, combining their powers Benjamin would not have a hope of succeeding. As they killed, he would take each aside and inflict pain upon them. Steal some of their power; it became a give and take until they were crazy. It was then they decided to join as a unit. And then your Rebecca called, paving the way for Benjamin's demise."

Robert stopped at the end of Florence's street. He would grant her the desire she had requested. Were he to be honest, he would admit to being curious as to why she wanted him fed from; he wasn't honest, not for this.

Robert turned to the others and nodded before facing John. "What you experienced was wrong, John. I hope you will believe that and accept that it is not the way you have to or should live. This is your chance; your turning point. Listen carefully as he teaches and choose wisely. We do not give second chances."

John offered a semblance of a smile. "There will be no second chance needed, Elder. I am a Somnias Vagus; one that will follow the ways of a true Wanderer."

Robert clapped him on the back before weaving into the shadows. "Be safe; be thorough and be quick."

He glanced up to the window, following the moonlight that bathed the room in its gentle glow. As he remained along the edge of the sill he allowed his eyes to close; to reach out to the "old coot" as Florence referred to him as. "Allow me enter," He whispered to the man who snored loud enough to wake the dead. Robert barely heard the word "enter" with all the rumbling noises being emitted. "Ah Florence you owe me one for this," he thought as he melded into the shadows along the wall and reached into his mind.

Instantly the energy began to flow, increasing his strength; the clarity within his mind and thought. Power began to surge through him as he walked along the fabric of dreams. And then he stopped. It took all of his self-control to hold back the howls of laughter as he realized who the man was dreaming of.

"Well I understand now, Florence," he chuckled as he exited in the same manner that he had entered.

Chapter 18

Robert chuckled the entire way back to the camp; laughing outright as he shared the thoughts with the others. The image of Florence with her neighbour was unfathomable; especially considering the dream Robert had invaded involved an attempted stolen kiss and Florence's handy dandy frying pan upside his head. She was well and truly in love with her husband and would hurt any that tried to interfere.

"Beautiful," Jerard chortled, "Absolutely beautiful."

"I'm on my way back," Robert informed the others. "Be quick and safe please."

For just a moment he revelled in the freedom of the night; the slight caress of the wind against his steel like flesh, the pure abandoned joy of the freedom of movement. And for just this moment in time he felt no fear for Rebecca. He felt nothing but peaceful slumber from her. Robert knew there was much he still had to explain to her; atonement to be made for placing the mark on her without seeking her permission but within all of that; he had never felt so utterly complete or alive than he did at this moment. He enjoyed the reflection on each memory that had been stored away in his mind. From her first call to the last kiss before he went to feed. She was vibrant; alive with fire and beauty, and most importantly-she was his.

She was also somewhat of an enigma to him. Robert was never quite sure what to expect when it came to Rebecca. She was impulsive, annoying with her continued placing others before her own safety, and ugh, Robert thought- that sassy streak went up one side of her and down the other. Controlling her was tantamount to controlling a wild bear. It was a good thing he enjoyed a challenge. Three marks, he mused; just three had tied them more completely than many with four. Would she accept the fourth mark from him? Allow him to bring her to the brink of death where she would hover before being drawn back as one of his kind.

Robert slowed as he entered the clearing, his thoughts a little cluttered though very clear in the path he must take. First and foremost was Rebecca's safety and if he had to bind her to the couch he would ensure she remained safe this time. He took just a brief moment to watch her sleep so peacefully before leaving the house to head towards the cavern.

Power radiated not only from him but from within the walls of the cave. He had not felt it as strongly before. Perhaps it was having not fed that was the cause; or Rebecca had absorbed the brunt of it. Either way it now pulsated around him like a living, breathing entity. His eyes drank in every crevice along the passage, noting the droplets of water that rained down along the cracks in the thinner sections of the ceiling. The lights weren't needed for him to be able to see though he did enjoy the mysterious dances that played along the wall as the flames flickered with the slightly stuffy breeze. So many things he had overlooked for some reason he now too notice of. Miniscule motions of ants that crawled along the rough uneven rock formation floor; the scent of history; of secrets held carefully within the walls. He revelled in each new vision; seeing everything again for the first time.

"We are almost at the cavern," Markus announced; breaking the spell that held Robert.

"Excellent, I will meet you at the circle. How did John do?" The young one seemed genuine in his devotion to Rebecca. He could not fault that and would guide John in any way he could-as would the others.

"Outstanding of course; with my expert tutelage," he chuckled as he spoke. "John is a natural, Robert. He was Kind and gentle and very non-invasive. And at the moment he is flying high on energy and what it actually feels like to be fed."

"Good." Robert answered automatically as he entered the chamber itself. He heard the other Elders behind him before feeling them at his side.

Within the circle lay a tall, very slender man. His hair was matted and greasy, eyes a smouldering black. They didn't shimmer with light or fear; they breathed fire and anger. Loraine and Florence remained outside of the circle their hands intertwined, chanting softly as the other cursed and threatened. Loraine held the frying pan leaving the Elders to assume Florence had tried to use it on the man. They shook their heads. Robert gave Florence a knowing look and a grin before speaking. "I visited your neighbour. He still remembers feeling the whap from your pan on the back of his head."

Florence blushed. "What else did you see?" she hoped he would say nothing or old Jones would be getting another smack upside his head.

"Absolutely nothing of importance, Florence." Robert thought discretion the better part of valor. He turned his attention to the man writhing in the center.

"Is Benjamin dead yet?" Robert questioned.

The man laughed in response; a laugh that would cause goose bumps to rise on the flesh of humans. The elders were no humans, and combined would annihilate the young one quickly and viciously.

Robert nodded to Leonard. He knew that Leonard loved the battle, the skills involved within the mind.

Leonard stepped forward, remaining just out of the circle itself. As he closed his eyes he drew on the power that exuded from the room; the ancient secrets held in bondage for centuries. As the young one had ripped at Rebecca's mind; Leonard began to return the favor.

Slowly; making each strike one that would last a lifetime he began to chip away at the outer layer of the man's diseased mind.

"He is not well," Leonard's voice sounded distant; matter of fact as he struggled with the young one. His smile was cold as he turned it towards the man lying in the circle. "Within moments I will strip away the remaining exterior that contains the secrets you wish not to share. Spare yourself the agony, young one; tell us what we wish to know. Is Benjamin dead?"

The light began to flicker in the young ones eyes. Bravery was best felt when in combination with the other three. Now; as he lay in this circle of magic, surrounded by the formidable power of the five Elders, he understood defeat. There would be no remorse given without compromise; without answers. Slowly he nodded.

"Benjamin is a shadow of himself now." The words were slurred as Leonard held his grip on the shredding of his mind. "We drained him; as he taught us to drain others- as he taught us to drain portions of him that included souls."

"Dead or alive?" Robert pushed forth his power causing the young one to scream out in agony.

"I don't know. That is the truth," He cried out as Markus began to probe his mind as well. "When the woman called; Benjamin sent me along with those that were compelled to follow her whisper song. They were enchanted; felt freedom and peace which he had never allowed. He sent me to kill her."

Again he screamed as Robert forced his powers deep into the man's mind; offering no quarter.

"Benjamin was close to death as I left. The other three retain his powers. Upon my return I was to take the remainder. Four; divided equally. Spreading ourselves around the country making it difficult to be found; that was the plan until the woman sang. The beauty within the music drew many; we had to kill a dozen before the others remained behind. I suspect I was left here to die. They will not come; they no not where I am. "

"So your intent was to kill Rebecca?" Robert's eyes glowed ominously, his breathing slowing as he focused on the man.

He shook his head. "It was Benjamin's desire. He knew with your marks he could no longer touch her. With four combined, we knew we could. Our intent was to have her; not kill her."

"Where are the others?" Giles tossed the question at him while doing his best to hold Robert from entering the circle.

"We were supposed to meet at the barn where you first encountered us. If I was not to show; they would leave for destinations unknown, separate for a period of time before regrouping. They will maintain silence as they know the woman can hear them."

"So they are gone," Robert cursed loudly. "We will comb the area to be sure but I suspect that he speaks the truth. He has nothing to gain by lying except a more painful death."

"The old house of Catherine's, "Jerard spoke before glancing towards Loraine and Florence, "I believe it needs to come down. The others are drawn there for some reason."

Loraine locked eyes with Jerard as he spoke, shaking her head in response. "If I am not mistaken, the new ones of your kind that can become like John will be able to find comfort there." She turned her eyes to Robert, appealing to him before speaking again. "There is something that draws your kind there; you are right. I believe it is something that was meant to be; a reason for Catherine's death-for my grandchild's survival. Perhaps it can be used as a training place for the five of you?"

Robert glanced towards the others, nodding in response to their assent of Loraine's suggestion. "We think that is a wonderful idea,

Loraine; but perhaps you could help us in some ways-if you would be willing that is.

"How?" She looked genially confused.

"Creating those charms that I spoke to Florence about," Robert glanced towards both women. "Ones strong enough to protect the inner sanctum from those that carry the madness; keep those new to us a little safer while we train them."

"That we can do," Loraine nodded her head. "I would also like to spend time with my grandchild. She needs to learn to control the new powers she gained these past days. If she doesn't, it will consume her."

"Our homes are in Woodstock; I'm sure that we could all benefit from your guidance and since Catherine's homestead is here, I suspect you will be seeing more of us than you perhaps would like." Robert chuckled.

They turned back towards the one in the circle. Already he looked drained; pale flesh almost transparent. He had not been strong enough to survive the gifts; or curse, whichever way one chose to look at it, on his own. His mind was becoming ravaged; powers he was not in control of being drained within the circle of blood, binding it within the clay it rested upon. More secrets for the cavern to hold, Robert bent down to place his hands upon the earth. He could feel it tremble beneath his power; offering nothing yet promising so much. "So many moments of history this holds," his voice was quiet in respect to the ancient history he intended to learn.

"Many indeed," Loraine watched him carefully, knowing few others that could feel the magnificence that flowed beneath the dirty red, hardened clay. Perhaps there was hope for them after all.

He glanced at his hands as he stood tall again; the rich wet soil coating both of his palms. Energy still flowed into them; the tingling sensation not nearly as powerful as it had been when he had pressed his hands against it-but it was there. Carefully he brushed his hands together; not wanting to take any of it with him; knowing its secrets were safe here. Robert tilted his head as he felt a stirring; something deep inside pulling him away from the circle.

"Rebecca wakes," his eyes moved over to his friends. "Would you spare this soul the painful end? Please ease his suffering and allow him peace. It is what Rebecca would ask us for."

They nodded, turning towards the shell of a man that lay curled within the circle. Offering peace to one that wished to kill them was difficult, but perhaps they had learned something as well.

She was waiting for his arrival, her eyes languid; cheeks flushed, and she wore the most beautiful smile Robert could ever remember seeing. As he opened his arms she rose, eagerly fitting herself within the perfect circle as they closed around her.

Amazing, she thought, that arms could be the home she had searched for all of her life. Unable to resist, she rubbed her nose against his shirt to inhale his scent. Angling her head so she could see his face she stood on tip toes to kiss him before drawing back. "Why do you always smell like sunshine? "

Leaning down he kissed her with everything in him. "Because our lives are lived within the shadows of night; we were given a scent of warmth-of day, of sunshine and light.

"It's beautiful," Becca murmured as she inhaled again before sighing and drawing back. "I need to find Benjamin, Robert."

"He is gone, Rebecca," Robert informed her as he watched her make a coffee.

"He isn't fully gone; I have felt him since I woke."

"What!!" Robert was by her side instantaneously; hovering unnecessarily.

"Oh stop; his powers are as weak as he is. There is little time left before he will breathe no more." Becca turned to look up at Robert, her eyes imploring. "Please, Robert; I need to do this. He has fragments of souls that need to be released. One of them belongs to Catherine." She heard him sigh; felt his body tense and she straightened, preparing herself for an argument that was about to ensue.

"Fine, but only if we are all with you, Rebecca," Robert acquiesced knowing it would haunt her forever should she not try. "Though our connection should keep your mind safe from the rest, there is no guarantee that you will not call others again. The other Elders will be able to keep watch."

She nodded as she blew on the coffee before taking a drink. "Thank you, Robert." Again she smiled that melted even the coldest parts of him.

"When you are done, please would you come into the house. Rebecca seeks to contact Benjamin; apparently he is still alive though barely, and she would like to be able to have him release the shards of souls he holds. Her powers are unpredictable; she may call all others to us, we don't know."

"On our way," Markus was already moving as he spoke.

"They are on their way, Rebecca."

"I know; I can hear the five-well actually the six of you as well."

"What will you be like, my Rebecca," Robert mused as he stroked the pale, smooth flesh of her face, "when you are given my fourth mark."

"I don't know, Robert," Becca stepped back so she could look at him, already missing the sense of closeness. "But it will be some time before the fourth mark is given." She watched his eyes narrow; could feel an unsettling within him. "Please, allow me to explain." She waited until he reluctantly nodded.

"The fourth mark will take us down a path neither of us knows right now. The results of the third mark have been more unpredictable than expected right?" Again he nodded. "Ugh," she thought, "and he thinks I'm stubborn."

"According to the journal; once the fourth mark is given, I will become what she did-a creator or something. Are you ready; really ready to begin that life without fully exploring this one?" Becca blushed as she spoke. "There are so many things I don't know yet; I don't understand, things I don't know about you. I need you Robert; you are my life and my love. I want to do this right, to savor each moment of being together; to make love without worrying about spontaneous combustion."

His lips compressed; not in anger but amusement. With her luck she probably would catch everything on fire. "Rebecca," his voice was hesitant though he smiled when she moved back into his embrace. "When we consummate our relationship you will receive the fourth mark."

"Well," she coughed. "I've kind of been thinking about that. The journal said he poured his gift into her, correct? What if…." The blush that stained her cheeks was fiery red and Robert was finding it far more difficult not to laugh. "Well what if we used… protection?"

"Protection." The word came out with a choked sound. Gripping her hand he dragged her over to a chair, settling down before drawing her onto his lap. "There will be no protection, my Rebecca; no protection from me or this fourth mark. "He paused to kiss the nape of her neck, feeling the tremors working their way down her body. "It is inevitable, my love. In order for our souls to unite completely; we must have all four marks.

His touch was so damn irresistible the thought of dragging him in the back was about all she could think of. She writhed as his hands roamed over her slender form, cupping her breasts. Need, hot and intense ripped through her. How the hell was she supposed to resist this? "Bastard."

"Can you," she shifted on his lap, burying her head against his chest as she spoke. Can you..." God why was this so hard. "Can you have sex without erhm, offering the fourth mark? I mean is that controllable?

"I don't know Rebecca. Union between us will be extremely powerful, intense and will most likely unite us."

"Yes; I understand that, but I mean," shoot me now Becca thought." Can you control which um... parts are released when we consummate our relationship." She fumbled for words. "Um, what I'm saying is; this won't be your first time having sex, right?"

Finally he was beginning to understand though he considered feigning ignorance while he enjoyed her squirming. "Yes, Rebecca, we do enjoy sexual pleasures."

"Then why can't we..." she stammered. "Try that until we are ready for the mark?"

"That is simple, Rebecca," His voice dropped a tone, becoming sensual, hot and arousing. "Because you are mine."

She hugged her stomach, trying to stop the somersaults that were tumbling around inside. Her breathing became ragged as she tilted her head up to look at him. "All or nothing huh?"

"All or nothing."

She placed the cup on the table as she slid from his lap. "Hope you enjoy celibacy then Robert."

Gales of laughter echoed in his head. The other Elders were close enough to hear the conversation though they were holding back

234

entering until they were finished their discussion. "Hold back my ass, "He stood, gathering her into his arms.

"Celibacy is. Not. An. Option." Each word was enunciated with a forceful, lingering kiss that stole her breath- and resolve. She clung to him, returning each kiss with wild abandon; arching her body into his, her nails scraping along his hard skin. Her lips were swollen when he pulled back. "When you are done speaking with Benjamin, we will finish this discussion." Reluctantly he released her; feeling the pulsing in his own body. "Asses; "he spoke in his head to his friends. "Get in here; let's get this over with."

Rebecca looked nowhere but down as the others entered the small kitchen area. She wasn't sure she would ever grow accustomed to hearing voices in her head; well except for her sub conscious who at the moment was in a blissful state after those kisses.

"Just remember all of you," Rebecca turned towards them, "my grandmamma is never wrong; soon the positions will be reversed and it will be us chuckling at you." With a smug look she moved to the couch, leaving them standing there. "I am going to reach out to Benjamin, if you all are done the laughing."

They laughed harder as they watched her; admiration and respect flickering within their ebony eyes-along with incredible humor. "Bastards."

"Ok, I need to do this now before he expires."

Chapter 19

Sitting cross legged on the ground she let her fatigued eyes drift closed. It took some moments for her to be able to focus; the riotous emotions Robert stirred ran deep and strong; lingering long after his lips had left hers. Pushing the thoughts away for now she imagined her mind opening slightly; like a window was slowly being drawn up to allow the breeze in She was hesitant; the pain from last time still fresh and pulsing. She turned her thoughts to Catherine as she called out to him.

It was quiet; almost too quiet for her, shaking her head as she felt Robert place his hand on her shoulder, keeping the connection between them alive and beating-its own entity. Again she called to him; conjuring the image of Catherine as she opened her mind inch by inch.

"Do you seek to mock me upon my death?" The voice was barely a whisper; haunting, a man realizing there would be no peace upon his death.

"No," Becca spoke the words aloud as well as in her mind. "I can't hold you responsible for what madness began."

Benjamin tried to laugh; the sound more like a person's last breath. "What then?"

"To offer a peaceful passing, Benjamin," she spoke slowly and with complete conviction and compassion.

"You? Why?" It took his energy to speak, she could feel the laboring.

"Because no one deserves to not have peace; though I will ask something from you in return," Becca was firm in her responses to him.

Robert tried to sense the presence of others, gripping her shoulder before speaking to her. "Do you sense any young ones, Rebecca?"

Her head tilted as she pushed outwards; straining to feel any other Wanderers. Her brows furrowed; her head moving in the directions she felt them. "A few; they come this way-seeking release."

Robert nodded, glancing towards the other Elders. They were gone before his head rose.

"What do you want from me?" Benjamin strained to talk. She could sense the fear in him. Drained of power; of life, he was slowly fading into nothing.

"My ancestor and others, Benjamin; you carry essence of them. Release the remains of the souls and I will offer comfort and peace to you."

Again he tried to laugh, coughing instead. "They are mine."

"They haunt you, Benjamin. I feel each one of them straining for release. I feel their pain and anguish. It will be nothing in comparison to what you will feel should you not accept. I do not say this to threaten; I simply speak the truth."

"She was my caller." Again he coughed his breathing shallow and raspy. "Didn't know it though… Every year… went to her… mark called me."

"I know, Benjamin; I know. It is why it now runs in our genes. Do you not wish the one you loved to have peace and to unite both complete souls upon death? It is time for you to offer goodness and hope, Benjamin. Reach out to me; feel the love and forgiveness as you release the shards. Know that as you offer these gifts back to those they belong to; you will find peace."

Quiet reigned. Fear that she was too late ate at her insides though she prayed not. Her eyes rimmed with fresh tears, spilling over as she blinked.

"Your eyes water for me?"

"Yes, Benjamin; they do."

"Why?"

"Because to me there is beauty within each person; some saving quality that will ultimately define who they truly are."

"Reach your hand out, Becca," nothing more than a hoarse whisper.

She reached out with both arms, wrapping one hand around Robert's arm as she held the other out to him. Coldness flowed up her arm and through her entire body as she felt his skin. Robert was positively hot in comparison to this unbearable chill.

Benjamin felt her hand; warm and soft, pleasant. It reminded him of Catherine's.

"You aren't alone Benjamin. Please I beg you; allow those that have passed to the other side be reunited with the slivers of life you hold."

With concerted effort Benjamin raised his other hand until he could place it atop of Rebecca's. She could feel a weight that didn't belong to him. "Be at peace, Benjamin," Becca whispered as his hand dropped away from hers. Tiny glittering shards sparkled with trapped life in the palm of her hand. Within each one was the last spark of life.

Carefully she pulled back her hand; her eyes wide with wonder and glistening with unshed tears. Lifting her other hand she lovingly cradled them; drawing them closer. "Be free," Becca spoke in soft gentle tones before blowing to release them. She watched as they danced along with the breeze; lifting higher and higher until they were no longer visible.

It was over. She closed her mind and opened her eyes as she leaned back against Robert.

"That was the most beautiful thing I have witness in more than six hundred years." His voice held the twinge of awe.

Becca tilted her head back to gaze into his beautiful eyes, a grin forming. "Aren't you a little old for me? Old man! Geez," peals of laughter escaped as he lunged, pinning her to the ground.

"Old huh; I'll show you old," he slowly lowered his head until his lips gently touched hers, his fingertips tracing her face causing shivers to race up and down her spine. It was the hot and cold again.

She shifted beneath him, tugging at his shirt; lifting it until she could slide it from his body, gasping as she saw his exquisite chest. Eagerly he swallowed her gasps and moans as his lips covered hers once more. She ran her fingers over the broadness of his shoulders before trailing them down his flawless skin.

Clothing began to fall in all directions as their hands discovered one another. Heat pooled deep inside of her, moistening her flesh for him. She arched and cried out as his lips found first one breast, then the other, suckling gently; drawing each tight nipple into his mouth. He hovered above her, resting his weight on his elbows as he parted her thighs with his legs.

Every touch inflamed her even more until she thought she would burst with the need. Her fingers clawed at his back, pulling him towards him as she writhed and cried out. "Now; please Robert, now."

"Are you sure Rebecca," Robert held back as he locked eyes with her.

"Now; now, yes," she raised her hips, feeling him at the juncture between her thighs. And then he was inside; filling her more completely than she ever thought possible.

Everything stopped around them as he slid inside; breathing no longer mattered, nothing mattered but this moment as their souls merged together. Each thrust drew them closer together; their cries and shouts muffled as their lips locked hungrily, their tongues beginning an intricate dance. Their hips moved in perfect synchronization, burning; driving the passion and needs to places neither had visited. When his lips closed over her nipple she fell over the edge; her body spasming and rocking against him as she screamed with pleasure. The flames of need licked over the entirety of her body as she writhed beneath him; uncaring that she couldn't catch her breath.

And then she saw him as he rose slightly. He was glorious in his nude form; his face a picture of intensity as he stroked and rocked against her, pushing deeply inside, stirring the flames again. She watched as each muscle strained as he plunged in fully, holding himself there as he released. His cry was sharp as pleasure exploded inside; feeling the pulsing as he leaned down to kiss her again.

Cold began to enter her body as he released. Fire against her lips; icy fingers reaching inside of her womb before spreading throughout her body. She screamed and arched, her nails digging fiercely into his back as the frozen sensations expanded even more until it encompassed the lower half of her body, moving upwards over her belly to her breasts and upwards.

Robert drank in her screams as he held her with his body; using his free hand to calm and soothe her. Pulling back from her lips as her body ceased to move he watched; wiping the perspiration from her forehead as his mark began to take effect, changing her. He held himself inside as she changed; whispering words of love and encouragement as her world began to grow dark; distant. Soon, he prayed, soon the pain would end and her new beginning would start.

She felt the pain; as though her insides were being frozen to the point that any movement would snap every bone in her body. Her eyes were wild and terrified as they held his gaze. She could barely feel his body against her or inside of her. Focus on his words she chanted; focus on his words. Dimness; darkness-slowly evolved into nothing. She couldn't feel her heart beating; her lungs felt empty, and she had no voice as she tried to scream.

It was time. She was as close as he would ever allow her to be. Without care he ripped away the flesh at his wrist before bringing it to her parted lips. Drops of blood trickled into her now dry mouth, moistening it; coating it with life. He tilted her head so it would flow downwards until she could swallow again. "Come back to my Rebecca; come back to me, my Love."

Silence had become her world. Ice; quiet and fear. She couldn't feel her body; fairly sure at this point she wouldn't want to. Something warm dripped into her mouth chasing away the numbness from the cold. If her throat weren't frozen she would have moaned with the sensation of heat after the frigid temperature her body had dropped to.

The warm drops trickled effortlessly down her open throat; every place it touched began to thaw. And then it reached her blood stream; surging through her veins as quickly as the ice had. Now she screamed with the heat, arching as she began to breathe again; to feel her heart beating again. Hot, now she was too hot, it was consuming her. She began to panic, her body shaking and writhing to move from beneath him.

She began to glow; her skin pink as she released the fire inside; allowing it to cover her body with its heat. The pain eased as she allowed it to expand outwards. Now she could think; she could see and hear better than she had ever been able to.

The first place she looked was towards him; standing there watching her; concern etched on every feature. She gloried in the new feelings; the new sensations; the fresh need for him that now raced through her body.

She reached for him and smiled as he lay on the ground, rolling her on top of him.

I love you my Rebecca," Robert groaned the words out as she settled herself on top of him; beginning a slow rhythm.

"Told ya; it's Becca," her voice cracked as she leaned down and kissed him thinking he could call her anything he wanted. "I love you; Robert."

Hope you enjoyed the Robert book 1 of Adlucinor Chronicles
Please check out:
http://dreambigpublishing.net
for more info on the books in our collection.

Made in the USA
Charleston, SC
12 August 2015